RISE
OF THE
SNAKE
GODDESS

JENNY ELDER MOKE

RISE OF THE SNAKE GODDESS

A SAMANTHA KNOX NOVEL

HYPERION

Los Angeles   New York

First Edition, June 2022
10 9 8 7 6 5 4 3 2 1
FAC-004510-22089
Printed in the United States of America

This book is set in Fairfield LT Std/Adobe
Designed by Phil Buchanan

Library of Congress Cataloging-in-Publication Data
Names: Moke, Jenny Elder, author.
Title: Rise of the snake goddess : a Samantha Knox novel / Jenny Elder Moke.
Description: First edition. • Los Angeles : Hyperion, 2022. • Series: Samantha Knox ; 2
• Audience: Ages 14–18 • Audience: Grades 10–12 • Summary: Samantha Knox
goes to the island of Knossos where she discovers the ancient Snake Goddess's
golden girdle that has a magical power.
Identifiers: LCCN 2021027083 • ISBN 9781368067270 (hardcover)
• ISBN 9781368081948 (ebook)
Subjects: CYAC: Adventure and adventurers—Fiction. • Archaeology—Fiction.
• Magic—Fiction. • LCGFT: Action and adventure fiction. • Novels.
Classification: LCC PZ7.1.M639 Ri 2022 • DDC [Fic]—dc23
LC record available at https://lccn.loc.gov/2021027083

Reinforced binding

Visit www.hyperionteens.com

For Lily,
My partner in crimes figurative and literal

CHAPTER ONE

Samantha Knox was not lurking.

At least, she tried to tell herself she was not lurking. She was simply waiting. But the longer she paced the short stretch of hallway outside Professor Atchinson's office, the less it felt like waiting and the more it felt like lying in wait. The paper she carried had long since crinkled into a withered white flag more suitable for blowing her nose than for triumphantly presenting to the professor as Sam intended. But it was the content of the paper, not its physical state, that mattered most to her.

"Professor Atchinson, good afternoon, so good to see you," Sam rehearsed softly to herself mid-pace. "I know we had a rocky start, sir, what with you kicking me out of your class on the first day of the semester and humiliating me in front of all my peers. You might be thinking I'm here now for revenge, but I assure you, sir, that idea hasn't occurred to me in months. Hmm, maybe not the most auspicious start."

Better not to bring up that awful day, already cemented in Sam's memory among other such denigrating experiences as falling in the mud pit outside of her schoolroom back in her hometown of Clement, Illinois, or that time she ate with the wrong fork at her best friend's house and had to be quietly corrected by the serving girl. No, if she wanted to win over the man who held her academic future in his hands, she would have to put aside the past and forge a new future.

Sam paused, her sensible loafers squeaking as she changed direction physically and mentally. "Professor Atchinson, sir, good afternoon! I am sure you are as excited as all your students are to begin your summer field school at Knossos. I know I am, because I will be one of them! Your students, I mean. For the summer. Because I did it! I made top of the class for first-years. Does that sound like bragging? That might sound like bragging. Professor Atchinson, if you would kindly read this paper for me, you will see . . . well, now it just sounds like I don't know how to read for myself."

She let out a sigh, slumping against the wall of the empty hallway. It was the end of the spring semester—her first semester at the University of Chicago—and the students had scattered faster than the pollen on the trees outside as soon as final exams were complete. She should have been off celebrating along with the rest of her peers—well, the ones that hadn't bought into the rumors about her—but instead here she was, certainly not lurking, but perhaps doing an approximation of it.

Sam fumbled with a little figurine in her pocket, drawing it out to hold it up in the electric lights of the hall. A misshapen lump of metal, nothing more than a bit of mangled tin. The front half of it was crushed and distorted, the back half giving the impression of hind legs. Once upon a time, it had been a toy horse, carried along in her father's pocket as he fought on the front lines in France, a gift he intended to send home to her. But it had been destroyed along with the rest of her father when a shell hit the hotel where his regiment had been sequestered.

"Oh, Papa," she said, petting the lump of tin where the horse's head would have been, the metal there tarnished and slightly indented from all the times she had invoked its comfort. "I wish you could see me now. At a real university, just like we always dreamed! And top of my class, besides. I know *you* wouldn't think I was bragging."

There had been a letter sent back along with the horse, half-written and half-burned. Her father had found the trinket buried under rubble, and he'd detailed to her how he had used the tip of his bayonet to excavate it, applying the techniques she had taught him. It had made him feel closer to her, the letter had said, on his own little treasure hunt just like the ones she was always so obsessed with back home.

He'd had dreams for her, Sam's father. Dreams she had put away for seven long years after he died. Dreams that hurt too much to have after he was gone. But that all changed six months ago, when a mysterious diary appeared at her shop and sent her on a journey that upended her life. Now all she wanted was to recapture that lost time and do right by her father's memory. She wanted to make him proud.

There was only one thing standing in her way, and he should have been done with office hours fifteen minutes ago.

"I should just knock, shouldn't I? I am a student with a question after all. Is that not what office hours are for?" Sam marched up to the door, lifting her fist and willing it to knock. Except all it did was hover there, uncertainly.

"Maybe I'll give him five more minutes," Sam said, pacing back toward the opposite wall. She dropped her forehead against the cool stones, shaking her head. "Or maybe you're just being a coward, Samantha Margaret Knox."

Or perhaps she was just hungry. She *had* elected to skip lunch in the hopes of catching Professor Atchinson after office hours. Her mother had often told her growing up that her stomach was more reliable than the dinner bell. And it was certainly ringing all the alarms now, gurgling loudly enough that a passing student gave her a worried glance.

"Happy end of semester!" she called to the boy as she hastily pulled her forehead off the wall to frown down at her stomach. "Hush, would you? I promise to give you an extra helping of mashed potatoes at dinner if you would just let me talk to the professor without embarrassing me."

"Too late for that," came an obnoxious male voice. Theodore Chapin, one of Professor Atchinson's graduate students, smirked at her from the doorway of the professor's office. He played full-back for the University of Chicago football team, and it showed in the massive span of his shoulders and the blunt thickness of his nose that had seen its fair share of breaks.

"Hello, Theo," Sam said to the boy, aiming for polite and landing closer to apprehensive. She had grown up around plenty of rude boys in Clement, but Theodore Chapin strained even her patience. Professor Atchinson had a reputation among the undergraduates for dispensing his favor to the students based on their worth to him, and Theo played the perfect heavy. He fell into the role now, crossing his arms and puffing out his chest so that she could hardly see past him into the professor's office.

She went up on tiptoe to peer over his shoulder, her hopes that she might have been spared some measure of embarrassment falling as she spotted Professor Atchinson standing just behind him. Still, she forced enthusiasm into her voice. "Professor Atchinson, hello!"

"Not you again, Miss Knox," said Professor Atchinson, his British accent lending a knife's edge to his annoyance. "I thought I made my feelings on your presence perfectly clear the day you attempted to infiltrate my anthropology lecture and sow your chaos among my students."

Well, so much for not bringing up the past. Sam cleared her throat of the lump that suddenly formed there, determined not to let it ruin her moment. "I know we started off on the wrong foot, Professor—"

"The wrong foot," Professor Atchinson snorted. "As if you did not conspire with Barnaby Wallstone on his harebrained scheme to undo all my tireless work here, traipsing halfway across the world to Dublin with no credentials and no experience and debasing the good name of our program at the University of Chicago."

That was not at all what had happened, or even how it happened, but she could hardly make that point to the professor. Sam, Bennett, and Joana had given their official version of what happened in Dublin enough times over—to the authorities in Ireland and those here at home, to the official inquest opened by the school, not to mention in dozens of informal settings to gossip-hungry peers—and she couldn't claim anything to the contrary without opening herself to more questions that she did not want to answer. So she gritted her teeth, willed the corners of her mouth to lift in a smile, and focused all her energy on the future.

"I hope we can start fresh—well, start at all, really—this summer during the field school at Knossos."

"What could possibly make you think you would be part of my field school?" Atchinson asked with a sniff. "It is for graduate students only, Miss Knox, those handpicked by me for their skills and dedication. Students like Mr. Chapin here, who has earned his position among my elite disciples with hard work and dedication."

And kissing up to you every chance he gets, Sam added silently.

But the thought must have made itself plain on her features, because Professor Atchinson's tight expression soured.

"This is what the prestigious University of Chicago has come to, letting in any riffraff from the cornfields on bloody scholarship," he muttered, as if to himself but loud enough that Sam and Theo could hear.

Sam stiffened, her face going red as Theo let out a loud laugh. "Not going to start in with the tears now, are you?" he taunted her. "You're just like my girl, Evelyn, getting misty-eyed at the thought of a wounded bird."

Sam rather thought his girlfriend, Evelyn Hamilton, must get teary-eyed at the prospect of having agreed to date someone like Theodore Chapin. But Evelyn was not her concern today, and her attempts to start anew with Professor Atchinson were about as fresh as curdled milk.

"I made top of the class," she blurted out, thrusting the wilted piece of paper at the professor. He eyed it with distaste, and she gave it a little shake. Or maybe that was just her hand shaking with the attempt to keep her frustration at bay. "First among the undergraduates."

She waited for her meaning to sink in with him, waited to see it change his opinion of her. When he made no move to respond, her confidence faltered.

"The . . . the open position, in the field school," she continued, glancing between the professor and Theo. "For the undergraduate student who shows the most promise in the field. It's a tradition. Top of the undergraduate class gets to join the graduate summer field school excavations. Don't they?"

Theo's smirk only got smirkier, which didn't bode well for Sam. Professor Atchinson sniffed and straightened, the small motion as dismissive as if he turned his back on her. "That position has been eliminated."

Sam lurched a half step forward. "Eliminated? But . . . how? Why?"

"The costs would simply be too prohibitive," the professor said, looking past her at some distant point down the hall. "Were we making our normal excavations at the Kincaid Mounds, perhaps it would have been possible. But we are traveling to Knossos, on Crete, as part of the twenty-fifth anniversary of Sir Arthur Evans's discovery of the Minoan civilization that built the palace. There are a great many details to consider—passage to Crete, accommodations near the palace, invitations to the gala celebrating the anniversary. The undertaking is great, and we can hardly extend our scholarship considering the added costs of such an endeavor. Perhaps next year, if you can manage such a feat again."

"But I earned that spot," Sam said, her whole body trembling. She couldn't stand to look at Theo, whose haughty expression practically glowed. Instead, she focused on the professor. "I worked hard for it all semester. I followed all the rules. You can't just take it away from me now. It's not fair."

Professor Atchinson stepped past Theo to come toe-to-toe with her. He wasn't an impressive man in appearance—he was small and round, his hair grayed and drawn back sharply along a receding line from his temple, his nose slightly too large for his face. But what he lacked in physical prowess he made up for in presence. He knew how to hold a room's attention, whether it was a lecture hall filled with students or a boardroom of university trustees. He used that power now on Sam, giving her such a hard stare that she felt she must have shrunk three sizes in one look.

"What is not fair is that I have to contend with untried, overeager amateurs like you, trampling through my carefully laid plans and disgracing all the hard work I have done. Your kind does not belong here, Miss Knox, no more than a cow would belong in the White House or a chicken on the throne of England. The sooner you learn that your place is not here but out in those cornfields from which you grew, the faster this sinking ship of a department will be righted and set back on course."

Desperation sucked at Sam's shoes, holding her fast when all her wounded pride wanted her to do was run and hide. "That's not true," she whispered. "I deserve to be here, same as everyone else."

"The only place you deserve to be is in that lunatic asylum alongside Barnaby Wallstone," snapped Professor Atchinson. "You've wasted quite enough of my time, girl, and I have no more of it to spare. Better luck next year. Come along, Theodore."

"Better luck," Theo echoed cruelly, trotting after the professor down the hall and disappearing around the corner, taking all of Sam's hopes along with them.

CHAPTER TWO

"**A**rsenic in his tea," said Joana Steeling, slamming her empty glass down on the bar top for emphasis. Her bright violet dress glowed in the dim light of the Green Mill speakeasy, drawing the attention of several of the young men in their pin-striped suits and spats along with the girls hanging off their arms. Joana had that effect on a room, that effortless Steeling charm like a magnet. She looked as fantastic as she always did, her dress fresh from next season's catalogs and her hair styled in short finger curls framing her gorgeous face.

"Jo, arsenic is a poison," Sam said glumly, swirling the full contents of her own glass. She wore a gold dress that was the height of fashion six months ago, before she tore the hem climbing out a ship's porthole window. The hem had been repaired, but the dress was showing signs of wear after being Sam's only evening attire for the past semester. "It would kill him."

"We don't give him enough to kill him, just enough to make all his weaselly hair fall out," her best friend said, giving a little wave to the man behind the bar and shaking her empty glass at him.

Sam frowned. "Does arsenic do that?"

Joana gave her a determined look. "Let's find out."

"I don't want to poison him, Jo," Sam said with a sigh. "I just want him to give me a chance."

"The only chance that man will ever give you is a fat one," Joana said, gracing the barman with a winning Steeling smile. "Another one if you would, Leland. Sam, you know Atchinson's reputation. Self-thinkers need not apply. If you can't worship the ground he walks on, you might as well be made of wallpaper for all he'll see you."

"But it's not fair!" Sam protested, finding a new fount of energy in her outrage. "I earned my place in that field school, same as every top undergrad who came before me. But it's only me that's being denied. And I don't believe it could be about the budget, do you? What difference would one student make among thirty others?"

Joana took her glass from the barman with a little wink, only wincing slightly as she threw it back in one gulp. "If you want to call his bluff, you could offer to pay your own way."

Sam gave her a flat look. "With what money?"

"You could always ask Daddy for the funds. He'd be pleased as punch to send one of us off on a dig."

Sam slumped back over her drink. "I couldn't ask that of him. He's already done too much for me. He's practically paying my room and board here, along with sponsoring my scholarship. Never mind that I can only afford the rest of it because of the money I saved working at the bookshop all those years. Taking any more from him would be egregious."

"It's practically your right," Joana said. "You know Daddy considers you a second daughter, and if you asked him after a few tumblers of the good stuff, he'd tell you that you're his favorite."

"But I'm *not* his daughter," Sam said. "I love your father, you know that, but he's my employer. It's not the same."

"Well, don't let Daddy catch you saying that—you'll break his heart."

"I want to do this for myself," Sam insisted, wishing she could make her point to Joana.

Their friendship had always managed to bridge several divides, but sometimes those gaps in their upbringing came to light with frustrating clarity. Sam was the daughter of a washerwoman and a farmer killed during the Great War, while Joana was the daughter of a textile magnate and a former actress turned socialite. Sam only owned the dress she now wore and drank the swill she now pretended to drink because Joana had bought them both. If it were not for the Steeling family's generosity, Sam would be burning her arms hauling out steaming piles of laundry to dry on the line alongside her mother. They had given her every opportunity she'd ever had except this one. This one she had earned herself, only to have it snatched right from under her.

"Well, good luck convincing that old windbag of anything. You know he hates us because of Old Man Wally and the Dublin incident," Joana said, surveying the club around them. The Green Mill was on the famous side of illegal, thanks to a payoff to the local police by the mobster who leased the place, Al Capone. His booth sat in the corner with a clear view of both doors, and legend had it the band would stop whatever they were playing when he entered the joint to play *Rhapsody in Blue*, his favorite tune. Luckily there was no *Rhapsody* in earshot tonight, just the easy croons of singer Joe E. Lewis. Sam didn't mind accompanying Joana on her lawbreaking excursions, but she wasn't interested in getting mixed up with any real mobsters. She'd done her time with dangerous men.

"He thinks we conspired with Wallstone to try and make some great find in Dublin and take over the department from him," Sam said, shaking her head. "No matter how many times I tell him that's not what happened, he's convinced of it. And it's not like I can say what *actually* happened either. He had everyone's opinions of me set before I ever stepped on campus, and no matter how hard I work to change their minds, they choose rumors and lies."

"You and Bennett are going about this all wrong," Joana said, leaning back on her elbows against the bar as her tone turned expansive. "You keep looking at your reputations like a liability instead of an opportunity. You're not embracing all the possibilities. Just this past week I started a rumor that we were hired by the new Irish government to track down a cult of blood drinkers within their own ranks. I heard the Russo twins repeating it during library hours on Friday, and now I've got seven invites to end-of-the-year soirees this weekend, so you know it made its rounds."

"I'm glad you can find the fun in it," Sam said, turning her back on the room to glare at the clear liquor in her glass. Joana swore it would help ease her troubles, but Sam could never get past the dried-flower taste of it. "With Wallstone on indefinite leave and Atchinson firmly set in his intentions to blacklist me, I'll be lucky to have a career as a trench digger on an excavation site."

"Cheer up, here's Bennett," Joana said, taking pity on Sam's neglected glass and sipping from it herself. "If anyone can un-dol your drums, it's him."

Sam perked up and spun to face the room once again, her whole being coming alive at the sight of Bennett Steeling entering the Green Mill. He wore a suit that would have looked casual on any-one else but managed to look crisp and perfectly fitted on his wide shoulders and trim physique, his raven hair glimmering with deep rivers of warmer brown in the low light of the speakeasy. The lights flared a little brighter, the music swelled, the temperature of the early June night raised the heat in the bar. Or perhaps that was just Sam's reaction whenever Bennett entered a room, despite having spent plenty of time in plenty of rooms with him over the past six months. She wasn't the only female in the vicinity to notice him either, but his gaze skittered over the collected painted lips and sparkling dresses until they found her. His expression softened and warmed, his eyes swirling to a light golden brown as he sent her a small, private smile. Joana gave an audible sigh beside her.

"Hot looks," she said as Bennett moved through the tight crowd of the bar toward them.

"Hmm?" Sam asked, the single sip of gin she'd taken that evening suddenly hitting her.

"If I stuck a marshmallow between the two of you, it would roast," Joana said, rolling her eyes. But her tone was good-natured.

Sam smiled shyly. "I'm mad for your brother and you know it."

Joana made a playfully retching sound. "I've told you not to bring that up with me. It's bad enough I have to experience it with my own peepers. I don't need you waxing poetic about his brain or other less appropriate parts."

Sam gave a dramatic sigh, looking dreamily through the swirl of lace and sequins and slick suits on the dance floor. "He really does have the best brain."

"Sam," Bennett said as he reached them, taking her hands to help her up off the stool. "You look incredible as always."

"Bennett," Sam said, shivering at the sound of her name spoken so intimately from his lips. Would there ever be a time that he called her name and she did not respond in such a manner? She doubted it.

He kissed her softly, his hands lingering at the base of her spine, his fingers warm and strong through the thin lace and silk of the underdress. Joana cleared her throat loudly, slapping her hand on the bar top.

"And I'm here, too, brother," she said, dry as sand.

Sam stepped back, a fierce blush crawling up her neck as Bennett gave a discreet cough. "Yes, Jo, hello to you as well."

Joana held up a hand. "I don't require the same greeting, thanks."

His expression flattened. "I hope that's a club soda, Jo."

Joana gave him a brilliant smile, swirling her glass. "Of course, brother. Alcohol is illegal after all."

Bennett's nostrils flared on a sigh before he turned back to Sam, his expression growing serious. "I heard about Professor Atchinson."

Sam deflated back on the stool with a groan. "It's all over the school already? I thought I'd at least have the summer to recoup my dignity."

"I bet it was Theo Chapin, that worm," Joana said. "He got that big by feeding on other people's misery. I'd lay money on it."

"Sam, I'm so sorry," Bennett said, running his hands along Sam's bare arms and making her shiver once again. "I know how hard you worked to earn that position. It's unfortunate they didn't have the budget to include you this year."

Sam snorted. "You actually believe it's about budgets?"

"You think otherwise?" Bennett asked in surprise.

"I think it's flimsy at best and an outright lie at worst," Sam said. "Atchinson hates me."

"He doesn't hate you, Sam," Bennett said. "Atchinson is the old guard, and with the university president dying unexpectedly last month and throwing the administration into confusion, he's just trying to protect his position. I'm sure it's not personal."

"It felt very personal when he told me I don't belong here," Sam muttered, but her words were lost in the smother of Bennett's jacket as she burrowed into his chest.

He linked his arms around her back. "I know it's a low blow after all your hard work, but it's only your first year. Your first semester, really. And after the Dublin business, you were lucky to get into the university. But you overcame all of that, stuck to the rules, and came out top of the class. I'm sure you'll be top of the class next year as well, and the year after that, and you'll be so sick of the Kincaid Mounds by the time you graduate that you'll be begging them to send you anywhere else in graduate school."

"What good is following all the rules if Professor Atchinson is just going to rip the pages of the rulebook right out from under me?" Sam shivered at the idea of the worst torture she could imagine—purposely mutilating a treasured book.

"I'm sure that's not what he's doing," Bennett said, smoothing one hand down the little ripples of her spine. "Atchinson is a stickler for the rules, especially the ones he created himself. This is simply a budgetary constraint, you'll see."

"And anyway, why are we letting the old codger steal our joy?" Joana piped in. "Tonight is not a night for moping—it's a night for celebrating. Sam came out top of the class and I survived an entire semester without even the whiff of a scandal. Gold stars all around."

"You mean besides the rumors everyone keeps passing around about why we were in Dublin and what happened when we were there?" Bennett asked dryly.

"Those don't count," Joana said, pointing a finger at him around her fresh glass of gin. "That technically happened before the semester started."

"I can't believe I'm saying this," Bennett said, shaking his head. "But for once I agree with Joana. You did a brilliant thing, Sam, and you deserve to celebrate. Atchinson can go hang."

"That's the spirit, brother!" Joana declared, hopping off her stool and taking Sam by the arm to drag her upright. "Come on, kid, let's twist."

Sam sighed, doing her best to breathe out the disappointment weighing her down. It helped, maybe a little—or maybe that was simply the effect of being bolstered between the Steeling siblings. Either way, they made a decent point. Professor Atchinson could absolutely go hang. If he meant to deny her the opportunity she deserved, she would find a way to make her own.

CHAPTER THREE

"I won't be able to walk for days," Sam groaned, pulling her heel loose of her shoe and wedging it off with a sigh. She held her leg out, wriggling her toes and stretching her calf muscles. "I don't think I've ever danced so much in my life."

"You'll ruin your stockings like that," Joana said, though she did the same and slung her shoes over her shoulder, hanging by her index finger. When Sam gave her a pointed look, she shrugged. "I never much cared for stockings anyhow."

They walked through the quiet campus toward Foster Hall, the women's dormitory where both Sam and Joana lived. Bennett looped his arm casually around Sam's waist, the heat of the day and the sweaty atmosphere of the speakeasy giving way to the soft breath of night as they wandered home. They took a meandering, easy path to get there, the dark obscuring most of the buildings around them. But Sam didn't let that stop her from admiring them as if it were full daylight, for she knew all the buildings by heart now. Encapsulated as the university grounds were, it was easy to forget the bustle of downtown Chicago honking and clattering just beyond its borders. Sometimes if Sam let herself think about it—about how far she had come in the last six months—it gave her a dizzying feeling like she'd shot up into the atmosphere.

But a familiar voice rebounding out of the darkness brought her plummeting right back down to earth. Joana and Bennett heard it as well, all three of them pausing under an electric lamp to frown at the slightly slurred, boasting tone.

". . . you shoulda seen it, Evie girl," said the voice with a snicker. "I thought she'da cried right there on the spot. Figured they made them out of sterner stuff in the cow pastures or wherever she's from."

"Chapin," Joana said, her face screwing up as if she'd just bit into a rotten piece of fruit.

Sam went rigid, and Bennett's grip on her waist tightened. "Let's cut through the grass here," he said in a low tone.

But it was too late, for they had been made standing under the lamplight like that. Theodore Chapin came swaggering into view, a young woman tucked under his arm. She had soft brown curls and a pinched expression, like she was half-crushed trying to support his bulk.

"Speaka the devil," Theo slurred, grinning stupidly at Sam. "Aw, look at her, Evie girl. She's still twisted over it."

"Go chase yourself, Chapin," Joana said, setting her bare feet apart like she was about to charge.

Theo sneered at her. "What are you gonna do, Jo, blow me over with a kiss?"

"Right in the kisser," Joana said, holding up her free hand in a fist.

"That's enough, both of you," Bennett said, using the same tone his father used when conducting his business. "Chapin, you're drunk. Go sleep it off somewhere, and I'll walk Evelyn home with the girls."

"Don't you lay a hand on my girl," Theo snarled.

"Theo, please," said Evelyn, grunting as she tried to keep him from lunging for Bennett. "I can walk back with Sam and Jo. It's no problem. We're in the same dorm after all."

"Yeah, only because Daddy Steeling picked up the tab for the two of them," Theo said. "The three-a them. Think what a brain like mine coulda done with that kind of bread."

"Rot," Joana said succinctly.

Theo bared his teeth at her. "Says the princess in her brand-new dress."

Joana's expression turned hot. "Let me get one good swing in," she said, stepping forward. Only Bennett's hand on her arm pulled her back.

"Don't lose your gold star on his account," Bennett said. "Evelyn, will you be all right?"

"You don't need to ask her nothing," Theo slurred, but Evelyn nodded.

"I'll be all right," she said softly, giving a grateful smile to Bennett. She turned her face up to Theo, her expression so pleading it made Sam's hands ball up into fists. "Theo, don't you think you might want to get some air before you walk back to your place? The campus really is its loveliest at night. And the dorm is only right over there."

"You just wanna walk with *him*, don't you?" Theo growled.

Evelyn blushed, but her expression didn't change. "Of course not, Theo. You're the only one I've got eyes for. Promise. I'm only thinking of you. You know how much you like the walk past the Classics building."

Theo attempted to straighten up, weaving slightly as he did so. "I'll be in charge of the whole place one day, you mark it, Evie girl."

"I know you will," Evelyn said soothingly, petting his arm as if he were a caged dog and not a man.

"Spoken like one of Atchinson's sycophants," Joana muttered.

Theo's eyes homed in on her, a sneer creasing his upper lip. "At least I'll have an advisor come autumn. Where do you think princesses like you go when their money won't stretch no further?"

"Theo, why don't you walk?" Evelyn said. "I'll be fine, really I will. Go on."

Theo eyed Bennett as if he might try to snatch Evelyn there and then, despite Bennett's arm secured around Sam's waist. Bennett gave no more indication of his attention than a soft sigh, and Sam had never loved him more. Finally, Theo snorted, dragging his arm off Evelyn's shoulder and staggering to the edge of the light.

"I'll come check on you in the morning, Evie girl," he said, making it sound like a threat.

"Good night, Theo," Evelyn said with a little wave. When he was out of earshot, her shoulders rose and pulled back.

"I don't know how you stand him, Evelyn, really I don't," Joana said. "He must be the worst kind of boyfriend, and I ought to know about the worst. Boys with more spit than shine."

"He's not so bad when it's just the two of us," Evelyn said, folding her hands together. "He's like my father was. Too much emotion and not enough body to hold it, my mother always said."

Joana surveyed the broad expanse of Theo's retreating shoulders. "I don't know how much more body his bones could possibly stand. He's enough for the three of us put together."

"Don't let him get to you," Evelyn said, turning to Sam. "Theo told me what happened with Professor Atchinson. I'm so sorry, Sam. If I'd have known he would do that, I never would have told you about the position in the first place."

"You were only trying to help when you did," Sam said. "I'm still grateful you even spoke to me that day. Most of Atchinson's graduate students act as if I've got the pox or something. It's not your fault he pulled the rug out from under me."

"Professor Atchinson is a brilliant man," Evelyn said, earning a snort from Joana. "I think sometimes he forgets everyone else has a brain, too, and he doesn't like being reminded of it. It's why Professor Wallstone infuriates him so much. They came up together at Oxford, you know, along with Sir Arthur Evans. I think Atchinson is looking for his own Knossos to make his name."

"Oh hell," Bennett breathed out suddenly.

Sam looked up in alarm. "What is it? What's wrong?"

"The competency hearing," Bennett said, pinching the bridge of his nose. "Between finals and meeting you out at the Mill, I completely forgot about it. Atchinson insisted that Professor Wallstone be subjected to a competency hearing before he's allowed to return to teach next semester. He's got to submit his paperwork for consideration by the end of the semester, but I left it in the office."

"But that's . . . today," Sam said.

"I'll have to go to his office and get it tonight," Bennett said, shaking off the fatigue. "You girls can make it back to the dorm on your own from here, can't you?"

"Of course not," Sam said. "I'll go with you."

"Sam," Bennett said with a slight frown. "It's already late, and—"

"You're wasting time arguing with me about it," Sam said firmly. "It'll help Wallstone and rankle Professor Atchinson at the same time. You can't rob me of such an opportunity."

"Well, I'm not walking home alone," Joana said before glancing at Evelyn. "No offense."

"None taken," Evelyn said, though she looked a little smaller when she said it.

"It's not a picnic at the park," Bennett said, but Sam could already tell he was capitulating in the way he checked his watch and glanced around. "I really do need to hurry if I'm going to get it returned to the dean's office."

"Shake a leg and get the lead out, then, brother," said Joana, linking her arm through Sam's and dragging her down the sidewalk.

"I love your enthusiasm, Jo, but the Classics building is in the opposite direction," Sam said, suppressing a smile.

Joana did a quick pivot, wincing as she did so. "Forgot I didn't have shoes on. I did say I hated the stockings."

"Evelyn, we can drop you off at the hall on our way there," Bennett said, holding out a hand cordially.

Evelyn blushed, walking along with them. "It's really all right, I can find my way back myself. I do it often enough, even though Theo likes to play the protector."

"Is that what he was playing?" Joana muttered.

"It's no trouble, really," Bennett said as they walked. "I wouldn't be comfortable leaving you out here alone."

"That's very kind of you," Evelyn said shyly.

"Bennett is a true gentleman," Sam said, giving him a smile over her shoulder, one he returned in full force.

"Hot looks," Joana said in a stage whisper.

"What was that?" Bennett asked as Sam flushed a deep red.

"Nothing," Sam said firmly, doubling her pace toward Foster Hall and the Classics building looming just beyond it in the dark.

CHAPTER FOUR

"It looks like somebody beat us here and tossed the place," Joana said, surveying the perilously stacked piles of books leaning against furniture left at random locations throughout the office. One wingback chair sat right in the middle of the space, as if someone had started across the room with the intention of relocating it and forgotten their purpose halfway across the carpet. There was even a plate with a sandwich resting on top of a pile of folders on the desk, looking for all the world as if it had been petrified.

"No, I'm afraid it's always like this." Bennett sighed, picking his way through the chaos with a speed that made it clear he'd had to traverse that same path many times before. "The professor refuses to let the cleaning staff in his office because he's convinced they will—and I directly quote—'muck it all up.'"

Joana snorted. "The place is certainly an apt expression of old Wallstone."

"I left the paperwork on his desk," Bennett said. "You two can just wait there, and we'll be out in a minute."

"How was the professor the last time you saw him?" Sam asked, gently lifting an open book from the top of a stack and closing it to preserve its spine. It had been six months since she last repaired a book, but that didn't make them any less precious to her.

"He is in and out," Bennett said, thumbing through what looked like a stack of exams. "Some days his mind seems focused and present—well, as present as it ever was—and other days it's like he's lost in the fog. Last month when I visited him in the facility, he had smuggled a blackboard in during lunch and was giving a speech on Doric versus Ionic pillars to the residents. He seemed genuinely surprised when I told him it was a cafeteria and not a lecture hall. Sometimes I worry he'll never shake what happened to him in Dublin."

"Poor Professor Wallstone," Sam murmured, a chill overcoming her when she thought of their adventures through the Dublin Mountains. Best to leave such things in the past and forge on with a more promising future.

Well, what was once a more promising future before Professor Atchinson dumped a cold cup of bitter coffee all over it. But she would make it promising again, somehow.

"I for one would be far more amenable to a lecture on columns if it came with lunch," Joana said, picking her way over to a chair stacked with letters and packages and shoving them to the floor to make room for herself.

"Jo," Bennett said, his tone censuring. "Try not to—"

"What?" Joana interrupted, sinking down into the leather and closing her eyes. "Muck up the place?"

"The professor will return," Bennett said. "Eventually. And I'd like to keep everything as it was for when he gets back."

Sam frowned at the cascade Joana had caused on the floor, squatting down to retrieve an envelope that had skated close to her stockinged feet. "This letter is postmarked two months ago, and it's unopened."

Bennett sighed. "The professor still gets a healthy amount of mail from colleagues and amateurs seeking his insight on all kinds of things. People believing they've cracked Linear B, farmers who dug up strange bones in their back fields wanting him to come do an excavation, things like that. I did my best to keep up with it at the beginning of the semester, but there was too much. I tried to open any urgent-looking mail, but with final exams, I've been swamped myself this past month."

Sam sifted through the pile, the stamps and far-fetched mail addresses reminiscent of her time receiving books at the antique shop. She began to sort them on instinct, pulling together a large pile and putting them in chronological order. Any that looked more official—such as the ones that came from other professors at other universities—she put aside in a separate pile. She had made progress on her two tidy stacks when Bennett raised his hand triumphantly at the desk.

"Found it," he proclaimed, giving it a little wave. "I'll just slip it under the dean's door and walk you girls back to your room."

"At this point, you're going to have to carry me," Joana murmured, nestling deeper into the chair.

"Sam, what are you doing?" Bennett asked, picking his way across the room to crouch beside her.

"Organizing the professor's mail," Sam said absently, putting a letter from Brooklyn College in the "personal/important" correspondence pile.

"You don't have to do that," Bennett said, but he reached for another pile and sat beside her, intuiting her sorting method and joining in. They worked in relative quiet for a few moments, only the soft slide of paper and their breathing filling the quiet space. And then, slightly louder, Joana's snoring.

"I thought she'd aged out of that," Bennett said, glancing up at her.

Sam smiled. "I've got a pair of wax-coated cotton balls back in our room. It's the only way I get any sleep."

Bennett chuckled softly, leaning over her to place a letter in the important pile. The brief brush of his jacket against her shoulder sent her thoughts skittering in all directions, and it took five read-throughs to figure out where the letter in her hand should go.

"I really am proud of you, Sam," Bennett said quietly. "Not at all surprised, though. I've known you could do anything you put your mind to since the treasure-hunt days back home. This business with the summer field school is just a setback. I envision plenty of field schools in your future, so many you'll be sick of the dirt and digging."

Sam smiled. "I wouldn't make much of an archaeologist if that were the case, would I?" She sighed, letting the stack of letters in her hand drop to her lap. "It's not just Atchinson, I think. It's everyone. Everyone has heard some rumor about what happened in Dublin, and why we were there, each one more outlandish than the last."

"I don't think Jo is helping that any," Bennett said. "I'm positive she's started half of them."

Sam's mouth quirked to the side. "Her rumors are at least entertaining. It's everyone else who thinks I'm . . . I'm just a treasure hunter, or a gold seeker, or a foolish amateur with stars in my eyes. I worked so hard to get here, and I've worked so hard since I came here, but people have already made up their minds about me over something I can't control. It's not as if we can tell anyone what really happened in Dublin with Phillip. But without the truth, people have invited themselves to fabricate the details. How am I supposed to make these people my colleagues, much less my friends, if they choose to believe such lies about me?"

Bennett lowered his own stack of letters, reaching out with one hand to rub her knee affectionately. "If anyone could win over their detractors, I would put my money on you. They don't know the real you, not yet. When they do, they'll wonder why they wasted time believing anything else."

Sam smiled at him hopefully, the friction of his hand against her bare knee like a tonic. She laid her own hand over his, trapping his fingers against her skin. "Do you think so?"

"Of course I do, otherwise I wouldn't have said it," Bennett said, drawing his hand back with a flush. "Now come on, we can't spend our whole evening sorting mail. Let's get you girls back to the Hall."

Sam's gaze drifted down to the stack of letters still left in Bennett's lap, her instinct to leave the place tidier than when she came battling against her fatigue. But there was a letter sticking out from the pile, the address catching her eye even in the dim light. She plucked the letter loose from the stack, squinting to make out the full name on the return address. She sucked in a soft breath, her exhaustion evaporating like a mist.

"Bennett," she said, adrenaline pumping through her system. "This letter is from Crete."

Bennett leaned forward, glancing at the address. "That's not all that unusual. Like I said, he gets letters from amateurs across the globe seeking his expertise."

But Sam shook her head. "No, this letter is from Hector Killeen."

Bennett drew back in surprise. "The director of the Heraklion Archaeological Museum? Why would he send the professor a letter?"

"I don't know, but it's postmarked three weeks ago. Bennett, this could be important! We need to open it."

Bennett shook his head. "I'm sure it's just a question about some new artifact. I'll take it along with the other important letters next time I visit Wallstone."

He reached for the envelope, but Sam pulled it away. "Bennett, this isn't some associate professor or a clerk at the museum. This is *the* Mr. Killeen, director of the greatest collection of Minoan artifacts in the known world! Do you think he would waste his time sending letters on trivial matters?"

"I wouldn't begin to know how he conducts his affairs," said Bennett, bemused. "If you think it's that urgent, I'll make a trip to visit Wallstone first thing tomorrow."

Sam sighed, struggling to keep her patience while trying to make Bennett see the importance of this letter. "It's already three weeks old. What if Mr. Killeen needed something immediately, and it's just been moldering away here on the professor's floor?"

"Technically it was in a chair," Bennett muttered. "And it's already gone three weeks. What's one day more?"

"Exactly, one day more that he does not have the answer to whatever problem plagues him," Sam said, already sliding her index finger under the flap. "And you said it yourself, the professor has good days and bad. There's no guarantee tomorrow will fall under the good column . . . er, pardon the pun. What I mean is, it would be most helpful for all involved if we look at the letter and assess its importance for ourselves. It could be a small matter that we can help him with; no need to trouble Professor Wallstone."

Bennett hesitated, the look he gave her long and heavy. "Sam, are you sure this isn't—"

"We'll just open the letter and check," Sam said hastily, ripping through the top of the envelope before Bennett could come up with any additional arguments. A single sheet of paper had been tri-folded within, covered in a tight but neat handwriting. Sam unfolded the paper, and a small photograph fell out, dark and blurry in the dim lamplight. Bennett picked up the photo as Sam read the short letter out loud.

"'Dear Barnaby Wallstone, I write to you out of a great sense of frustration and urgency. I have discovered something I believe to be of great significance—indeed, a discovery that could reshape the very foundation of what we currently know about the Minoan civilization. I seek to protect and preserve it for future generations, but there are those who seek it only for the fortune and notoriety it could bring. I entreat you to lend your noted expertise on iconography and lost languages to further my cause before these men can desecrate it.

"'As part of my duties as director of the museum, I often investigate claims of found caches of antiquities. Many are identified as frauds, shysters seeking a quick payday. But there have long been rumors about a cave here on the island, a place called Skotino cave. Or Agia Paraskevi, as the locals call it, after a church built above the cave that was dedicated to the saint Paraskevi. The church was constructed in the late 1800s, but the cave has had a reputation for religious observance that stretches back to the Bronze Age. It has been linked to the goddess Britomartis.

"'I made my routine inspection, expecting to find no more than trinkets or baubles. But what I found instead exceeded all expectations. Deep in the recesses of the cave was a symbol, etched into the wall, that has defied all my attempts at intuiting its meaning, but that I am sure indicates something of great significance. It is only after months of attempting to decipher its secrets on my own that I reach out to you in desperation, for you are certainly known for your more unorthodox approach to the rigors of due process in our field.'"

Bennett grunted, interrupting her. "He must be talking about the article Professor Wallstone wrote, criticizing Sir Arthur for keeping the Linear B tablets under lock and key and not allowing anyone else to examine them to attempt to decipher the language."

"If I recall, that didn't earn him any friends in Sir Arthur's camp," Sam said. "That must be why Mr. Killeen wrote this letter, rather than reach out through more official means. Look here, he even indicated that Professor Wallstone send his reply to a different address than the museum."

Sam scanned the remaining contents of the letter, her breath catching in her throat. "Oh, Bennett. I think Mr. Killeen's life might be in danger."

CHAPTER FIVE

"**W**hat do you mean?" Bennett asked, his back going ramrod straight.

"Listen to this last part of the letter. 'I am afraid I must press you for a swift reply if I am to protect whatever it is the symbol hides. This area of the country is rife with looters, treasure hunters seeking their black-market wares in the statues and relics they recover from caves and shrines. There is one group of vicious men in particular who have set their sights on Skotino cave. They have already done extensive damage to potential archaeological remains in their search for treasure. Should they become aware of my discovery and uncover the symbol's secret, any hope I have of protecting the artifacts will be lost in a haze of dynamite and malice. They have already threatened me once, and I shudder to think what they might attempt should I make the discovery too late. Please, Mr. Wallstone, do send your thoughts posthaste so that I might preserve the past and protect the future. Sincerely, Hector Killeen.'"

"That certainly doesn't sound good," Bennett hedged, glancing down at the photograph in his hand. "Though I don't know how we could help him."

"We need to figure out what that symbol means," Sam said, tucking the letter away and reaching for the photograph.

"That's easier said than done," Bennett said, handing over the small square of glossy paper. "The quality is blurry and grainy at best, and I can barely see anything."

Sam rose from her sitting position, shaking out the pins and needles in her legs as she headed for the desk. She laid the photograph beneath the lamp there, squinting as if that might turn the shadows and blurred lines into something more legible. The symbol appeared to have three parts, as near as Sam could tell. A labrys—a double-headed axe ubiquitous in Minoan symbology— etched vertically at the top of the symbol. Below it was a pair of horns—the horns of consecration, as Sir Arthur Evans had coined them in his discovery of the palace of Knossos. Symbolic of the importance of bulls in Minoan society, included in sacrifices and bull leaping as depicted in their frescoes. All routine symbology in most Minoan sites of worship, even if it was exciting to see it so intimately.

But the most striking thing about the symbol was an elaborately carved snake curled in a figure eight around the horns of consecration. It was obvious, even in the poor rendering of the photograph, that every scale had been painstakingly crafted, the head rearing up in front of the handle of the labrys with fangs bared. There were snakes in Minoan hieroglyphics, to be sure, but they were usually no more than a squiggle of lines, a suggestion of a head or a tiny forked tongue. This snake was intricately chiseled, detailed and etched with reverent care. Even through the shadowy under- exposure of the film, it almost seemed to glow. It was so lifelike, as Sam leaned in closer to examine its head, that if it had flicked out its tongue she might not have even been surprised.

"This is extraordinary, Bennett," Sam said, holding the photo closer to the lamplight. "A terrible photo, to be sure, but I suppose that's what comes of taking a picture in a dark cave when one's life is in danger."

"I've certainly not seen anything like it," Bennett said, leaning over the edge of the desk. "Mr. Killeen was right to contact Professor Wallstone, though I'm afraid he might not be much help in his current state. Still, I could take the photo to him tomorrow, see if it might shake something loose from the fog."

Sam squinted harder and tilted her head to the side, something about the angle and shape of the snake's tongue—blessedly stationary—catching her attention. The half glass of gin and the yellow of the light conspired to make her head ache, but she pushed both annoyances aside.

"Bennett, the professor wouldn't happen to have a magnifying glass anywhere abouts, would he?" Sam asked. "I think there's something odd with the tongue here, but I can't quite make it out."

Bennett looked around the mess with a slightly bewildered expression. "I'll see what I can dig up."

It took several minutes and more than one toppled stack of books—the racket eliciting a mumbled complaint from Joana before she shifted position in her chair and promptly dropped back into sleep—but Bennett managed to find a highly decorated magnifying glass from what Sam suspected was the king of Egypt. She held the glass over the photograph as Bennett crowded in beside her, his presence a delicious distraction.

"What is it?" he asked, the warmth of his breath on the back of her neck doing nothing to help her concentration.

"I'm not sure it's anything," she murmured. She pulled the reading lamp closer and tilted it toward the picture while holding the glass a few inches above the photograph. "There's something odd about the tongue, I think. Look, see there? The end of the tongue. It should be forked, but it's—"

"Not," Bennett finished, leaning in closer and once again distracting her with his scent of fresh paper and ink and soap. Even after six months of dating, she still reveled in these little stolen moments. She took in a deep breath, which earned her a strange look from Bennett.

Sam flushed, quickly returning her attention to the tongue. "Look, the split in the tongue should be along the front, making it a traditional fork shape. But this one, the splits are on the side, the reverse of a fork tongue. It almost looks like . . ."

Bennett took in a sharp breath. "An arrow."

Sam tapped the picture, straightening in her excitement and nearly bashing Bennett on the nose. Luckily, he had plenty of experience with Sam's breakthrough moments and managed to step out of the way to avoid disaster.

"That is not just a symbol," Sam said confidently, a buzzing starting in the back of her teeth that made her breath come quick and light and her chest tighten with excitement. "That is a clue. We need to find where that arrow is pointing."

"You mean Mr. Killeen needs to find where that arrow is pointing," Bennett said, crossing his arms on a frown.

"Bennett, do you know how long a letter would take to reach Mr. Killeen at this point? When this one has already been collecting dust for the past three weeks on Professor Wallstone's floor?"

"About as long as it would take a person to travel there as well," Bennett said dryly. "Sam, I can feel the argument you're working up to, and the answer is absolutely not."

"Bennett, look at this!" Sam said, picking up the picture and waving it in his face. "A hidden symbol buried in an ancient cave used by the Minoans as a place of worship? The potential for a discovery of a *lifetime*, the kind of discovery that could put us on the front page of newspapers and make us star lecturers instead of social pariahs. And you want to send a *letter*."

Bennett's expression did not improve over the course of Sam's speech. "I'm not interested in archaeology for the front page of the newspaper, and I didn't think you were either."

"Of course I'm not," Sam said, stung more than she was willing to let on by his implication. "But you must admit, a bit of flash and attention brings in the donors. Donors like your father, who make this education possible for the both of us."

"Sam, what you're suggesting is madness. We can't go to Crete. Mr. Killeen wasn't even writing to us! He was seeking Professor Wallstone's expertise."

"And the professor is currently three puddings and a chalkboard deep into his recovery," Sam countered. "Besides, he's not the one who spotted the arrow. I am. And if I found that, I could help Mr. Killeen find whatever it is the arrow is hiding. You know I can, Bennett."

"I know you *can*, but that doesn't mean you *should*."

"Why not?" Sam reasoned. "Just think of it. What if we discover something? Really discover something great, something that changes what we know about Minoan civilization. Think what it will do for us, for the field of archaeology! Isn't that what drew us to this course of study in the first place? The promise of a discovery that would change the world?"

"Last time we discovered something, it nearly *ended* the world," Bennett pointed out.

"Are you going to let that keep you from ever seeking adventure again?" Sam asked.

Bennett's brows drew down defensively. "No, of course not. But

I will let it teach me to take more than a minute to decide to travel halfway across the world on a whim. And did you miss the part where Mr. Killeen said dangerous men were after the same thing? When you got tangled up with dangerous men previously, it cost my father a bookshop and it cost someone else their life. *You* might be cavalier with it, but I'm certainly not."

Sam sucked in a breath, coughing unexpectedly when it felt like something caught in the back of her throat. Something that tasted of ash and carbon, that singed her throat like it had been only yesterday when she felt the hot press of those flames trapping her inside the bookshop. But Sam had survived those dangerous men, and she had stopped the end of the world before. And she would be damned if she let it hold her back like her fear of the world after her father's death had held her back for so many years. She came to the university to make change, not to cower at the first sign of opposition.

"It is precisely because of those dangerous men that I believe Mr. Killeen needs our help," Sam said finally, when she had regained her breath. "If he were to have figured out the mystery of the symbol, he would have done so long before sending this letter off to Professor Wallstone. He might be the greatest authority of Minoan artifacts in the world, but he's not a code breaker. What if there are other symbols that require deciphering? What if there are greater obstacles within the cave? What if those dangerous men discover it first? I thought you got into archaeology to preserve and learn from the past, to protect it from robbers just like these men."

"You know I did," Bennett says begrudgingly. "That doesn't mean I agree with this ludicrous plan. I think this has far more to do with Professor Atchinson's summer field school at Knossos, and showing him up as revenge for not including you on the trip."

"It does not!" Sam said, a little too sharply. Bennett's only response was a slight crease in his forehead as he raised his eyebrows, but he had the good sense not to press it further. "Would it bring me a great deal of satisfaction to see the look on the man's face when we announce the discovery of whatever is hidden in that cave? Well, I would have to be a stone-cold statue to say it wouldn't. But that's not why I'm suggesting we go. I'm suggesting we go because this is exactly why we're here, isn't it?"

Bennett leaned back against a bookshelf, pressing his fingers to the bridge of his nose. "Even if I . . . *considered* such a ludicrous idea as going to Crete, there are more practical matters to consider. Securing passage across the Atlantic, for one. Accommodations once we get there. Visas to secure. Planning a trip like this can take months, Sam. You can't just gallivant off at the drop of a hat. There are costs."

"Costs that your sister has assured me your father would be pleased as punch to cover," Sam reasoned.

Bennett cocked his head, giving her a sardonic look. "If you tell my father about this, he'll book passage for himself first."

That was . . . a valid point. "Well, then we just won't mention the photograph bit. We'll tell him . . . we'll tell him Mr. Killeen invited us, personally. As students of Professor Wallstone. If anyone can make a rush order of tickets and papers, it's your father."

"I don't know, Sam," Bennett said, shaking his head. "This feels like Dublin all over again, heading off pell-mell into unknown dangers against my logical protests of caution. Mr. Killeen won't be expecting us, and we only know the man by reputation besides. And who are these men after the same thing? I can't in good conscience send you and my sister into such a situation with so many unknowns."

Sam had to admit, when he put it like that, it did sound a bit . . . impetuous. But then she remembered the sneer on Theodore Chapin's face when Professor Atchinson told her there was no budget to include her on the summer field school. And she remembered the hot slide of shame that sat in her stomach like a lead weight when the professor told her that people like her didn't belong in the field.

She would show them. She would make a discovery so great, they would be begging her to join their study groups and field schools.

"Bennett, this could lead to something extraordinary," Sam said, her voice soft and inexorable. "Something we could actually *tell* the world about, unlike Dublin. Don't you want to be part of that?"

Bennett's nostrils flared on a deep inhale, but he didn't protest. "I just don't want to see you or Jo get hurt again. I almost lost you both once, Sam. I can't let that happen again."

"I know, Bennett, and I understand," Sam said. "But this won't be like the last time. I promise."

It wasn't a promise she could make or keep, but that hardly mattered now. She was so close, she could feel it in the soft bend of his head toward hers.

"This is a bad idea," he said. "I shouldn't let you go, much less agree to go myself."

"But?" Sam said hopefully.

"I know I can't keep you from going, short of locking you up," Bennett said. "And considering your history, even that isn't a guarantee that you'll stay put. And lord knows Joana won't keep you safe. They don't even have Prohibition there. Someone has to keep the two of you from disaster."

Sam gave him a brilliant smile, feeling the electric spark of a new adventure all the way down in her sore toes. "I'll wake Joana and get started. She'll want an entire new wardrobe for the trip. Thank you, Bennett. You won't regret this."

But Bennett could only sigh. "Seeing as I already do, that's not possible. I hope you know what you're doing, Sam."

"Of course I do," Sam said, filled with the confidence of ignorance. "It'll be fantastic, you'll see."

CHAPTER SIX

"**S**teerage class?" Joana hissed at her brother as they walked up the gangway to the massive steamer waiting at the docks in New York City. "You booked us in steerage class?"

Bennett spread his hands, nodding to the thick smokestacks that belched black plumes into the bright blue sky of a June morning. "It was the best I could do on such short notice, and we were lucky to get those tickets. The *Mauretania* is a smaller vessel than the *Olympic* we took to Dublin and has fewer staterooms. Steamers book up months in advance, and as we planned this trip with less than a week to spare . . ."

"But steerage class," Joana said, looking up in horror. "Why didn't you just ask if there were any positions shoveling coal in the boiler room?"

"I would have if I thought you had the discipline."

"Steerage will be fine!" Sam piped in, anxious to move on from any lingering doubts Bennett harbored. They reached the main deck of the ship, the narrow crush of the gangway opening out to the wooden boards as the crew directed passengers to their decks. "I'm just happy to be on a different ship this go-round. And I hear the portholes on the *Mauretania* are too small to fit a body through, so that works in my favor as well."

She said it to be lighthearted and funny, but all their expressions soured at the memory of the last time they took a transatlantic trip together. Sure, the stateroom on the RMS *Olympic* had been grand, the smoking rooms and dining halls the height of elegance. But Sam had also been forced to escape through the porthole window of that stateroom to avoid intruders and nearly gotten herself dumped in the freezing ocean for it. It was only by falling into a friend's room that she had been saved from a resting place in Davy Jones's locker. A friend who . . .

Sam shook off thoughts of Dublin, determined that they would face no such tribulations this time. "I plan on spending the majority of the trip studying up on Minoan symbology and hieroglyphics, personally. And, Jo, you'll still have access to all the bars on board, won't you?"

"I'll certainly need it," Joana muttered, glaring at her brother as they reached the stairs leading to the lower decks. "Steerage class, what a brute."

"Glad you're handling it well, Jo," Bennett said dryly.

Sam thought the accommodations on the lower deck were quaint, if a bit tighter than their last trip. There was a common area for taking meals or cigarette breaks, and each door led directly off the main area. Joana found their room number and swung the door open, her expression twisting up in disgust.

"Bunk beds," she said, like they'd just personally insulted her. "As if we were participating in some kind of sleepaway camp. Bennett, I swear, if we run into anyone we know on this trip, I'm chucking you overboard. Anna Marie Duncan would love nothing more than to have my head on a pike outside her town house, and this would be just the cut direct to hand it to her on a silver platter."

"I thought you declared Anna Marie to be a puff with all the cream squeezed out and you wanted nothing more to do with her," Bennett said, stopping at his own room.

"Of course I don't, she's a chicken with all the bones stripped out," Joana replied. "But that doesn't mean I want to give her any ammunition to spit at me over watered-down lemonade at Mama's next interminable party."

"The bunk beds will be fine," Sam said, laying a hand on Joana's arm. "They could even be a bit of fun, like when I used to stay over at the Manor during a treasure hunt. I'll take the top bunk."

"Obviously," Joana said, giving her a bewildered look. "I wouldn't disgrace myself by climbing a tiny ladder to sleep."

"Let's just get settled into our rooms, shall we?" Bennett said, already sounding tired. "I'm sure with a few gin cocktails and some decent food in your belly, you'll be far more amenable to our accommodations."

"That's a bet I'll take and you'll lose," Joana muttered.

But before they could squeeze themselves into their shared room, a shadow fell over Sam and Joana. "What in hell are you two doing here?"

Sam did her best to smother the groan in the back of her throat, but some of it leaked out through her pressed lips. "Theo Chapin," she said, glancing up at his looming bulk.

"Master Chapin, what is the delay?" came Professor Atchinson's voice down the narrow stairs leading to the common area. "You're blocking the walkway and holding up the class."

Theo crossed his arms over his chest, stepping to the side without breaking his glower. "You're going to want to see this, Professor."

Sam sighed, looking heavenward for patience but meeting only the plain white ceiling. She knew there was a possibility of being on the same departure as Professor Atchinson's field school, but she had hoped the ship would be large enough to avoid direct contact with them. Well, best to tear off the bandage clean.

"Hello, Professor Atchinson," Sam said, trying to muster a tone of nonchalance.

"Miss Knox?" the professor said, shock making his mouth go slack. "What do you think you're doing here?"

"Isn't that part obvious, Professor?" said Theo. "The deluded girl thinks she's going to sneak onto the field school roster."

"I do not!" Sam protested. "That's not what we're doing here at all."

"Really, Miss Knox, this is beyond the pale," Professor Atchinson said, frowning severely. "You will explain yourself and your presence this instant, or I will be forced to report you to the university board for this little stunt."

More students descended the stairs behind him, including Evelyn, crowding the small common area with wide eyes and whispered comments behind their hands. They weren't the same students who had been there when Professor Atchinson humiliated Sam on the first day of class and forced her to leave his lecture, but she felt the same clench of panic in her gut, the same prickles along the back of her neck as the opinions and rumors swirled. Like a Greek chorus, come to witness her demise.

"I . . . There was a letter, and we noticed . . ." Sam swallowed, so loud that several students close by snickered at the sound.

"We were invited," Joana said brashly, always to her rescue. "By somebody named Killeen, who I gather is a bigwig on Crete."

"Hector Killeen invited you?" Professor Atchinson scoffed. "I very much doubt that."

"It's true, Professor Atchinson," Bennett said, coming to stand beside his sister. "Well, mostly true. Mr. Killeen wrote to Professor

Wallstone about a bit of symbology he couldn't decipher, but it was Sam who figured it out. And since Professor Wallstone is still convalescing, we're traveling there now to share our findings."

The professor had been less "convalescing" and more "accusing his roommate of stealing his stash of cafeteria puddings that he himself had stolen" when they brought him the letter from Hector Killeen. But Sam figured that part was best left out of the current conversation.

Professor Atchinson sniffed. "And where is this letter now, Master Steeling?"

"We left it in Chicago," Sam said quickly, before Bennett could answer with the truth that he had stored it in his luggage. He gave her a look of mild confusion, but she shook her head once. "So Professor Wallstone could review it and confirm our . . . er, my findings."

Professor Atchinson looked at her sharply, making the prickle along the back of her neck turn into a full sweat. He swiveled his gaze to Bennett, still just as piercing.

"Is that true, Master Steeling?" he asked.

Bennett hesitated, glancing once again at Sam, but all she could do was beg him with her eyes. She didn't want Professor Atchinson swooping in and stealing her chance before she even met Mr. Killeen and made her case for her findings. Bennett took a deep breath, and Sam teetered on the edge of disaster.

"Yes, it's true, Professor," Bennett said, the barest hint of disappointment seeping into his tone. Sam breathed a sigh of relief.

"You don't really believe that claptrap, do you, Professor?" Theo asked, still spoiling for a scene.

"What I believe remains to be seen," the professor said. He looked to Bennett once more with a sniff. "Master Steeling, I trust that you will keep these girls out of the way of my graduate students? They have worked hard and followed protocol to earn their place here, and I will have nothing derail their studies."

"I understand," Bennett said with a nod.

"So you will vouch for these girls and promise to keep them away from our field school activities and Sir Arthur's celebrations for the twenty-fifth anniversary?"

"Of course," Bennett said.

Joana made a gurgling noise in the back of her throat, her eyes narrowing to slits. But Bennett stepped in front of her, effectively elbowing her into her open room and stepping inside to keep her from leaping out in attack. Professor Atchinson leaned close to Sam so that only she could hear, lowering his voice to a menacing whisper.

"I shall hope, for your sake, Miss Knox, that I do not catch another glimpse of you on this boat or the island of Crete. Are we understood?"

Sam nodded tightly, clamping her back teeth hard to keep everything she wanted to say from burbling up. The professor stood back, waving his students to their rooms. They began to dissipate after it became clear there would be no further scene. Only Evelyn remained, hovering near Sam.

"Is that really true?" she whispered, glancing over her shoulder to where Theo stood only a few feet away, imploring the professor to make an official reprimand against the three of them. "You don't have to worry about me saying anything to the professor or Theo if it is. I know you deserved to be on this trip, same as us, Sam."

"It *is* true," Sam insisted, feeling defensive despite Evelyn's friendly tone. "Mr. Killeen really did write a letter to the professor, and I really did figure out something he missed on the symbol. And we really are traveling there to help."

"I believe you," Evelyn said, nodding. Sam thought if she really did believe them, she wouldn't have to say so. "But Professor Atchinson will be on the warpath after this, you know. He's desperate to impress Sir Arthur, though he'd die before he said so. He's planned for this trip obsessively all semester. He believes this will be his chance to convince the university to give him more control in the department. He won't tolerate anything interfering with that."

"He won't have to worry about us," Bennett said, popping out of the room just long enough to take Sam by the elbow and draw her inside. The space was already tight, but with the three of them wedged in, there was hardly room to turn around. Joana crawled into the lower bunk as Bennett closed the door and turned the lock.

"The nerve of that man," Joana seethed, glaring like she could burn a hole through the wood. "Asking you if you would vouch for us, like we're some kind of rabble-rousers or stowaways."

"Well, you *are* freshmen in the college," Bennett reasoned.

"I don't think that is what he finds so irksome about us," Sam said, working her jaw side to side to relieve the tension that always seemed to build there whenever Atchinson was around. "I think he takes exception to having to give his attention to anyone who cannot further his ambitions."

"I'm sure that's not true," Bennett said. "He's only trying to protect his students."

"What is he trying to protect his students from?" Joana asked, throwing her hands wide and slapping both Sam and Bennett on the thigh in the confined space. "Is he trying to protect them from Sam? What, is he afraid she'll outsmart him and show him up to Sir Arthur?"

"It's all right, Jo," Sam said, suddenly so tired that all she wanted was to drag herself up those three rungs and land face-first on the mattress above. "Professor Atchinson can try to embarrass me all he wants. When we find what that symbol is pointing to, we'll see who's embarrassed then."

"That's my girl," Joana said proudly, giving Bennett a look like she dared him to contradict either of them.

Bennett only sighed. "I'm beginning to see why he made me vouch for the two of you. I've got to get settled in my room. Will you be able to stay out of trouble until dinner?"

"No promises, brother, you know the routine," Joana said.

"We'll be fine," Sam said. "Go."

Bennett hesitated at the door. "You *will* be fine, won't you?"

Sam held back the lurch of annoyance that rose up at the doubt in his tone. "No going out porthole windows or sabotaging graduate programs, I promise."

Bennett nodded, hesitating only a moment more before disappearing through the door and closing it again. As Joana raged on about the nerve of Professor Atchinson, Sam set about wearily unpacking her meager belongings and stuffing them into the bureau situated beneath the small window. She wouldn't say so to Bennett or Joana, but the encounter with Professor Atchinson left her feeling more rattled than determined. All she could hope was that the symbol Mr. Killeen discovered really did lead to something profound, something so great the professor could no longer dismiss her. Because if it didn't, if it was a dead end, she feared her future in the field might be one as well.

CHAPTER SEVEN

S am had never cared for summer in Illinois, not in the hot stretch of endless fields of her hometown of Clement nor in the oppressive oven of the steel and glass of Chicago. The air turned people sluggish, the sun relentless in its pursuit as it bleached the blue out of the sky and the green out of the trees. The only relief from the heat had come in the form of the local watering hole in Clement, a site popular among the other schoolhouse children when they were young. But considering she had barely tolerated their presence in the schoolhouse, she had hardly wanted to extend their social interactions to the afternoon and evening hours. So she had spent months in a perpetual sweat, waiting for the cool relief of the first breath of autumn.

But summer on the Mediterranean was a *revelation*. Sam stood at the railing of the ferry carrying them from mainland Greece to its largest island, Crete, home of the great Minoan palace of Knossos. The heat was no less present here, but instead of feeling like a punishment, it came as more of an invitation. An invitation into the emerald-and-topaz waters of the sea, an invitation to shuck the heavy wool skirts and button-down shirts of her usual wardrobe for the lighter linen of the dresses she had seen throughout Greece when they first arrived. Every breath she took tasted of sun and sea salt, as rich and complex as the olive oil the country was famous for.

"I see now why your father has dedicated his attention to the classics," Sam said to Joana, who lounged against the railing beside her in a wide-brimmed hat and a sleeveless white dress that magnified the brilliance of the sun.

Joana smiled, tilting her head upward. "Beats the hell out of hiking sand dunes in the Valley of the Kings, wouldn't you think?"

"I imagine so," Sam said, doing the same as her friend and turning her face up to the welcoming kiss of the sun. "I could get used to this."

"I already am," Joana quipped. "Considering how many summer seasons Daddy has spent in Athens, I'm surprised he hasn't gotten Greek citizenship for the lot of us. It already feels like my second home. If we moved here permanently, I wouldn't weep too many tears in good-bye to blustery Chicago."

Crete rose up along the horizon like Atlantis climbing out of the sea, the mountains shrouded in mist and the beaches a blinding white wreathed in deep green. The port city of Heraklion dominated the center of the island in a kaleidoscope of colors. The brightly painted houses dotted the hillside as a massive stone fortress lurked along the coast.

"What is that?" Sam asked, pointing to the stone building that looked so out of place among the cheerful buildings perched above it.

"Koules Fortress," said Bennett, coming up behind her. "It was built by the Venetians who occupied Crete in the sixteenth century. They named it Rocca al Mare, which means 'sea fortress.' Brilliant builders, but not so creative in the naming department."

Sam slid a little closer as he leaned over the railing beside her, the calling of the seabirds overhead and the whip of the salt wind across her face feeling brighter and sharper than her existence back in Chicago. With the approaching city expanding along the horizon and the sun crisping her skin, she refused to give in to the apprehensions that had plagued her for the last week aboard the *Mauretania*. Back in Chicago, she might just be a washerwoman's daughter on scholarship, but out here in the wilds of the Cretan countryside, she could choose to be anyone she wanted to be. She could fashion herself into someone that the likes of Professor Atchinson could never dismiss so easily, and it all began with finding what that symbol led to.

The waters grew choppy as they pulled into port, the workers on the dock bustling to life as they caught ropes and guided the small ferry alongside a pier. The crew on the ferry pulled out the gangway and began directing the passengers off the small ship. Sam started toward the exit, but Bennett took her by the arm, holding her back.

"Let's let the other passengers off before we bother," he said, but he wouldn't quite meet her eye.

Sam didn't think there was much of a rush on their tiny ferry, but as soon as she spotted the group waiting to disembark, she realized what he actually meant. There was Professor Atchinson at the head, demanding that he and his students be let off first, as the highest-priority patrons.

"Why don't you just ask us to wait down in the hold with the luggage?" Joana said laconically, leaning against the railing.

"I'm just trying to avoid trouble before we even set foot on Cretan soil," Bennett said, exasperated. "Which would be a lot easier if you would cooperate instead of fighting me on every single thing."

"You basically held us hostage in that cramped little steerage-class cabin the last week," Joana said. "So you can understand if we're a little fevered."

"Sam, you get it, don't you?" Bennett asked. "It's not as if you want another confrontation with the professor, do you?"

"Of course not," Sam said, but she crossed her arms rather than taking the hand he proffered her. "And the matter is settled anyhow, since they're already off the ferry. I assume it's all right for us to disembark now. Or did you want to wait until they leave the harbor so there's no chance of our paths crossing?"

Bennett sighed. "I'll get the bags and meet you on the dock."

Sam felt a twist of guilt at the slouch in his shoulders as he departed, but she refused to let it make her feel bad for being upset. In her head, she knew Bennett was only trying to avoid any fights that could endanger their futures at the university, much less their expeditions here. But in her heart, she could only be hurt that it seemed Bennett took the professor's side every time they clashed. Why couldn't he see how unfairly Atchinson was treating her?

"Come on, Sam, maybe we can sneak in a quick shot of raki on the beach if we beat Bennett out of here," Joana said, taking her arm and steering her toward the gangway.

Sam made her way down to the rocky shore, the water lapping in gentle waves against the port, so close she could reach a hand down and scoop it up if she wanted. Bennett managed to wrangle their possessions before Joana could make a run for it and they headed into the city. As their car climbed into the twisted labyrinthine streets, they passed open-air cafés, partially hidden courtyards, brightly painted buildings with low-slung terra-cotta roofs, and street vendors selling everything from bottles of oil to raki, the local liquor made from crushed grape skins. They passed several street vendors selling trinkets inscribed with a mishmash of Linear B, Linear A, and Minoan hieroglyphics. Had Sam not been on a mission, she would have risked a dive-roll out of the car door to purchase a few of those trinkets for herself.

It took them more than a few wrong turns to locate the address provided by Mr. Killeen in his letter, but eventually they found their way to the outskirts of the city, the buildings spread farther apart and the yards filled with all manner of domesticated chickens and goats. They were far from the tourist center, and it showed in the cracked roof tiles, weathered paint, and rough patches of haphazard cobblestone giving way to dirt road.

"Your Mr. Killeen lives here?" Joana asked as they parked the car and walked the short stretch of road down to a small building. "I thought the antiquities business would have paid a prettier penny than this."

Bennett looked up at the house with a frown. "I have to say, I find myself in agreement with you. Surely Sir Arthur would have provided better accommodations for the man responsible for inspecting, repairing, and cataloging his findings at Knossos. Sam, are you sure we shouldn't seek him at the museum first?"

"He said the men would be watching the museum," Sam said, waving the letter at him as proof. "That's probably why he chose somewhere far out of the watchful eye of the city center. And anyway, I think it has a . . . unique charm. Not all of us grew up in a manor house."

Joana and Bennett exchanged a quiet look of surprise as Sam stepped up to the door, giving it a solid knock. She waited a moment, but when there was no answer, she knocked again louder.

"Mr. Killeen!" she called out. "Mr. Killeen, are you home?"

"Sam, if Mr. Killeen is in danger as his letter says, maybe we shouldn't be so loud about announcing that he's here?" Bennett suggested.

"Oh, you might be right," Sam said, chewing one corner of her lip in concern. She knocked again, her knuckles stinging from the insistence, but lowered her voice. "Mr. Killeen, are you there?"

"I don't think he is," Joana said. "Such a shame. Shall we hit a taverna now?"

"We could always check the museum as I suggested," Bennett said, glancing at his watch. "It is the middle of the day, the likelihood is high that he'll be there."

"I don't understand it, " Sam said, stepping back from the door and down to the street level. She looked up at the house in consternation. "He said to write him here, so why isn't he here?"

"Maybe he stepped out for a drink," Joana said. "Let's check all the local joints, just to be sure."

Sam had no intention of giving up, but she had to admit—if only to herself—that Bennett and Joana were right. Maybe they could travel to the cave on their own and search for the symbol, find what it was leading to, and bring the discovery back to Mr. Killeen. Or better, they could publish their findings in *Archaeological Digest*. She was sure Mr. Steeling could get them a full-page spread. She could see the title now: "Budding Archaeologist Discovers Find of the Century, Earns Her Place in History." She'd have it framed and hung up in her room.

"Sam?" Joana asked, tapping her on the shoulder. "What say you?"

"Say me about what?" Sam asked, still dreaming of what pose she would strike for the photographs.

"We've lost her in there," Joana said to Bennett.

Something off to the side caught Sam's attention, and she

hurried to catch a glimpse behind the house. Through the narrow gap between homes she could see down to the alley that ran behind them. Someone was there.

"Wait!" she called.

The man—who had presumably emerged from a back door, which she now realized she should have checked for—paused and glanced at the three of them in fear, a knapsack slung over one shoulder. Sam frowned at the odd picture he presented, a rather formal-looking man with a tidy mustache and light-brown hair just graying at the temples, his tweed suit well tailored if a bit worn around the cuffs and lapels.

"Mr. Killeen?" Sam called. "Is that you?"

The man's ice-blue eyes lit in surprise, just before he took off running down the alley.

CHAPTER EIGHT

"**W**ait!" Sam cried again, scrambling up the stairs and around the back of the house with Joana and Bennett close behind. The man was already at the other end of the alley, where he disappeared between two houses. "Why would he run?"

"Why does anybody run?" Joana asked. "He probably owes somebody money."

Sam ran after him, her youth and enthusiasm overtaking the man's haste to make his escape. She caught up with him just as he reached a cross street, where a passing cart forced him to stop and face her.

"Mr. Killeen, please wait!" she huffed, leaning over slightly. "You *are* Mr. Killeen, are you not?"

"Who is doing the asking?" the man inquired, his eyes darting side to side as he crouched against the wall, taking stock of his disadvantages in the alley.

"Please, sir, my name is Samantha Knox," she said, sucking in deep breaths. Six months huddled over library tables took the stamina out of a body. "I'm a student of Barnaby Wallstone. You wrote to him? About the symbol?"

"Shhhh!" Mr. Killeen hissed, taking her by the arm and steering her back into the alley away from the main street. He tensed up immediately as Bennett and Joana reached them, his gaze cutting. "Who are you?"

"They're students of Professor Wallstone as well," Sam said hastily. "Bennett and Joana Steeling."

"Steeling?" Mr. Killeen said in surprise. "As in Steeling Textiles?"

To Bennett's credit, he only gave the slightest impression of a sigh. "That's our father, yes."

The man's nostrils flared on a quick intake of breath. "You are to be trusted, then. I thought you were sent by *them*."

"Them?" Sam asked, before lowering her voice and leaning in. "You mean the men you mentioned in your letter?"

He nodded, watching the far end of the alley. "It's not safe to speak here. Where is your professor now? We must go to him immediately."

"Er," Sam hedged, glancing at Bennett. He only returned the stare, waiting for her to build her own ladder out of the hole she had dug. "He is . . . indisposed, I'm afraid. It's why it took so long for your letter to be discovered. We only found it in his pile of neglected correspondence recently, but we came as soon as we could."

Mr. Killeen frowned. "I don't recall requesting his presence in person, though I would admit that I wrote that letter many weeks ago."

"Yes, well," Sam said, gliding right past that, "here we are. And I believe I've found something in the symbol that will be of help to you."

"What is that?" Mr. Killeen asked, his gaze suddenly zeroed in on her. He had an intense way about his stare, his eyes so light and blue that looking into them was like being dunked in a cold lake at sunrise.

"It would be better if we could see the symbol, up close," Sam said. "Can you take us to the cave?"

Mr. Killeen's gaze shuttered. "I am not sure how possible that will be. The situation has rather . . . deteriorated since I wrote that letter."

"Deteriorated how?" Bennett asked, suddenly on guard. "They haven't destroyed the cave, have they?"

"Not yet, though I'm sure they have grown desperate enough to try if I do not stop them soon." Mr. Killeen tapped his fingers against his trousers, his gaze darting around once again. His eyes suddenly lit like a shaft of light striking the depths of the lake. "That might very well be the answer, though. Get the jump on them before they jump us. Yes. Yes! Come along, we have a great deal to prepare."

"Prepare?" Sam asked, bewildered. "Prepare for what?"

"We must make haste," Mr. Killeen said, energetic now. "If we are to make Skotino cave before nightfall."

"They attacked you?" Sam asked in surprise, the rocky terrain of the road they traveled giving her exclamation an extra oomph as they hit a rough patch. "Why would they do that?"

Mr. Killeen touched one side of his face tenderly, and now that Sam wasn't chasing him down a back alley, she could see the blossom of greenish-yellow highlighting his cheekbone. "I am afraid they have grown rather bold in their actions since we discovered that symbol. They have pressed me for weeks now to decipher its true intention, but as you know from the letter I rather desperately wrote to your professor, I have been unable to divine its meaning."

"So you hired these men to help you excavate, but they turned on you the second the prospect of treasure was written on the wall?" Joana asked, twisting from the front seat to look at Mr. Killeen.

"Jo, eyes on the road, please," Bennett said, his voice strained.

"Oh please, what am I going to hit out here? A stray goat?" The look she tossed back at Mr. Killeen was shrewd. "I would have figured you'd know every digger on this island, considering all the work you do with Sir Arthur up at Knossos."

Mr. Killeen tilted his head in acknowledgment. "Normally, I do. But with the twenty-fifth anniversary of his great discovery rapidly approaching, we have engaged all our usual laborers out at the palace. Sir Arthur is on the hunt for a new chamber to unveil during the festivities. I was forced to search for workers outside our usual pool of trusted associates. And I have paid for it dearly now."

"Why have you not contacted the local authorities to alert them to these would-be thieves?" Bennett asked. "Surely this can't be the first time you've encountered such men."

"No, it is not. But they have not technically broken any of our laws here yet, so while I have put the local magistrate on notice, he cannot do anything to them unless they actually steal something. The cave is open to the public, and they can easily claim they are tourists taking in the sights. Besides, the magistrate is busy with the preparations for the anniversary celebration. He can hardly post a watch on the cave day and night. I have had to do that work myself, until they caught me the last time. Hence why they attacked me."

"How do we know they won't be there now?" Bennett asked. "I'll not risk the girls' safety by confronting them."

"I have been watching them the last several weeks, learning their patterns and behaviors should I need to report them to the magistrate accordingly. They labor in the mornings, doing their diggings and excavations in search of treasure, but they leave in the early afternoon to return to Heraklion. We won't have much time before evening falls, but it should be enough to reach the symbol within the cave."

Mr. Killeen turned his ice-blue gaze on Sam, the rugged terrain of the Cretan countryside whipping along outside the car window behind him in a dizzying fashion. It was hot and sunny, the temperature growing unbearable the farther they moved away from the refreshing sea air of the city.

"Now tell me, girl, what was it you found in the picture I sent to your professor?" he asked. "And let us pray those men have not discovered it for themselves."

"Oh, well," Sam said, digging through her satchel to unearth the letter, "I can't be entirely sure of it, for the picture quality is somewhat blurry. Not through any fault of yours, I'd imagine, sir! Just that it must be difficult to take photos in a dark cave all by yourself with unscrupulous men haunting your steps."

"Yes, quite," Mr. Killeen said, his tone admirably mild.

She pulled the photograph loose, holding it out to him. "If you look, here, at the tongue, the proportions are rather odd. Normally, one would see a forked tongue, split down the middle into two parts. But on this one, the cuts are along the side, and flared at either point, so it looks more like—"

"An arrow," Mr. Killeen interrupted with a tone of wonder. "Brilliant. I don't know how I could have missed this!"

"Might have been the fellas giving you a good roughing-up," Joana piped in from the driver's seat.

"Do you know where that arrow is pointing in the cave, Mr. Killeen?" Sam asked. Tall, slender cypress trees stood sentinel over their drive along the meager dirt roadway, the shorter and more lush olive trees interspersing their watch.

Mr. Killeen scratched at his cheek, wincing as he remembered the bruise there. "I would have to see it again to be sure, but we found the symbol deep below, nearly to the end of the system. For all I remember, that might have been pointing at a back wall. But it really is extraordinary. What could it mean?"

"I suppose we'll find out soon enough," Sam said, watching the placid passage of the countryside to calm the fizzing energy of excitement burning through her blood.

It was nearing late afternoon by the time Joana pulled the car to a halt on a rocky bluff, the hills hazy and indistinct in the distance. The little village of Skotino they passed through on the way there was long since gone, the sky a deep blue and tufted with cottony clouds that floated past on a nonexistent breeze. Joana tilted her head back after they piled out of the car, pulling at the collar of her dress to unstick it from her neck.

"I'm almost looking forward to the cave to get out of this heat," she said, not so discreetly blowing down her bodice. When Sam gave her a look, she spread her arms wide. "Who's here to see it?"

"You'd be surprised," Bennett said grimly, approaching the ruins of the old church and crouching behind the stones.

A steep cliff led to the cave entrance below, mostly obscured by trees with only a half-moon of black yawning above the tree line to indicate the opening. Sam shivered at the sight of it, like a hungry mouth ready to devour the earth. But then a movement among the trees below distracted her, drawing her attention.

"Are those the men?" she whispered to Mr. Killeen.

"I am afraid so," Mr. Killeen said grimly.

There appeared to be four of them, the type of men who would fit right in with the mob heavies working the door back at the Green Mill in Chicago. Sam couldn't quite see their faces from this far up, but she could vividly imagine they were hard and lined with scars, maybe with a missing tooth or two for extra menace.

One of them even held a bright red bundle under one arm, and Bennett sucked in a breath as he caught sight of it.

"Dynamite," he said, his voice soft with shock. "Surely they don't intend to use that down in the cave? They're just as likely to bring the whole place down around them as they are to excavate anything. Not to mention that dynamite has fallen far out of favor since the days of Heinrich Schliemann excavating the lost city of Troy."

"I wouldn't suspect they know anything of Herr Schliemann or the advancements in our scientific methods of excavation," Mr. Killeen said. "These men are blackguards, treasure hunters through and through."

"I don't see much treasure lying around down there, though," Joana said.

"That's good!" Sam said. "It means they haven't found whatever that symbol is leading to yet. We still have a chance."

"We're not going down there," Bennett said, quietly but firmly. "It's too dangerous."

"Bennett, we've come all this way!" Sam said. "And Mr. Killeen said these men always take off in the late afternoon. We'll just wait them out."

"Sam, those men have dynamite," Bennett said emphatically. "Who knows what they've rigged up, or what kind of detonator it's got. For all we know, they could be setting traps for anyone trying to enter the cave while they're away. It's too dangerous."

"If I'm going to be buried in anything, it's going to be silk," Joana said, watching the quick movements of the men below. "Certainly not ten tons of dirt and rock."

Sam turned to Mr. Killeen, desperate for an ally. "Surely this is not the first time you or Sir Arthur have come across unscrupulous people who threatened violence to get what they want. But you always managed to persevere, did you not? Sir Arthur lived through two wars out here on Crete. We cannot let a few . . . blackguards stand in the way of a discovery that could change the world, can we, Mr. Killeen?"

"No, of course not," Mr. Killeen said, his eyes lighting with the fire of her whispered speech. "Miss Knox is right. If we let them blow up Skotino, we could lose whatever chance we have of discovering what that symbol is hiding. As I told you, I have watched them go about their business for several weeks. The sun is getting low. They shall depart any moment now."

"Which means we need to get out of here before they do," Bennett said, an edge of exasperation to his tone. "Unless you mean for them to run us off the road and over a cliff instead of dynamiting us to oblivion. Sam, be reasonable."

"I *am* being reasonable," Sam said, stung by the words and the little spot of guilt that bloomed where they planted in her chest. "I don't pretend that going down there is without danger. But, Bennett, if we let those men set off a charge, think of the damage they could do. Think of someone dynamiting the grand staircase at Knossos, or the boy king's tomb in the Valley of the Kings. Think of the history we would have lost. Do you really want that to happen here?"

"No, of course not," Bennett said, but it sounded as if wild dogs had to draw the concession out of him. "Though at the moment I'm thinking more of our lives than of a piece of history."

"Well, there's certainly no need to worry on that account," Mr. Killeen said, his voice suddenly chipper. He stood up, sweeping his hand toward the steep drop-off leading below. "Because the men have gone. Just as I said. Shall we proceed?"

Joana sighed. "Miles of beaches and you two drag me down to a slimy old cave."

CHAPTER NINE

The descent was tricky, the rocks slippery underfoot and the ground uncertain in places. As Joana cursed her impractical skirt, Sam was at least grateful that she had opted for the jodhpurs Joana purchased for her back in January. She couldn't imagine trying to navigate the course in a dress as Joana had to do. The trees, at least, provided some semblance of shade as they came down to the level of the cave entrance.

From above, Sam had only caught an impression of the top of the entrance, obscured as it was by the trees. But once they made their way to the ground, it gaped high and wide like a cathedral arch. Even the first few steps into the cave shifted the atmosphere, the shade provided by the cave a blessed relief after hours under the relentless sun. The walls seemed to amplify and distort the sound of their every step, each little rock sliding under their boots echoing back with the warning of boulders.

Sam caught her breath at the hushed reverence of the interior of the cave, the rocky and uneven ceiling vaulting a hundred feet overhead. It dwarfed her with both its size and composition, the stalagmites looming out of the shadows as the four of them cautiously made their way down the rocky path into the cave's interior.

She'd never felt so small or so new, the makings of the cave a careful collection of time and patience. She could well understand why the ancient Minoans would have used Skotino cave as a site of worship. It reminded her of the ethereal solemnity of the medieval cathedrals she had visited while in Dublin.

"Bit like being in church, doesn't it feel like?" Joana whispered as if reading her thoughts. She glanced around the first stalagmite they passed. "I keep waiting for Pastor Jonathan to leap out and try to redeem me with a spray of holy water."

Sam looked at her in horror. "He didn't really do that, did he?"

"Got me right in the eye," Joana said solemnly, tapping her left cheek. "Really did burn like the devil. He might have had a point."

"There's a great deal of equipment still here," Bennett said, lifting a pile of rope and a shovel. "They might be gone for now, but there's no guarantee they won't be back soon."

"Trust me, I know these men," Mr. Killeen said, examining a bundle of dynamite as if it were a vase to be appraised and not an explosive. He took hold of the leads and pulled them out with one swift movement. "They are off for their evening libations and entertainments. We shall be fine."

"Mmmm," Bennett grunted. He located a flashlight and flicked it on, casting long shadows over the collection of stalactites and stalagmites. Several of them took on imposing shapes, and he stepped closer to examine one that looked like a bear.

"This chamber is the Mega Nao," Mr. Killeen said, sounding for all the world like he was launching into a lecture at the museum. "Or the Great Temple, as some would call it. Many of the stalagmites here show evidence of treatment, like that one you are examining, Mr. Steeling. There are others, supposedly, though their purposes are unknown. These carvings are what drew me to investigate the cave in the first place, and what I can say for certain from my brief surveys is that it was obviously occupied at some point."

Sam took another flashlight from the pile, wrestling with the switch that seemed to be jammed in the off position. When she finally managed to force it on, the light exploded out, illuminating a looming stone figure before her. She squeaked in surprise, stumbling back a half step and nearly turning her ankle on a large rock in the path. The stone figure was only a collection of stalactites reaching down from the ceiling above and nearly touching the ground. They looked like teeth, the cave baring its fangs in warning at the intrusion.

"Sam, are you all right?" Bennett asked, taking her elbow to stabilize her.

She nodded, doing her best to push back the panicky feeling. It was just the cave, the spooky feeling of abandoned worship that permeated the stone. And the idea of being under what was probably thousands of pounds of earth and rock that could crush them all in an instant if it chose. Bennett might have had a point about being more cautious around so much explosive material. But she could hardly tell him that now without losing face. And besides, there was still the symbol to locate and its meaning to decipher.

"Lead us to where you found the symbol, Mr. Killeen," she said, straightening up. She lamented the loss of Bennett's hand at her elbow, but they had a job to do.

Mr. Killeen led them out of the Mega Nao and down into a lower chamber, the terrain growing more difficult to navigate. It took all their concentration to descend the formations in the lower chamber, and several times Sam nearly dropped her flashlight as she slipped on a surprise slide of loose earth or caught her foot on the edge of a rock. Joana blew out a muttered curse behind her, making Sam grateful that at least she wasn't the only one having difficulty maintaining her footing. They stopped when Mr. Killeen did, at the edge of a steep drop.

"I am afraid the going gets considerably more difficult from here," he said, holding up a length of rope he had taken from the supplies the men left behind.

Joana leaned heavily on Sam's shoulder, huffing out a breath that blew a stray lock of crimped hair away from her face. "You're telling me all that was the *easy* part?"

Mr. Killeen handed the end of the rope to Bennett. "Mr. Steeling, if you would tie that off? We'll need to rappel to get down to the next chamber."

Mr. Killeen did not lie when he said the going would not get easier. Even with the ropes and flashlights, the way was treacherous. They helped each other down the steep drop, a chain of hands and ropes and unsure footing that left them all sweating and breathless by the time they had passed through more lower chambers. Any semblance of light from outside was gone, the meager reach of their flashlights the beginning and end of the world. Sam found that she didn't care for the dark down here—the totality of it, the uncertainty it bred within her. She was used to knowing where she was going before she went, but here she only existed one cautious step at a time. And the low, sloping roof of the cave, with its teeth of stalactites, did little to settle her nerves.

"Mr. Killeen," she said when they had descended into yet another chamber with yet another collection of startling formations. "Are we getting close to where you found the symbol, do you think?"

"We'd better be," Joana muttered behind her. "If we go any deeper, we'll have tunneled our way to the other side of the world."

"I . . . am not sure," Mr. Killeen's voice said, slightly chagrined. "I thought I knew where we were, but it's possible I've gotten a bit turned around."

The three of them sent up a groan in unison, Joana going so far as to throw her hands wide in frustration and slump back against the nearest stalagmite. Her flashlight beam bounced wildly over the surrounding natural architecture, casting shadows and illuminations and making frightening shapes across the nearby cave walls. But one shape passed under the beam that had nothing to do with shadows, and Sam reached to still Joana's swinging arm.

"Jo, wait, I think you did it," she said, moving the beam carefully over the uneven surface of the cave walls until the darker shape edged back into the light.

"Well, sure I did," Joana said. "I'm always having to save you guys."

Her words were flippant, but her tone was not. They all crept carefully toward the far wall, where the symbol adorned the rock. The photograph they had seen had been grainy and dark, slightly blurry from Mr. Killeen's efforts to hold both a flashlight and a camera still. But here, in person, in the holy dark depths of Skotino cave, the symbol was perfectly rendered. The points of the horns of consecration glinted with a bit of the moisture that permeated the cave walls, and the double-headed axe curved wickedly. Whoever had carved the symbol had executed the image with great skill, not that Sam expected any less. The Minoans were famed for their artwork—their murals, their writing, it was all advanced and painstakingly rendered.

But still, these incredible details paled in comparison with the serpent. The intricacy of the scales, the perfect curvature of the head, the round eyes—she had suspected they would be stunning in person. And so they were. But they were beyond that, too. If she stared at the symbol too long, trapped there in the concentrated light of their quadruple beams, it was almost as if the snake . . . *moved*.

Sam squeezed her eyes shut, willing her heart rate to slow, willing her lungs to bring in air and release it. When she opened them again, the symbol was still just as lovely but no longer looked alive.

"Sam?" Bennett asked.

"I think the cave air is getting to me," she said, attempting a laugh and ending up with something that sounded like a wheeze. "It's absolutely exquisite. The craftsmanship, the preservation . . ."

"I've never seen anything like it," Mr. Killeen said, his voice hushed but still buzzing with excitement. "Not in all my years of searching."

"It's creepy," Joana said, ever practical.

"It's leading deeper into the cave," Bennett said, only the faintest hint of wonder edging into his voice. He tapped against the tongue, the arrow shape clear.

Sam shook herself. She had almost forgotten why they were there. "Right. We should follow it."

"Counterpoint, should we, though?" Joana muttered, but she didn't lag behind as they continued on.

They made their way cautiously downward, farther into the chamber, the rocks growing slippery with the peculiar moisture that collects underground, making it even harder for them to descend. The walls disappeared around them as the air grew thicker and more oppressive, as if the earth were exhaling and pressing down on them. Sam had never considered herself claustrophobic—after all, she had found herself in some tight quarters during the treasure hunts Mr. Steeling would put on for them in their childhood. She'd once had an unfortunate run-in with a family of raccoons living under the porch of the old schoolhouse. But down here was different, the air swallowing up their light like a black hole.

"I don't think I like caves," Sam said when she couldn't stand the drip of some unseen water source any longer.

"That's because you're human, and not a patch of lichen and whatever else makes a cave its home," said Joana.

"Actually, there were plenty of human civilizations whose people dwelled within caves," said Bennett. "Especially here on Crete."

"Spare me the lecture when I'm ankle-deep in cave slime, brother," Joana sniped.

"I wasn't lect—" Bennett started, but stopped as they came up against a wall. "This looks like the end of the chamber, and I don't see another one branching off anywhere."

"We need to spread out," Sam said. "Bennett and Jo, you search that way. Mr. Killeen and I will go this way. Look for anything out of the ordinary."

"For a cave, you mean," Joana said dryly.

"You could stay here, Jo," Bennett said. "It will be easier for me to look without having to worry about you getting lost or stuck."

"And let *you* be the one that makes the big find?" Joana said with a snort. "Stuff it, Bennett. Let's go."

"Are they always so argumentative?" Mr. Killeen asked Sam.

"Oh, no, this is them being kind," Sam said, though she smiled as she said it. "You should see when they fight."

They scoured the back walls of the chamber, Sam searching the low reaches of the rock while Mr. Killeen did his best to look at the curve overhead. She wasn't sure how long they looked, her eyes straining in the poor light, but other than a startling collection of snails on one stalagmite, they came up with nothing.

"Anything?" Sam asked hopefully as they rejoined Bennett and Joana.

Bennett shook his head. "Nothing of import. No symbols, or

hieroglyphics, or even graffiti. It doesn't seem as if anyone has ever inhabited this part of the cave."

"But the symbol pointed in this direction," Sam said, surveying the blank wall before them in consternation. "Didn't it?"

"There's nothing here, Sam," Joana said. "Unless that creepy snake has some other secret message hidden in its scales, we're at a dead end."

"The snake," Sam said, the gears of her mind biting into an idea and cranking slowly. "Why a snake?"

"I thought that was the question on hand," Mr. Killeen said.

"Just let her talk," Bennett advised. "It's how she works things out."

Sam tapped a finger against her lip. "Mr. Killeen, what do you know of the snakes here on Crete?"

"Not much more than the average inhabitant," he mused. "Snakes factor prominently in Minoan symbology and worship, but most of the snakes here are harmless. There is a myth about Heracles clearing the island of harmful snakes to pay honor to the birthplace of Zeus, which is allegedly in another cave on this island."

"Like Saint Patrick driving all the snakes out of Ireland," Bennett added.

"I thought islands weren't supposed to have snakes," Joana said. "I was banking on that being the case, actually. I hate snakes."

"Oh, that's not true at all," Sam said absently, still searching the cave walls. "There is an island off the coast of Brazil nicknamed Snake Island because the snake population is so high humans can't live there. They have the world's deadliest snake there. They say its venom is so poisonous that it melts your flesh where it bites you."

Joana pointed an accusing finger at her. "Don't make me regret our friendship."

"We don't have anything like that here," Mr. Killeen said hastily. "There is the whip snake, the leopard snake—which is actually quite beautiful, red and spotted—the cat snake, and the dice snake."

"That sounds like a lot of snakes," Joana said ominously.

"They really are harmless," said Mr. Killeen. "Well, the cat snake does have venom, but it's too weak to cause any damage to humans. And none of the species native to the island are cave dwellers. We're quite safe in here."

"The arrow in the tongue—it wasn't meant to be casually discovered," Sam reasoned. "Whoever carved that symbol meant to hide something. We've been looking for a big 'here you go!' sign. But it must be something more secretive than that. Something meant to stay hidden. So why the snake?"

She let her flashlight beam drop to the ground, tracing it over the misshapen stones underfoot, the water sluicing into little rivulets and carving paths that were millions of years in the making. One such path curved down into a deep well near the edge of the cave wall, the opening no larger than her hand. She crouched down, something about the little well drawing her attention.

"Sam?" Bennett crouched beside her, looking into the small black hole. "What is it?"

"What do you notice about that hole?" she asked, pointing.

"It's filling with disgusting cave water?" Joana offered.

"It looks like a snake den," Bennett said.

"Exactly!" Sam said. "No one would notice a small, natural hole like this. Except this one is not natural."

"It's perfectly round," Mr. Killeen said, huffing as he squatted behind her.

"*Too* perfectly round," Sam said. "Where in nature have you seen anything so perfect?"

"You think someone carved this hole?" Mr. Killeen said in surprise. "Why?"

"There's only one way to know," Sam said resolutely. "We reach in and find out."

CHAPTER TEN

"**I**n the history of ridiculous things you've said to me, I didn't think it was possible to top yourself," Joana said. "But here we are."

"No one is sticking their hand in there until we know what it is," Bennett said. "If we're wrong and it is a snake hole, we're miles from any kind of help."

"Mr. Killeen said none of the snakes are poisonous!" Sam protested. "And this is where the symbol was pointing. Whatever we're looking for, it's in that hole."

"Or it's a booby trap that'll bite your hand clean off," Joana countered. "I'm not losing a hand to test it."

"I'll do it," Sam said.

"No!" Bennett and Joana exclaimed in unison.

"Perhaps it should be I who does it?" suggested Mr. Killeen. "As the resident expert here."

"No," Bennett said, shaking his head. "It's too dangerous without more information."

"We don't have time for more information!" Sam exclaimed, annoyance bubbling up. "We have come this far, and we are so close, and you would rather putter around and make charts and draw risk analyses. Is this not why we're here? To make such a great discovery as lies right here at our feet, right now, if we would only reach for it?"

Bennett gave her a strange look. "*Is* that why you're here, Sam?"

"Well, I'm certainly not here to listen to you lecture me like a . . . like a stuffed shirt," Sam said, her anger offering up the first word that came to mind. She thought it was a rather mild insult, considering some of the more colorful ones Joana had invented for Bennett over the years, but that wasn't the effect it had on Bennett. He dropped his arms, his face going slack like she had landed one in the gut.

"Sorry to drag your happy-go-lucky adventure down with my drab logic and reasoning," Bennett said, his jaw stiff.

"I didn't mean—" Sam began, but Joana shoved between both of them before she could finish.

"Oh hell, we'll all be fossils by the time you two finish hashing this out," she said, glaring at Sam and pointing a finger at her. "You owe me for this."

She drew up her sleeve and shoved her hand down in the hole before either of them could stop her, drawing an exclamation of surprise out of Sam and one of fear out of Bennett. But the deed was done, and her arm disappeared nearly up to the elbow. Her face contorted in a grimace.

"Well, I was right about one thing," she said. "It's full of disgusting cave water."

"No snakes?" Sam asked.

Joana's gaze narrowed on her. "Why would you even bring that up right now?"

"Sorry," Sam said. "Do you feel anything else? I mean, besides the cave water?"

"The cave water is a bit distracting," Joana said, but she tilted her head in concentration. "It's a small hole. I can't open my hand all the way. Wait, hang on. I think I feel something."

The rest of them leaned in eagerly, accidentally pressing against Joana's side and making her squeak in alarm.

"What is it? What have you found?" Mr. Killeen asked, and even he couldn't keep the youthful excitement out of his voice.

"It feels like . . . well, I don't know. Something different. It's like a bit of rock sticking out or something. It's got a shape to it, too. Long and skinny up the middle with two little fat arms on each side. The arms are wide, though. Much wider than the middle."

Sam sucked in a breath. "Are they curved? Up and down?"

"Yeah, it feels that way, maybe."

Sam looked at Bennett over Joana's head. "A double-headed axe."

"The labrys," Mr. Killeen filled in. "Same as the symbol on the cave wall. Can you remove it?"

"It's pretty far down there," Joana said, torquing her arm around and grunting. "It's stuck, I think. Hang on, let me get a better grip, and I'll see if I can't pull it loose."

She maneuvered until she was flat on her chest, her arm fully extended down the hole. She grunted as her shoulder flexed, pulling at the object and crying out in surprise as her arm came several inches out of the hole. The earth rumbled and groaned beneath them, an ominous sound that had all of them scrambling backward.

"Dynamite!" Bennett said sharply, grabbing for both girls as Mr. Killeen gave a very undignified yelp.

"They really did booby-trap it!" he cried.

The earth continued shuddering and groaning, and for a terrifying moment, Sam imagined a detonation going off and the rock ceiling crashing down on them. No one even knew they were there. Some perky upstart like herself would probably find their bones in a few hundred years and wonder about their demise.

"Run!" Mr. Killeen cried.

"Wait!" Sam said, pointing at the wall above the snake hole. "Something is moving."

Perhaps it was an earthquake, cracking the wall before it swallowed them up. But the opening was too perfectly round to be caused by natural disaster, same as the snake hole. The rumbling stopped, and as Mr. Killeen stepped forward, his flashlight beam illuminated what looked for all the world like a set of stairs inside. All of Sam's nervous, fizzing energy sparked to life.

"It's a secret passage," she breathed in wonder.

"I've done it," Mr. Killeen said. "We, I mean. We've done it."

"Says the man with two dry arms," Joana muttered.

"See?" Sam said, unable to help the smirk that twisted up her lips as she looked to Bennett. "No booby traps."

"It's not as if I was hoping for one," Bennett said.

Mr. Killeen moved into the opening, quickly descending and taking his flashlight with him. Sam caught only a brief flash of the walls within the passage, but it was enough to spur her forward. The narrow stairs were etched into the cave floor, the rock surprisingly dry after their passage through the rest of the cave muck. Sam put out a hand to steady herself, her flashlight beam concentrated on the ground before her. But something was odd about the wall where she touched it, and as she brought the light up to investigate, she sucked in a breath in wonder.

"Bennett, look at this," she said, running her fingers through the grooves that had been carved there.

"Is that . . . Linear B?" Bennett asked in shock.

Sam shook her head. "No, I think it's older. Minoan hieroglyphics. Their symbols were more elaborate and detailed, more pictorial."

The image she touched was a beautifully rendered ship in

miniature, the craftsmanship as evident here as it was on the serpent symbol. There were rigging lines coming from the mast, and even small oars that poked out of the side. There were dozens more on both sides of the passage, telling a tale that led them down to wherever the stairs ended.

"What do they mean?" Joana asked, crowding into the space behind them as they continued after Mr. Killeen.

Sam shrugged. "Most of the symbols have never been translated, though some are obvious. The ship, for instance. Minoans were renowned seafarers, and they traded as far as Egypt and Italy. And here again are the horns of consecration. The bull was sacred to Minoan culture and often depicted in their murals. But what they all mean together, and where they're leading? I couldn't say."

"Where did Mr. Killeen go?" Bennett asked, peering down the stairs.

"He moved awfully spritely once the hard work was done," Joana said. "They're all the same when there's treasure on the table, aren't they?"

"That's not kind, Jo," Sam said, though she had to admit her friend had a point. "Even Mr. Carter broke open a hole to view the inner chamber of Tutankhamen's tomb when he first discovered it and patched it up to be reopened officially afterward. Finds like these are less than once in a lifetime, and most men work their whole lives without such a reward. You can hardly fault his enthusiasm."

"Just don't forget to pat down his pockets when we leave," Joana said.

They made their way slowly, Sam wishing she could take more time to explore the symbols marked into the walls. She had seen some of them in Sir Arthur Evans's book *Scripta Minoa*, the definitive volume on Minoan symbology. But seeing Sir Arthur's sketched interpretations or the small photographs contained in the book's pages was nothing remotely close to standing in this secret tunnel, most likely undiscovered since the time of the Minoans themselves, her fingers fitting into the grooves etched by names and faces lost to history. For that brief moment, standing in the dim light, feeling the soft edge of a four-thousand-year-old chisel mark, Sam could almost imagine herself there, the iconography whispering its secrets to her.

"It keeps going," Bennett called from a few steps down.

Sam thought they might descend forever, right into the center of the earth. She even began to imagine she could see the glow of its molten core emanating up from below.

"Is that . . . fire?" Sam asked, breathless. Because now that her eyes had had time to adjust, she could make out the distinctive flickering movement. She gave a shudder; the last time she found herself in the presence of a room filled with fire, she had been trapped in an inferno of burning books. And while she was fairly certain the room below did not contain a library of eighteenth-century European philosophers or medieval illuminated manuscripts, she still felt a strong desire to turn tail and scrabble back up those steps as fast as possible.

"I think Mr. Killeen has lit a fire below," Bennett said, ignorant of Sam's hesitations.

"But how?" Joana asked.

"It seems there is . . ." Bennett began, but trailed off. Sam reached the bottom of the steps just behind him, peeking out from around his shoulder to discover exactly how Mr. Killeen had lit a fire and—more importantly—why.

"My goodness," she breathed in wonder.

The chamber was small, the circular walls only wide enough to hold the four of them as long as they didn't stretch their arms too far. Sam might have found it more than a little claustrophobic, if she hadn't been so completely distracted by the chamber itself.

"It's a bench shrine," she said, taking in the low benches carved from the stone walls. The walls themselves were painted in a mural of such brilliant colors Sam would have sworn it had been done only recently instead of thousands of years ago. She nearly reached out to touch the nearest swath of red to test its tackiness before reminding herself she might cause damage to such a find if she did. Still, the paint glistened, the colors thick and bold and stark in the flickering firelight. There were four shallow bowls placed around the chamber in a diamond pattern, their bottoms filled with a liquid that burned cheerily.

"Kerosene," Mr. Killeen said, not turning away from his examination of the far side of the mural. "At least, some ancient form of it, I believe. I smelled the substance as soon as I entered, and as luck would have it, I had a book of matches on me. I thought I might find something significant, but I did not imagine . . . *this*."

This, Sam felt, was an understatement. The mural that covered the walls of the small chamber was more complete, more detailed than any of the frescoes Sir Arthur had discovered at Knossos. They were like a panorama, the paintings on either side of the entrance mirrors of each other. First there were ships, not just symbols but actual depictions with individual wooden boards making up the sides and tiny seafarers working the rigging above.

Then the edges of the island rose from the waters, showing fields of grain and jars of what Sam assumed were olive oil or wine, showing the abundance of the Minoan agricultural production. There was also a bull, with a young woman riding joyously on its back, her grip firm on its horns. Converging on the back wall were women in elaborate headdresses bearing armloads of goods. All of it painted a picture of prosperity, of plenty, of pleasure and perfection.

But the ships, stalks of grain, the bull, and the women bringing offerings all bent toward a point on the back wall as if it exerted some inexorable pull. There, stretching from the floor of the cave up across the arch of the ceiling overhead, was a glorious female figure. Her skirt was stacked like a patchwork quilt, each tile beautifully decorated. Her torso gleamed in a yellow so brilliant it looked like gold in the firelight, with a girdle cinched around her waist as a belt. Her breasts were exposed, her arms stretched out to each side as a writhing snake curled over her wrists, their gazes directed at the entrance. The head and headdress of the female were lost to the curve of the ceiling overhead, shadowy and distorted as if looking down from a great distance.

"My god," Bennett said, awestruck.

"I think you mean *my goddess*," Joana quipped, but she quickly cleared her throat. "Uh, apologies, your . . . grace? Goddess? Needling my brother is a habit. No offense intended."

"The Snake Goddess," Mr. Killeen said, shaking his head. "I have only ever seen her in fragments, in suggestions. They guessed at her arms and the headdress. Pieced it together from other locations, from what I have heard. But this, this is . . ."

"Extraordinary," Sam finished. "This will change history. This will *make* history, and we'll all be part of it."

CHAPTER ELEVEN

"**W**ho exactly is the Snake Goddess?" Joana asked. "Besides being unspeakably tall and imposing, I mean."

"She is the mother goddess of Cretan mythology," said Mr. Killeen. "Goddess of home and hearth and fertility."

Joana gazed up at the indistinct features of the goddess looming overhead. "She doesn't look very . . . motherly to me."

Sam couldn't help a small sound that slipped out of her as she ran her fingers lightly over the panels of the goddess's skirt. Even though they were part of the rock, same as the surrounding mural, someone had taken the time to deeply carve each section as if they were separate stones placed into the wall.

"I know that sound, Sam," Joana said.

"Hmm?" she said, turning slightly. "What sound?"

"That noise you made. Like you swallowed a fly and tried to snort it back out. Or like you're trying to swallow a dissenting opinion so you don't snort it back out."

"Oh, that's not . . ." Sam glanced at Mr. Killeen, quickly darting her gaze away. "No, I haven't got anything . . . dissenting to say. It's all speculation anyway."

"Based on solid evidence gathered from decades of research," Bennett said.

"Sure, if you believe *The Golden Bough*," Sam muttered. "And the theory of a mother goddess of fertility and her king-consort who is constantly dying and coming back to life."

"There is a great deal of evidence to support it," Bennett said as if they were debating the merits of such a theory in a classroom. "There are several instances of a goddess with a smaller male consort on seals and decorated beads recovered here on Crete. Sir Arthur is not so out of line to assume the Snake Goddess is a manifestation of a mother goddess type."

"Yes, but doesn't it all seem a bit pat?" Sam countered. "The theory that every goddess must be a fertility goddess, and every ancient culture must have been a matriarchy? And all of it proves a linear progression to a patriarchy, which is the true utopia of human civilization? You accept these hypotheses as credible?"

"Well, not exactly," Bennett said, frowning. "I only meant there is a good body of evidence that possibly corroborates that belief."

"But . . . is that all women are? Vessels for king-consorts? Ruled by an unenlightened, outdated political system? Do we really have nothing else to contribute to a society except to bear the next generation and tend the hearths?"

Joana strode over to Bennett, leaning one arm on his shoulder and looking up at him with barely suppressed glee. "Go on, big brother. What have you got to say to that? I'm dying to hear."

"Well, that's not . . ." Bennett fidgeted under the pressing weight of her elbow digging into his shoulder. "I didn't say that's what I believed. Of course I believe women can do more and be more. I believe they are more."

"And yet you believe the Snake Goddess's only interpretation could be that of a fertility goddess?" Sam asked. She swung her arm up at the imposing figure above her. "Joana's right. She doesn't look motherly at all."

"Whatever her manifestation, she is exquisite," said Mr. Killeen, his accent growing softer and rounder as he spoke, almost to himself, his fingers caressing the lines of her belt. His fingers trailed up the side of the goddess's torso, brushing along the edges of her ample bosom so proudly displayed.

"Typical," Joana muttered, rolling her eyes.

But Sam didn't reply, because her attention had been drawn down from the goddess looming above to the plain dirt floor at their feet. It sloped slightly, but the slope was so uniform it was almost unnatural. Starting from the walls and leading to the center of the room, the floor seemed slightly depressed in the middle. She moved to the center, brushing her foot over the dip and scraping some of the accumulated dirt away. One small divot appeared in the floor, and she squatted to wipe away more of the dirt.

"Mr. Killeen, look at this," she said.

"Hmm?" Mr. Killeen said, his attention still riveted on the goddess.

"There seems to be a drain cut into the floor," Sam said. She sat back on her haunches, studying the chamber walls more closely. "Where is the altar?"

Bennett looked around in surprise. "You're right. Most of the bench shrines discovered on the island so far have similar features. The benches, of course, but also an altar with figurines of the goddess as well as other ritual objects."

"The benches go all the way around the chamber, but they stop at the goddess's skirt," Sam said, following the line of the seats with her finger before pointing at the tiles of the skirt. "Shouldn't there be an altar there, then?"

Bennett shrugged. "Maybe the depiction of the goddess is its own altar."

"Or maybe there's more to the chamber," Sam mused, looking back down at the drain. "This could be a sacrificial drain. Jo, you wouldn't happen to have any refreshments on you?"

Joana's expression grew guarded. "I'm sure I don't know what you're insinuating. I am a good girl."

Bennett snorted. "Right, as if we aren't fully aware of your predilections."

"Predilections?" Joana echoed. "Who are you, Auntie Neem? Next you'll be lecturing me on hair length and hemlines."

"Jo!" Sam said, exasperated, holding out a hand. "Please. I know you must have a flask on you. You wouldn't come out to the middle of nowhere without a little liquid fun."

Joana rolled her eyes, reaching for the hemline of her skirt. "Fine, but you owe me a refill. And keep old Bosom Eyes over there from peeking."

Quickly she lifted the skirt to bare her thigh, a small metal flask tied there by a leather holder. Bennett gave a grunt of disapproval, but Joana only stuck her tongue out at him. She unscrewed the top and kicked back a bolt of the liquid before handing it over to Sam.

"Just in case," Joana said with a shrug.

Sam wrinkled her nose at the vapors of pure grain alcohol that escaped the top of the flask before tipping a little bit out over the drain. The dirt seemed to melt away along with the alcohol, the cut edges growing sharper and more distinct. The walls of the chamber shook and groaned, but this time it was Mr. Killeen who gave a shout of surprise as he hopped away from the wall before the goddess.

The panels of her skirt shifted and sank back into the wall one at a time, parting through the middle until another small alcove appeared. Within the alcove was a table carved into the wall, a wide, shallow bowl sitting empty on the top. Behind the bowl was a statue, presumably made of ceramic, a simple rendering of a female with her arms lifted above her head. There was also a small stone tablet, the face blank, hung from the wall behind the statue.

"The altar," Bennett said, giving Sam an appreciative look. "You were right."

"Cor," breathed Mr. Killeen, kneeling before the altar as if he meant to offer up a sacrifice. "There are inscriptions here."

"More hieroglyphics," Sam said, stepping over the drain to kneel beside him and examine the markings.

"Look here, the bull again," Mr. Killeen said, tapping the symbolic figure toward the center of the altar. This one was more detailed than the horns of consecration, including the bull's head with decoration along the top, the horns curving down along the side. "And the labrys. And this symbol here represents a man or woman. The rest are unknown, but I believe it is fair to assume this chamber was meant as a ritual site for the Snake Goddess."

This, here, was history in action. And for once Sam was in the thick of it, not reading about it in squatty print five thousand miles away or playacting at it during one of Mr. Steeling's treasure hunts. Professor Atchinson be damned, she had done this. She had found this chamber, and all its secrets. She might be young, poor, and female, but she had just discovered something the professor had spent his whole life only lecturing about. Hang him and his accusations that her amateur attempts at discovery would lead to disaster.

"This bowl looks similar to the porphyritic basin in the throne room of Knossos," said Mr. Killeen, rising to stand before the altar. "Sir Arthur postulated that it would have been used to make sacrifices to the king who occupied the throne."

"Another sacrifice," Sam said, holding up Joana's flask excitedly.

"Hey!" Joana protested. "That's my one good stash."

"Jo, it's not Prohibition here," Sam said. "You can buy alcohol anywhere on the island."

"Well, sure, but that's from back home and I had to bribe three different shady characters to get it. It's got sentimental value. The finest bootleg money can buy."

"You'll have all the celebratory champagne you can guzzle when we report our find to the world," Sam said, her eyes glowing as she poured out the remaining liquid into the bowl. It sloshed around a bit, settling into the bottom. They held their collective breath, waiting for the next secret to reveal itself. But nothing happened.

"I don't understand," Sam said. "It worked on the drain. Why wouldn't it work here?"

"Perhaps that is the end of the chamber's secrets," Bennett said, giving a sigh. "And maybe it's for the best."

"Maybe it just needs more weight," Mr. Killeen said. "Or a different type of sacrifice."

He fished out a handful of Cretan coins, dumping them into the liquid at the bottom of the bowl. But still, nothing moved.

"I don't understand," Sam said again, shaking her head. "It should have worked."

"The chamber is an incredible find, Sam," Bennett said, stepping up beside her. "It will change the history of what we know about the Minoan culture. You should be proud to be a part of that."

Bennett was right; Sam knew he was. The chamber was exquisite. But it was still just a bench shrine. A perfectly preserved, highly decorated bench shrine that would give them far more material to study than the flakes of destroyed frescoes pieced back together by the restorers at Knossos, a father-and-son duo who everyone referred to as Émile Gilliéron, père and fils because they shared the same name. But her heart longed for more. For a crowning glory, something she could hold up in front of the Atchinsons of the world to say, *See, look what I can do. What I can be.*

She wanted a treasure.

"It's growing late," Bennett said, checking his watch. "It will be pitch-black by the time we reach the surface again, and we'll still need to make it back to Skotino village to find lodgings for the evening. We can close up the chamber when we leave so even if the men return, they won't be able to find it."

"I will need to locate a photographer and alert Sir Arthur's camp, of course," said Mr. Killeen, his expression animated as he checked off more items on his list out loud.

But Sam could not join their enthusiasm. There was something she was still missing. She was sure of it. Why put a sacrificial bowl on an altar if it was not meant to hold a sacrifice? A proper sacrifice to a great goddess.

But what kind of sacrifice did Sam really have to make? She carried no bundles of wheat, or vessels of oil and wine, or bolts of fine fabric. Sam had no gold, no precious gems, nothing a goddess would look twice at. She owned very little in the world that carried any value to her, but what she did have was more precious than any mineral or ore.

A proper sacrifice.

She dipped a hand into her pocket and pulled out her father's little tin horse, letting the meager weight of it drag her hand down as she extended it over the sacrificial bowl. The misshapen object held so many of her dreams and ambitions in every groove of its surface, in the incredible details of the horse's legs and the unformed potential of its ruined head. It wasn't just a toy to her; it was one of the only remaining possessions she had left to remind her of her father. For a moment she hovered there, hand poised over the basin, unable to let it go.

Most likely, nothing would happen. Most likely, she was wrong. Most likely, all that would occur was that her horse would get a little wet. But Sam could never leave a puzzle undone, and this was the greatest puzzle she had ever faced. How could she leave it be when she was sure there was still something left to be discovered?

"I'm sorry, Papa," she whispered to the tin horse, before turning her hand over and letting it drop. It plopped into the liquid and quickly settled at the bottom of the bowl, its shape even further distorted by the alcohol and the firelight. For a moment, nothing happened, and she felt foolish. She dipped her fingers just below the surface of the alcohol, intent on retrieving her horse before anyone noticed her foolish attempt, when the bowl shuddered and sank all the way down into the altar and disappeared.

CHAPTER TWELVE

S am stepped back in surprise, and the other three were there in a flash.

"What happened?" Mr. Killeen demanded. "What did you do?"

"I . . . It needed a sacrifice," Sam said.

She might have tried to explain or defend herself further, except that they were all distracted by a movement in the wall above the altar. A crack appeared where the wall had been smooth only one second before, the rock groaning as two paneled doors slid open. The four of them drew in a collective breath as the firelight illuminated the prize within. At first, Sam thought it might be a necklace, for it was long and narrow and looped around an ivory statue carved into the shape of the horns of consecration. The object was made of gold in overlapping panels that looked like the stripes of a snake, each one separate and fashioned to allow movement. But the bands were too wide and long to be a necklace, and she realized it must be some kind of belt. A series of holes dotted the wall behind it, perfectly round and hollow.

"It's a gold belt," Joana said. "Don't get me wrong, I love a good fashion statement, but . . . why a belt?"

"It's not a belt," said Mr. Killeen, his voice positively lusting. "It is a girdle. The girdle of the Snake Goddess."

"It must have been ceremonial," Sam said, her own voice vibrating with excitement. "A precious artifact of Minoan religious practice."

"Girdles appear often in Greek mythology," Bennett explained to his sister. "Take for instance the charmed girdle of Aphrodite, woven with her powers of love and seduction. She gave it to Hera to seduce Zeus and distract him from meddling in the Trojan War."

"This will be the greatest find since Knossos," Mr. Killeen murmured, almost to himself. He reached out a hand for the girdle, taking firm hold of one end. "And I will be the one who discovered it. Finally."

Sam drew in a breath to ask him exactly what he meant by that when a hissing filled the chamber. Mr. Killeen just had time to draw his hand back before a golden-headed snake slithered out of one of the hollow openings above the girdle, sliding down the belt and dropping onto the altar. It coiled in a tight knot, flicking out its tongue on another hiss before opening its jaws and baring fangs.

The four of them jumped back as another snake slithered out of a different hole, looping around the horns of consecration in a similar pattern as the girdle, and another came from below and reared up high behind the coiled snake. Sam and the others retreated all the way back to the opening of the chamber as more and more snakes dropped out, all of them golden in the firelight and hissing in warning.

"I thought you said none of the snakes here are cave-dwelling," Joana whispered harshly. The snakes didn't pursue them but simply piled up on the altar, forming a barrier between them and the girdle.

"They aren't," Mr. Killeen said, his voice shaken. "But those are unlike any of the snakes I've ever seen on this island."

"Maybe we can find something to trap them," Bennett said, though he didn't sound the least bit sure of it. "Or maybe we should take this as the sign it's meant to be and leave the girdle alone."

But Sam couldn't take her eyes off it. The way it gleamed, as if it had just come from under the metallurgist's careful hands. There was something so . . . compelling about it. She took a step toward it without realizing she had, and the girdle shimmered as if inviting her to take another one. The girdle was like a siren's call, and Sam was as powerless against it as the mariners who crashed their ships against the rocks. While the others debated their next steps, Sam approached the altar, watching the golden-headed hissing snakes. Some distant rational part of her screamed for her to stop, but her hands went out to the girdle nevertheless. Her rational mind threw up its hands, waiting for the snakes to strike.

"Sam, what are you doing?" Bennett asked, his voice sharp behind her. "Get back!"

"I think . . . it's okay," Sam said. "I made the sacrifice to reveal the girdle. I think it's me that's supposed to touch it."

"That's not a risk I want to take," Bennett said, but he couldn't get any closer to her without riling up the snakes.

But they did not strike. In fact, they coiled up along the altar's surface and tucked their heads within the folds of their length as Sam slipped her fingers under the weight of the girdle and lifted it, something like an electric shock running through her, visceral but not painful. The snakes seemed to sense the change, because they raised their heads in attention, watching her intently. The ground shuddered, and in her mind she heard singing, as if coming from a great chorus down the long passage of time. She gasped, dropping the girdle unceremoniously into the sacrificial basin.

"Sam!" Bennett said, his worry for her overcoming his fear of the snakes. They hissed at him as he took her by the shoulders and turned her to face him. "Did they strike? Are you injured?"

"No, no, nothing like that," Sam said, breathing as if she had just descended the full depths of the cave in the last five seconds. "I'm all right. I just . . ."

"Just what?" Bennett asked when she didn't continue. "What happened?"

She looked up at him, the concern in his eyes turning them dark and frantic. What could she tell him? That touching the girdle had been like a thrall come over her? Same as the bowl carved from the Tree of Life they discovered in Dublin. Only, that had been corrupted magic, dark energy that had poisoned her mind against him. The call of the girdle was even more like a siren's call now that she had touched it. Beautiful, enchanting, impossible to resist. Possibly leading her to her doom. Or possibly leading her to the height of existence.

But Sam knew that look in Bennett's eye. He had sworn he would never let another Dublin happen, and if she told him about the effect of the girdle, he would certainly never let her touch it again, much less carry it out of the chamber and declare their find to the world. He'd probably insist they close up the chamber, use the dynamite from the dangerous men, and blow the whole thing up—bury it in rubble so no one would ever find it again.

She couldn't let that happen, not when she was poised to be part of a discovery that would make Professor Atchinson eat his own hat. Besides, Bennett worried too much. Sam had fought off the bowl, and she could control whatever influence the girdle had on her as well. So she pasted on a smile, as best she could, and turned away from him to retrieve the girdle where she had unceremoniously let it drop.

"It's nothing," she said, dipping her hands once again into the little bit of alcohol. It had grown much warmer since she had last touched it, as if it had absorbed the heat coming off the girdle. "I was surprised, that's all. The girdle is much warmer than I expected, probably because of the fire. It's far too precious to leave it here. We'll have to bring it back with us to Heraklion for safekeeping."

"Yes, yes, safekeeping, excellent idea, Miss Knox," said Mr. Killeen, sounding relieved. He started to approach the altar, but the snakes flared their golden hoods, warning him back. "Ah, they don't seem to care for us menfolk, do they now?"

"Smart snakes," Joana said dryly.

"The girdle is meant for a female," Sam said almost unconsciously as her hands closed around the precious object once more. It was so warm, the links so smooth and expertly crafted it felt like holding a live snake made of metal. What an archaeological wonder, she thought in the rational—now distant—part of her mind. How did they achieve such craftsmanship?

But the forefront of her mind was singing again, the reverberations of it echoing like a stronger, more powerful heartbeat in her chest. It made her want to wrap the girdle around herself as if she were the Snake Goddess. She held the ends in her open palms, her fingers curling against her will as if they might complete the deed for her.

Sam had faced a goddess before, and she would not be cowed by another. She shook off the urge, closing her fingers and forcing the girdle instead into a coiled position within her palms. The snakes gave a short hiss of displeasure, but Sam stared them down.

"We'd better head for the village now if we want to make it before nightfall," she said.

Joana eyed the altar and its vigilant occupants. "Are we sure those things won't give chase?"

"They're not dogs, Joana," Sam said. Still, the snakes watched her. Their black eyes gleamed in the firelight as the party retreated toward the opening of the hidden chamber and climbed up the stairs, Sam the last of them. The snakes seemed to dip their heads in unison—whether in farewell, or acknowledgment, or some type of serpentlike warning, she didn't know. But she felt their eyes on her long after she had ascended the stairs and closed the secret entrance. She thought perhaps those eyes would not leave her for a long time to come.

CHAPTER THIRTEEN

Sam cradled the girdle like a child for the duration of their rocky ride back into Skotino village. It had been fully dark by the time they emerged from the cave, and they couldn't risk the trip to Heraklion before morning. Luckily, Mr. Killeen had already secured a room for himself in the village at a small inn, and they managed to negotiate with the proprietor to rent them out two more for the evening. They were all grateful enough for the prospect of a basin of clean water and a dry bed to lie out on.

There was a brief argument when Mr. Killeen insisted on taking charge of the girdle for safekeeping, and Sam couldn't bring herself to relinquish the thing to his grasp. Bennett had to intervene finally, giving the small British man his family's word of honor that nothing would happen to the girdle in the space of one evening. Mr. Killeen seemed reluctant to give up the fight, but he retreated to his first-floor accommodations.

Sam, Joana, and Bennett trooped up the narrow staircase to the two small rooms on the second level, Joana groaning from the step below Sam.

"I would give my entire inheritance for a hot bath right now," she said, holding out her arm, now dried and crusted over with greenish scum. "I feel like I've got lichen growing on me and my back cracks every time I bend over. I don't know how these rich old men do it, climbing through caves and digging up the earth all day."

"They don't, they pay other people to do it," Sam said, too tired to keep the edge out of her tone.

There was a time when such manual labor was second nature to her, helping her mother haul laundry and manage the chores around their family farm. But ever since she started working at Mr. Steeling's antique bookstore five years ago, she had eschewed the hard labor of the body for the more complex labor of the mind. And after a semester at the University of Chicago, she was even more unused to physical activity. Now the only calluses she sported were those on her thumb and middle finger from so many hours holding her pen.

"Is that a washbasin?" Joana asked as they reached their room. There wasn't much to it, just two narrow cotlike beds, a small old-fashioned washbasin with a pitcher of water beside it, and a tall shelf full of pictures and knickknacks. "No electricity and no running water, excellent. Why bother with the beds? We'll just find a nice soft field to sleep in."

"It was the best we could do at such short notice, Jo," Bennett said, dropping his knapsack in the room across the hall.

"As long as the water is clean and cold, you won't hear me complain," said Joana, making a beeline for the washbasin. "Sorry, Sam, but there's only enough for one person to wash up and only one of us stuck our hand in a hole full of cave water, so tough luck."

"That's all right," Sam said as she took up a seat at the small table with their only light source, a small glass lamp with a cheerily burning wick. "You earned it. Besides, I want to study the girdle a little more closely now that I've got the proper light to do it."

"I don't know why you'd want to be anywhere near that thing after those snakes," Joana said with a shiver. "I'll dream of them, I'm sure of it."

Sam unfurled the girdle reverently, sliding her fingertips along each link. It really was a remarkable feat of engineering, this girdle, the way the plates fit together and moved so seamlessly. She wondered what held them together on the inside. Her experience with jewelry was admittedly limited, but whoever crafted this piece must have been an artisan of the highest caliber. She turned the links over, the gold catching the light with a shimmering brilliance, and sucked in a sharp breath as she caught a good look at what she thought was the inside of the piece.

"Bennett, look at these," she said, already reaching for her notebook. "There are marks here! It looks like they span from the head to the tail."

"They could be decorative," Bennett said, hovering in the doorway instead of coming closer. "The Minoans were highly ornamental in their adornments."

Sam shook her head, the tail slithering through her fingers as she looked over the patterns. "This seems different. The pattern isn't repeating, so it's not a motif. Look, here at the head. It's the same symbol that was on the cave wall. The snake wrapped around the horns of consecration, with the labrys above it. Do you think the symbol could represent the Snake Goddess somehow?"

Bennett shrugged. "It's impossible to say without further study. What are you doing?"

"I'm copying down the symbols so I can study them more closely on my own. Look at this, three vertical lines, and then three on the next link. But then there's a circle, and ten lines, and another circle. And above each one is an arrow of some sort, but the pattern isn't repeating there either. Fascinating."

"Can I have a word with you when you're done making your notes?" Bennett asked, holding out a hand toward his room. "Privately?"

Joana raised a brow from where she was scrubbing her arm over the basin, the skin red and mottled already. "A little late for a tryst, isn't it, brother?"

Sam paused halfway through her notes, frowning at the expression on Bennett's face. "I don't think it's a tryst he has in mind, Jo."

"No, it certainly is not," Bennett said, though his ears turned slightly pink. His dark expression returned as he took in the girdle still cradled in her lap. "And leave that in the room."

Sam drew the girdle closer in a protective gesture. "Why?"

"Because it . . . I don't . . ." Bennett frowned, as if frustrated at his uncharacteristic loss of words. "Because it makes me uncomfortable."

A spear of panic cut clean through Sam's chest. Had he seen the thrall of the girdle in her eyes, in her expression? Did he know? Would he make her put it back?

"Uncomfortable? Why?" she asked, doing her best to keep her tone steady. "Is it the snakes? Are you worried they'll follow us here?"

"It's not the snakes," Bennett said. "It's . . . you."

"Me?" Sam swiveled her gaze back to Joana as if she might lend some support. But Joana would only look at her out of the corner of her eye, a bad sign from her forthright friend. Bennett stalked across the hall into his own room, and Sam scurried after, still clutching the girdle. "What's wrong with me?"

Bennett looked at Sam, the struggle still evident in the crease between his brows and the hitch of his shoulders. "Sam, your behavior today . . . your behavior over the past few weeks . . . it's not like you. To be so reckless and impulsive. To put your desires ahead of the safety of others. I know these puzzles get into your mind and take over, and you've always been . . . dedicated. But your singular fixation on solving this puzzle, to the exclusion of all else, has been dangerous."

"Bennett," Sam said, in a half-laughing, half-disbelieving scoff. "We found a ceremonial girdle for the Snake Goddess inside an undisturbed bench shrine. You know what this means as much as I do. All of Sir Arthur's conjectures on Minoan religious practice and the gods they worshipped has been based on heavily recon-structed pieces. Flakes of murals, crushed bits of faience statues. The chamber we found today is complete proof of the Snake Goddess's existence. Yes, there were some . . . some challenges, but was it not all in service to the greater good? Isn't this why we both pursued archaeology in the first place? To make a discovery so great it would change the world?"

"I study archaeology to illuminate the past," Bennett said. "To gain knowledge. Not notoriety. I thought you felt the same."

"I do," Sam said, withdrawing her hands as if he'd bitten her.

"Then why have you been so obsessed with making some great discovery on this trip? You know as well as I do that archaeology—true archaeology, not that treasure-hunting nonsense my father and his cronies subscribe to—is about the work. The pottery sherds, the leftover impressions of post holes, the small pieces of everyday existence. It might not have the gold or the glory, but it does a far better job at telling the full story of a culture. But this . . . this reckless pursuit you have to . . . I don't know, to prove yourself? It's not like the Sam I know. Is this because Professor Atchinson didn't have the budget for you to join his summer field school?"

"No, of course not," Sam said, running her fingers absently over the links of the girdle. She had managed to push the constant singing to the back of her mind, but she still had to fight against the urge to try it on.

"Then why? Please, help me understand why you were willing to risk all our lives today."

How could he possibly understand? He, who had been given every opportunity, every door opened for him, every path available to him. He had only to choose which one to step onto. But she had had to fight to even crack the same doors open the barest inch. And Professor Atchinson had shoved them closed that first day when he kicked her out of his class and humiliated her in front of all her peers. She couldn't let him have the last word.

"I wasn't risking our lives, not really," she said futilely, knowing it wasn't really true but not knowing how to put those big feelings into a container of words.

"The golden-headed snakes beg to differ," Bennett said. He stepped toward her, tucking one finger under her chin and lifting her gaze to his. Sam was lost to the dark depths of his eyes, turned a deep brown in the soft candlelight, mesmerized by the gentle stroke of his finger along her jawline. "Sam, if those snakes had attacked . . . We were miles away from any kind of help. Do you know what that would have done to me?"

Sam rubbed her chin against his caress like a shameless cat. "What would it have done?"

Bennett let out a slow breath, his head lowering toward hers as she tilted up to meet him. But there was no contact, and Bennett stepped away from her with a frustrated grunt, leaving her standing dazed in the middle of his rented room while he turned his back.

"You should get some sleep," he said, his voice distant. "I'm sure we'll have our hands full tomorrow."

"But, Bennett—"

"Good night, Sam."

Sam hesitated, but she knew better than to overstay her welcome, or lack thereof. So she left. Joana snorted awake at the sound of the door slamming shut, coming up off her cot like the creature in a German horror film Sam had seen recently.

"What in hell?" Joana asked, looking at Sam wildly. "What happened? Where are we?"

"Sorry, Jo," Sam said dejectedly, setting the girdle on the small table beside her bed. "I didn't mean to wake you. Go back to sleep."

"After that small heart attack you just gave me, who could?" Joana crossed her legs beneath her. "What happened with Bennett? Did he read you the riot act, or did you two kiss and make up?"

"No rioting or kissing," Sam said, unable to keep herself from running a hand over the links of the girdle. She still hadn't copied the full inscription from the inside. She leaned down, squinting in the meager candlelight to try and make them out and finish copying them to her notebook.

"Sam, you'll go cross-eyed doing that, quit it," Joana grumbled, waving a hand at her. "Tell me more about this lack of riotous kissing."

Sam sighed, sketching out the remaining symbols diligently. "Bennett's disappointed in me. I don't understand it, Jo. The discovery we made today . . . Most archaeologists spend their entire lives looking for a find like this. This is incredible. Beyond what we could have imagined. Everything we've ever worked for. Why is he so upset?"

"I think he's probably just worried about the idea of becoming a sacrifice for another goddess. Can't say I blame him so much either, regardless of how fabulous her choice of waist-wear is."

"That's not what's going to happen," Sam said, so forcefully she surprised them both. She took a deep breath, settling herself as she closed up her notebook and tucked it back into her stack of neatly folded clothes at the foot of her bed. "We'll take the girdle to the museum in the morning, have the find authenticated, and bring a full police force back with us to the cave if we have to in order to scare off those cave robbers bothering Mr. Killeen. Everything will be fine, you'll see. Better than fine. Extraordinary."

"Mmmm-hmmm," Joana said, eyeing her. "If you can keep Mr. Killeen from trying to steal all the credit for himself. The *eyes* on that man."

"I don't think Mr. Killeen would do that," Sam protested. "He's a man of knowledge, a man of learning. He's the director of the Heraklion Archaeological Museum, for Pete's sake. He was trying to protect the cave from robbers!"

"You trust him all you want," Joana said, lying back down and covering her eyes. "I saw that look on his face, same as every gold digger and treasure hunter that Daddy brings around to the Archaeological Society back home. These men would bury their grandmothers in a shallow grave to stake their claim. Don't be surprised when he cuts you out altogether."

Sam could hardly blame Joana for not trusting men, especially after their experiences in Dublin. But she had followed Mr. Killeen's successes as director of the Heraklion Archaeological Museum for several months, marveling at his expertise in organizing and displaying their collection. He had been handpicked by Sir Arthur Evans himself to manage the precious works. He was a professional.

"Put out that light, would you?" Joana said from beneath her arm. "I'm half-dead, and it keeps trying to revive me."

"Sorry," Sam said, turning down the lamp wick. The girdle lay on the table beside her, glowing softly despite any obvious source of external light. Sam longed to reach for it, to feel the smooth warmth of its links beneath her fingers once again. But Joana was not the only one fatigued by their excursions that day, and Sam was asleep before her hand could reach it, hanging instead down the side of the bed.

CHAPTER FOURTEEN

Oddly enough, Sam dreamed of trains. Specifically, the train ride they had taken earlier that year from Chicago to New York on their way to Dublin. She dreamed of the papers spread on the small table between her and Bennett, the air of the compartment warming with their shared breath as they pored over another mystery, the train car rocking steadily back and forth.

The papers slid to one side of the table, then the other, the motion of the car growing rougher and more unsteady as the train picked up speed. Sam looked up in fright as the car rocked even harder, Bennett's trunk clattering to the edge of the luggage store above their heads, hanging like a Damocles sword waiting to drop and crush them. She braced herself against the plush seating, planting her feet and digging her fingers into the fabric as the trunk fell open, raining down books and other objects on her. Something rattled and hissed, and when she looked up, a golden-headed snake bared its fangs in warning before darting straight for her.

She came awake with a shock as something very heavy and very real struck her in the face. She cried out, shielding her head as more objects pelted her. The knickknack shelf of their rented room was raining vengeance down upon them.

"Sam, wake up!" came Joana's voice from the dark, her hands grabbing Sam and pulling her toward the ground. "Sam, damn it, come on! We've got to get down!"

Sam looked up in a panic at patchy bits of starlight showing through the cracks in the ceiling. Those cracks widened as the walls shook back and forth like a runaway train.

"Come on, you loon, get down under the bed," Joana shouted right beside her ear.

"What is it?" Sam asked, bewildered, though her body followed Joana's command.

"It's an earthquake," Joana grunted, shoving aside a tipped-over end table to squirm under the bed and pull Sam with her. "The roof is caving in. We need to get under something or we'll get crushed."

Sam was fully, painfully awake now, a shower of dust choking her as she fitted herself under the thin mattress beside Joana. "But what if we get trapped under here?" she asked breathlessly.

The ground beneath them gave a sickening, rolling lurch, and Sam had to close her eyes and press her forehead to the floor to keep that wave from rising in her own stomach.

"It'll be over in a minute," Joana said, her voice high and thin but steady. She scrabbled for Sam's hand and linked their fingers, holding so tight it made the fine bones in Sam's hand creak.

"Oh my god," Sam moaned as the earth rolled again. The movement was smaller this time, though, and after one more rollicking movement, it seemed to settle into itself. The ceiling groaned, dropping a few more chunks of plaster and another shower of dust, but at least it didn't collapse on them.

"Wait," Joana said as Sam made to squirm out from under the bed. "Sometimes there are smaller ones afterward."

"More earthquakes?" Sam asked, her stomach executing a

dipping roll in anticipation. "Have you . . . Has this happened to you before?"

"A few times, when Daddy took us to Athens," Joana said. Her grip on Sam's hand loosened, but she didn't let go. "They get earthquakes a lot around here."

Sam had certainly read about some of those historic earthquakes, many of which had destroyed cities and leveled civilizations like the Minoans'. She just hadn't expected to *live* through one of them. She thought back to her dream, her stomach twisting and roiling again.

"Oh, Jo, what about Bennett?" she gasped. "We need to check on him!"

"Please, if anyone knows the proper precautions to take during a natural disaster, it's Bennett," Joana said. "I'm sure he's fine. Knowing him, he'll be directing the villagers on recovery efforts before we even crawl out of here."

Sam knew Joana was probably right, but that didn't stop the panic short-circuiting her system at the moment. Her chest was tight, her breath shallow and quick, and she knew she wouldn't be able to take a deep breath until she could put her hands on Bennett and know for herself that he was all right.

He apparently had the same concern, because less than a minute later, his voice filtered through the rubble in a shout, calling their names.

"We're here!" Sam cried, inching out from under the bed. "Bennett, we're okay! Jo and I are over here."

As she found her way out, she saw that the damage was far more extensive than she had imagined. The room was a mess, the furniture fallen over and the entire north-facing wall collapsed and open. The roof had mostly held, despite the cracks, though Sam didn't like the creaking coming from overhead.

"Sam!" Bennett said, climbing over the fallen washbasin to reach her. He pulled her into his arms, giving her a tight hug before holding her back for inspection. "You're okay? Thank god. Jo?"

"I'm here, too, brother," Joana grunted, shoving aside a piece of ceiling to make room to crawl out. "Sorry to disappoint you."

"Don't be ridiculous, Jo," Bennett said, stepping over more rubble to embrace Joana. Her eyes went wide in surprise before she patted him on the back awkwardly.

"All right, Bennett, don't get your knickers twisted," she said, pushing him away. But Sam caught the hint of a smile before Joana rearranged her expression into her usual armor. "I guess we're sleeping with the crickets and the stars tonight."

"You were planning on going back to sleep?" Sam asked.

Joana shrugged one shoulder. "Minor disasters make me sleepy."

The innkeeper called up to them in Greek, asking if they were injured or needed help getting out. Bennett helped Joana over the bigger chunks of ceiling toward the hallway that led down to the main floor, returning to help Sam navigate the new terrain. The inhabitants of Skotino had gathered in the street in their nightclothes, chattering and gossiping about the earthquake and the work that would need to be done. Sam overheard several of them remark on the intensity of the quake. She had found it rather intense herself and was glad it was not just her inexperience. If that had been a *minor* disaster, as Joana called it, she certainly did not want to find herself caught in a major one.

"Are you children all right?" the innkeeper asked, pulling a shawl tightly around her and watching their careful progress over the wreckage of her home and livelihood. Sam marveled at the practical tilt of her head as she assessed the damage and gave a grunt of annoyance. "This will take some rebuilding."

The inn seemed to have taken the worst of the damage, based

on what Sam could see in the faint light. The fault lines radiated out from the little building, cutting through neighboring homes and down into the road. It was a wonder they had survived, which gave Sam a shiver. How could these villagers live with the threat of this kind of disaster all the time?

"Whatever you need help with, please let us know," Sam said in her rudimentary Greek. "Clearing away the mess, getting food, anything."

"That's a kindness, thank you," said the older woman. "It won't be the first time we've had to do repairs from an earthquake, but this will be more extensive than previous ones."

"That's because it wasn't any ordinary earthquake, Elina, and you know it," said a scratchy voice behind them.

The innkeeper clucked her tongue in a dismissive manner at the frail old man who approached them, his hair a snowy white and his back curved like a question mark. He used a gnarled cane to walk, each thump of the wood against the ground making Sam wince in the aftermath of the earthquake.

"Go on, Lieke, and stop scaring my customers with your crazy old superstitions," said the innkeeper, waving the man away as if he were a cloud of gnats and not a human.

"They're not superstitions, you sour old woman," Lieke said, pointing an accusing finger at her. "The land is angry."

The innkeeper threw her hands up, rolling her eyes. "You've done it now. We'll be hearing this until the angels come for us all. Don't let Father Pasternost hear you speaking of this again."

"Speaking of what?" Bennett asked, frowning.

"The old gods," said the gnarled little man, his voice like a chill wind despite the humid night. "The ones who built this land, and who sleep beneath it now. Someone has disturbed one of them."

Sam drew in a breath, looking to Bennett and Joana in a mutual sense of dread. Most people would have dismissed the man's rambling as superstition, like the innkeeper had done. But they had seen an ancient goddess rise from the earth with their own eyes. For Sam, the man's theory wasn't so far-fetched.

Was that what Sam had done, when she took the girdle? Did she awaken the Snake Goddess? Did she cause this earthquake? But the singing had been so . . . inviting. So welcoming.

"Why would the land be angry?" Sam asked.

The old man took a deep breath, tilting his head as if trying to catch an elusive scent on the wind. "Someone has interrupted the ritual and thrown off the balance. The land will continue to erupt until the balance is restored and the ritual is complete. The goddess must be satisfied."

"Interrupted?" Sam echoed, shaking her head helplessly at Bennett and Joana. "What could that mean, interrupted? What ritual?"

But the man had wandered off, and when she began to follow, the innkeeper called to them from the house.

"Is your father all right?" she said, peering into the hallway where they had emerged a few moments ago.

"He's not our . . . Oh, blast, we forgot about Mr. Killeen," Bennett said, trotting toward the house and raising his voice in a shout. "Mr. Killeen! Are you there? Mr. Killeen, are you all right?"

Bennett disappeared into the rubble, emerging a moment later looking bewildered. "He's gone. Mr. Killeen. He's disappeared."

CHAPTER FIFTEEN

"The girdle!" Sam cried, clambering over the rubble and ignoring Bennett's shouts of protest as she made her way back to the precarious second level. In all the excitement from the earthquake she'd forgotten about it, but if Mr. Killeen was gone, that might mean . . .

She reached the landing, the wood creaking ominously beneath her feet as she gripped the doorframe for stability before picking her way gingerly through the minefield of broken porcelain and toppled books until she reached her bed. She searched the entire area as well as she could, considering the state of the room, but the heavy weight in her gut already knew the truth.

"Sam!" came Bennett's voice. "Are you all right?"

"I'm here, I'm all right," Sam said, extracting herself from the mess of the room and returning to the landing. It creaked under their shared weight, the floor listing slightly to the left and tumbling Sam into Bennett's chest. He grabbed her and steadied her.

"It's gone, the girdle," she said, her stomach twisting up tight. "Oh, Bennett, what if those men came back to the cave and somehow discovered the secret chamber? What if we carelessly left some evidence of our presence there, and they tracked us back here and kidnapped Mr. Killeen and stole the girdle? They could be anywhere by now! And poor Mr. Killeen, what will they do to him?"

"Sam, shhhh." Bennett smoothed a hand down her spine. "We won't do ourselves any favors panicking now. It's nearly dawn anyway. We'll find the car and drive back to Heraklion and do what we should have done from the beginning. We'll contact the proper authorities and report the find, and Mr. Killeen's disappearance. For all we know, he might have gotten an early start and taken the girdle back to the museum himself."

"But, Bennett, it's not just that," Sam said, stepping out of the comforting embrace of his arms. She didn't deserve it. "There's something about the girdle, something I didn't . . . I should have told you, back in the chamber when it happened. But you would have insisted we bury it without anyone ever knowing, and I couldn't stand the thought of it! But now, after what that old villager said, I'm afraid we've just made everything exponentially worse."

"What are you talking about?" Bennett asked, shaking his head in confusion. "What happened back in the chamber? What are you not telling me?"

"What are you two cuckoos doing up there?" Joana called from the bottom of the stairs, peering up from under the listing ceiling. "You're going to get yourself a headful of plaster if you don't come down from there. Oh, but do grab my overnight bag. I hate to lose a good pair of silk stockings."

"The girdle is gone, Jo," Bennett called back. "Your silk stockings will have to take the backseat for now."

"Like hell they will," Joana muttered, climbing the stairs with determination while clinging to the wall like it was the face of a cliff. "I'll get them myself."

"Sam," Bennett prompted when several quiet seconds had passed. "What happened? How have we made everything exponentially worse?"

Sam chewed at one corner of her lip, knowing she needed to tell them about the effect of the girdle but still agonizing over the actual telling. She already knew what Bennett would say, and she already knew he'd be right. But she had been right, too, hadn't she? The chamber and the girdle were far too precious a find to just bury and forget, weren't they?

"The old man just now, he said the ritual had been interrupted and it upset the balance," Sam said, evading Bennett's true question. "I think when the girdle was taken, when the wrong people laid hands on it . . ."

"You think *that's* what caused the earthquake?" Bennett said.

"How would you even know?" Joana asked. "This place gets earthquakes like Chicago gets snowstorms. What makes you think it had anything supernatural to do with it?"

And here it was, Sam's excruciating moment of truth. "Because when I touched the girdle . . . when I took it off the horns of consecration, I heard . . . singing."

Bennett took a long, careful breath, his eyes glimmering in the dark. "What does that mean, you heard singing?"

"I mean . . . I think the girdle is not just ornamentation. I think it's the real ceremonial garment of the Snake Goddess."

Bennett was so quiet for so long Sam began to fear she had broken him, or perhaps he had not heard her at all and she would be forced to repeat the damning information all over again. She opened and closed her mouth several times, starting and discarding a dozen different excuses. But when Bennett finally spoke, his voice was dangerously quiet.

"Why didn't you tell us?"

"Why didn't I . . . ?" It took Sam a moment to pick up the thread of what they had been discussing. "Well, Mr. Killeen was there. I couldn't very well say such a thing in front of him. He'd have had me hauled off to a mental ward."

"And after?" Bennett pressed. "When we made it back here, and Mr. Killeen was nowhere around to hear you, why not then?"

Why not indeed? "We had already taken the girdle out of the chamber by then," Sam hedged. "I thought . . . I thought if something were going to go wrong, it would have already happened. I thought . . . maybe I had imagined it."

Which wasn't exactly true, but she didn't figure Bennett was interested in semantics at that point. He had closed his eyes, his expression so rigid and still, he could have been carved from stone. Sam flicked her gaze nervously toward Joana, hoping for some support, but the other Steeling sibling looked more shell-shocked than supportive.

"What does it mean?" Joana asked. "If Sam is right, and this Snake Goddess is real, what happens now?"

"I don't know," Sam said, grateful for something practical to bite into. Bennett still wouldn't look at her. "The singing, it felt . . . like some kind of ritual performance, I guess. And I had this strange urge, to . . . to put on the girdle. Like it wanted me to."

"An epiphany," Bennett said, his eyes snapping open. "That sounds like an epiphany."

"Oh," Sam breathed, all the strange pieces suddenly clicking into place.

"What *oh*?" Joana demanded. "What am I missing? What's an epiphany?"

"The physical manifestation of a god or goddess on the earthly plane," Bennett said. "It was part of a ritual, usually, a renewal-of-power ceremony. The Minoans were supposedly ruled by a king named Minos, though that might have been his title and it might have belonged to more than one man. His power was bestowed by the blessing of a powerful goddess. But that power came at a cost. He needed his power renewed."

"Renewed how?" Joana asked, her voice sharp.

"The role of the king, Minos, was filled by a different leader every eight or nine years, supposedly," said Bennett, never one to pass up on a teaching opportunity regardless of the circumstances. "There are gold signet rings that have been recovered that show the connection between an epiphany of the goddess and the renewal of power of her king-consort. It ties into the myth of the labyrinth and the Minotaur as well. Some versions of the myth say the sacrifices from Athens were only sent every eight or nine years, as part of the renewal cycle. That the king needed to be replaced, or his power renewed, every cycle. And to renew such a power, one needs a goddess."

"The myth of the mother goddess and the king-consort," Sam said, burying her face in her hands. "Why didn't I think of that?"

"Probably because you were so busy tuning into her little song," Joana said, her voice dry as bones.

"I might deserve that," Sam said, frowning down at her feet. "I . . . I know I made a mistake—"

"A mistake?" Bennett said, incredulous. "Sam, a mistake is digging in the wrong location, or tossing out a pottery sherd with a heap of dirt. This wasn't a mistake. You did this on purpose. You *chose* this. After everything we went through with the Morrigan in Dublin, after what the bowl tried to do to you—to us!—you still chose to take that girdle out of the chamber. And for what?"

"I had no idea this would happen, you have to believe me!" Sam said. "The old man said that someone interrupted the ritual. I don't think the earthquake happened because I took the girdle. I think it happened because someone else touched it. Mr. Killeen, if it was only him. Or those men from the cave, if they found us here and took him and the girdle."

"So that earthquake might only be the start of it," said Bennett tightly.

"We can still fix this," Sam said. "If we just find—"

"*We* are not fixing anything," Bennett interrupted, turning his back on her and beginning the descent to the ground floor. "I am going to do what I should have done from the beginning and return to Heraklion to alert the proper authorities. They'll know far better than us how to find these men and return the girdle."

"But you can't do that!" Sam called after him. "They'll want to lock up the girdle, and we'll never get our hands on it. And who knows what kind of damage it'll do by then. We've got to do this ourselves."

"We've done enough by ourselves," Bennett said, not pausing as he passed Joana. "Come on, Jo, we'll need to see if the roads are still traversable."

"Jo, you understand, don't you?" Sam asked desperately.

"Oh, I understand," Joana said, following after her brother. "I just don't think that *you* do. Here's hoping we can find these mystery men before we learn what a half-awakened goddess considers appropriate punishment for stealing her jewelry."

CHAPTER SIXTEEN

They returned to Heraklion in the early afternoon, the sun glimmering off the waters of the ocean like scattered diamonds. The ride back had been tense and long, punctuated only by Joana's occasional quips that earned no more than a monosyllabic response from Bennett. And even those attempts from Joana eventually died away when she couldn't get a rise out of her brother. Sam, for her part, did not even attempt such conversation. She already knew what kind of response she would receive.

She had, at least, managed to convince Bennett to check Mr. Killeen's museum before they took their complaints to the magistrate. She had reasoned that since Mr. Killeen had hired the men, perhaps someone who worked there would know who they were or how to find them. Bennett had relented, but she suspected it was only because he didn't want to continue talking to her.

The Heraklion Archaeological Museum was still open when they arrived, and for a brief moment, Sam hoped she might be right and they might still find a way to stop these men before another earthquake hit. But her hopes sank right back down the moment they rushed inside.

"Professor Atchinson?" Bennett said in surprise as he entered the museum behind Sam. The small collection of graduate students glanced toward their intrusion in surprise, and Professor Atchinson gave them a sour look.

"I thought I made it explicitly clear what would happen to the three of you if our paths crossed again," said the professor.

"Professor, we need your help," Bennett said. "Something has happened with Mr. Killeen."

"Yes, Mr. Killeen," said Professor Atchinson, raising both brows. "Whom the three of you insisted sent a letter to request Barnaby Wallstone's help."

"Because he did," Bennett said, frowning.

"Yes, of course he did," continued Professor Atchinson. "Despite being completely baffled when I mentioned the three of you to him when we arrived at the museum earlier today."

"He's here?" Sam asked in relief, ignoring the professor's rude tone in favor of peering into the back reaches of the museum.

"Of course he is," said Professor Atchinson. "He is the one conducting our tour of Minoan artifacts."

"Oh, thank goodness," Sam said, heaving a sigh as she looked to Bennett. "If he is here, that must mean the girdle is with him. I told you we can still fix this."

"What are you on about now?" asked the professor, baffled. Before Sam could explain, a tall, thin man in an elegantly-turned-out suit approached their group from the back office of the museum.

"Apologies, Richard, Mr. Mackenzie requested a few pieces be transported to Villa Ariadne to be displayed during the gala celebration," said the man in a genteel British accent that was somewhat muffled by the impressive mustache that graced his upper lip. That mustache ruffled and stretched under the force of a jovial smile. "Shall we continue? Where were we?"

"Hector, these are the children who insisted you contacted

Barnaby Wallstone about some great discovery," said Professor Atchinson, waving in Sam's direction. "Perhaps seeing them face-to-face will clear up any confusion."

The man looked at them in polite ignorance, lifting his thick white brows in anticipation. "Yes, how can I help the three of you?"

"You . . . can't?" Sam said, shaking her head and looking back to Professor Atchinson. "I'm sorry, but where is Mr. Killeen?"

"Right here," Professor Atchinson said, looking at her as if she'd had all the sense knocked out of her. "This is Hector Killeen, director of the Heraklion Archaeological Museum."

Maybe she had been brained by a chunk of ceiling the previous evening, because this man was very obviously not Mr. Killeen. At least, not the Mr. Killeen who had led them to Skotino cave and then disappeared in the middle of the night . . .

"Oh hell," Joana muttered.

"We've been duped," Sam said.

Bennett looked just as stricken as she felt, his skin gone a pasty gray. "Professor Atchinson, we need to speak with you immediately," he said. "We've made a terrible mistake."

Mr. Killeen led them back to his office, the space wide and airy and neatly organized. Nothing like Professor Wallstone's cluttered office back in Chicago, nor Professor Atchinson's pompously arrayed office filled with awards and degrees. Mr. Killeen was a true professional, Sam could tell, exactly the kind of person she would have wanted to impress. And now, instead, she was about to be forced to admit her greatest embarrassment.

"Bennett, what are you doing?" Sam whispered as Mr. Killeen stepped outside of the office for a moment to direct one of his docents to complete the tour for Professor Atchinson's class before he and the professor dealt with them. "If we tell Atchinson about the girdle, he won't believe us."

"Or more likely, he'll tell us he doesn't believe us, then go find it himself and claim the discovery all his own," Joana said. "Bury us all in a deep hole somewhere so he can keep the credit."

"Professor Atchinson is a respected member of the faculty at the university," Bennett reasoned. "And what's more important, he's the only person of authority here that we know the *true* identity of. He may not believe us about the more . . . supernatural aspects of the girdle, but we have plenty of proof that the chamber and the girdle are real. And he can help us find Mr. Kill—the imposter formerly known as Mr. Killeen."

"But think of what Atchinson will do, if he knows we went off with . . . an imposter," Sam said, wincing at the fresh wound to her naïveté. "He's already threatened to have us up with the university board. This would be all he needs to put us on probation, or worse."

Bennett turned even grayer at that prospect, but it didn't change the firm set of his mouth. "Be that as it may, we have an obligation here. We opened that chamber against my better judgment, and we were the ones who removed the girdle and allowed Mr. Killeen, the fake Mr. Killeen, to abscond with it. For all we know, those men at the cave might have been working with him, as part of his scheme. It's only right we should be the ones to face the . . . consequences."

Bennett seemed to choke on getting that last word out, his grip tightening on the arms of his chair. Sam felt all her dreams, so recently excavated, now buried under the prospect of Professor Atchinson's reproval. But Bennett seemed steadfast in his decision to share their indiscretions with the professor.

"Now, what is it you three needed to speak with me about so *urgently?*" said Professor Atchinson, interrupting Sam's spiral of panic by plunging her straight into the deep end. Mr. Killeen joined him, only adding to the humiliation, the two of them lording over

Sam like high judges from days past. Now she knew what those poor girls on trial for witchcraft must have felt like.

"Something has . . . happened," started Bennett, straightening in his chair and doing his best not to look like he was terrified. He almost managed to succeed, thanks to his fine Steeling upbringing.

Quickly he ran through their predicament, starting with the letter they had received in Chicago right down to the stolen girdle and the coincidental earthquake that followed. He didn't outright link the two, but he let the question of their relationship linger in the air as he finished his explanation. A weighty silence filled the room after he finished, the two older men's expressions frozen in a state somewhere between surprise and disbelief. Sam longed to shout into that void, to raise defenses for herself and Joana and Bennett, but it was as if Bennett's unspoken recriminations sat on her chest, keeping her from speaking up.

Professor Atchinson had no qualms giving those recriminations voice, however.

"I had such high hopes for you, Master Steeling, when you first matriculated," said the professor gravely, shaking his head. "But I am afraid you have been far too susceptible to bad influence. It is one thing to align yourself with the likes of Barnaby Wallstone, but to let this . . . this overstepping, uneducated, dangerous young lady lead you astray like this is really beyond the pale."

"Is he talking about me?" Joana murmured.

"I think . . . I think he's talking about me," Sam whispered back, the words scratching her throat like thorns.

"Well, that's a disappointment," Joana said, slouching down into her chair.

"Professor Atchinson, I know how it all sounds, but I assure you—" Bennett began, but the professor held up his hand in a gesture that would tolerate no more interruptions.

"It is my fault, really," he continued, gazing over at the real Mr. Killeen with a look of long suffering. "I have been far too indulgent in allowing their ignorant ambitions."

"Now hang on," Sam said, her face flushing as her spine went rigid against the back of the chair. "You were the one—"

"You truly expect us to believe," the professor continued, looking pointedly over her head to Bennett, "that you three children found a—a what? A hidden Minoan chamber of such historical significance?"

He chuckled forcefully, and the real Mr. Killeen joined in.

"I assure you," said the real Mr. Killeen, his tone gentler than the professor's but no less patronizing. "If such a find were to be made, we would have made it already. Sir Arthur's men have conducted their own surveys at Skotino cave and found nothing more than a few bone pins and sacrificial beads. Nothing of such import, certainly. What a fairy tale! I'm afraid you've been duped in more ways than one here."

Bennett's expression froze. "Mr. Killeen, please give us the opportunity to prove our findings to you. If you could just—"

"That will be more than enough," said the professor, loudly and with a tinge of boredom. "The only thing you have proven is that I will have to take far more stringent measures to ensure your interferences no longer negatively impact the education of more dedicated students. I am afraid I have no choice but to call for a full investigation into your activities here on Crete. The university board will have to hear of this. I don't believe there's a check your father could write to save you from this terrible gaffe, Master Steeling. Now, Hector and I have actual students to attend to. I suggest, for your own good, that you find yourselves a trio of tickets on the next steamer out. Hector, shall we?"

Mr. Killeen hesitated, looking at them curiously. "This man you say was impersonating me, what can you tell me about him? I'd hate to think of such a character attempting to defraud more tourists like you in my name."

Sam shook her head; or was it that she was shaking all over? "I don't . . . He seemed perfectly ordinary. I mean, not that you are ordinary, sir. Of course not, you're . . . , you're the director of the Heraklion! Extraordinary. But he didn't seem . . . wrong?"

Though of course, now that she reexamined the facts, she could have drowned in the wave of embarrassment that crashed over her. Every flag was a red one, from the letter to the strange address Mr. Not Killeen left to the sneaking around the cave with no authorities. It wasn't just that she should have known; it was that anyone else *would* have known.

Professor Atchinson gave Mr. Killeen a look. "You see now what I mean."

"Yes, I believe I rather do," murmured Mr. Killeen. "Ah, well, I shall have to report such activities to the magistrate here."

Mr. Killeen exited the office, leaving them with Professor Atchinson's glowering presence. He drew in a deep breath, pinching his lips together.

"Good-bye, children, for what I expect to be the last time."

CHAPTER SEVENTEEN

"Whew, I'll never complain about another one of Daddy's lectures on how a proper young woman should comport herself again," Joana said as they skulked out of the real Mr. Killeen's office. "That man knew a disturbing number of ways to tell someone they're a failure."

"Let's just go back to the hotel and pack our things," Bennett said, all trace of emotion leached out of his voice.

Sam came to a halt. "Bennett, you're not serious, are you? We're not really going to just give up and go home. Not with the girdle still out there with Mr. Kill—er, the imposter. We have to do something!"

"Like what?" Bennett asked, holding his hands out. "What do you expect me to do, Sam? I tried telling the professor, and he didn't believe us. What do you think the authorities would do if we tried to tell them?"

"We can't just give up!" Sam exclaimed. "We've got to find the imposter ourselves, if Professor Atchinson won't help us."

Bennett closed his eyes, pinching the bridge of his nose as the furrow in his brow deepened even more than usual. "Sam, we'll be lucky to get out of this with a place at the university, much less a future in the field of archaeology. Do you understand the reach Professor Atchinson has? Everything in this field—*everything*—comes down to reputation, and we just squandered ours in there. We squandered it as soon as we followed that charlatan's letter to Crete."

"But the symbol," Sam protested weakly. "And the chamber. The chamber was real, and so was the girdle! Mr. Kill—er, whoever that man was might have been fake, but the chamber was certainly real enough. Professor Atchinson and Mr. Killeen might not believe us, but someone will. They have to!"

"Sam, it's over," Bennett said, running his hand through his hair and sending it curling in all directions. "Don't you understand? All we've done is create chaos since we arrived. At this point, the island is better off with us not on it. And you heard the professor. He won't stop until we're all expelled with dishonor. There will be no field schools in our future, nor can we count on any faculty endorsements for the graduate program. No doubt Professor Atchinson will use this as the final nail in Wallstone's coffin. All my hard work, the studying, the grades I fought for, it's all gone now. I might as well brush up on the ledgers at the Steeling mill, because that's where I'll be headed when all this settles."

Sam longed to do or say something—*anything*—to erase the intense pain from Bennett's face, but they were interrupted by a loud voice.

"Well, don't you three look properly horsewhipped," said Theo, blocking the museum exit with his prodigious form. He crossed his arms, gloating at them. "I've never seen Professor Atchinson as mad as he was at you. What did you do, knock over a pithos? Break the arm off a statue?"

"None of your business, Chapin," Joana said, the promise of a fight returning the heat to her blood. "Let us pass or I might mistake you for a door and make an opening myself."

Theo raised both of his brows. "That bad, huh?"

"Just move, Theo," Bennett said on a heavy sigh.

Theo's eyes widened. "Worse than bad? This must be my birthday."

"Theodore, please," said Evelyn from beside him. Sam had hardly noticed the young woman standing there, lost in his shadow. She gave Sam a worried look. "It's not so bad as all that, is it?"

Sam winced. "All that and worse, I'm afraid."

"Oh," Evelyn said on a soft sigh that was lost to Theo's crowing laugh.

"You lot got yourselves kicked out for good, didn't you? Oh, I always knew it. Didn't I tell you, Evelyn, from the beginning? These idiots and their crackpot professor were going to make fools of themselves and cock it up. And now they have, barely a day into the whole thing. What complete embarrassments."

"All right, Chapin, that's enough—" Joana began hotly, but the lights in the museum flickered and dropped out as the walls of the building began to shake. Evelyn screamed, and even Sam couldn't help a cry of surprise as the pottery knocked against the glass in the display cases. Bennett grabbed her on instinct, pulling her and Joana under a nearby bench as the earth roiled and bucked beneath them. Sam dropped her head and pressed in close to both of them, the terror of the previous night surging all over again.

The earthquake seemed even rougher this time around, although thankfully the ceiling didn't cave in on them. The ominous sound of shattering pottery filtered through the glass enclosures, and Sam nearly wept for the damage someone would have to repair when it was over. By the time the earth settled again, her breath was coming short and fast, mingling with Bennett's and Joana's labored breathing.

"Chapin, Evelyn, are you both all right?" Bennett asked, raising his voice. He craned his head out just enough to check that the building wasn't going to collapse before crawling out and helping Sam and Joana stand up.

"We're fine, Steeling," Theo groused, though his voice had lost plenty of its bravado. He came out from behind a display case where several urns had fallen over, Evelyn following close by as if he had been her shelter. And frankly, Sam thought, from the size of him, he probably had been. "It's not like earthquakes are uncommon around here."

"Was it too much to ask that a ceiling tile knock some decency into you, Chapin?" Joana asked.

"Well, you weren't crushed by a bull statue, so nobody gets what they want, Joana," Theo shot back.

"Evelyn, are you okay?" Sam asked, noting the girl's ashen features. She looked how Sam had felt the previous evening.

Evelyn gave a brief nod, but before she could respond, Theo took her firmly by the arm. "She's fine," he said. "We're both fine, and it looks like Mr. Killeen and Professor Atchinson will need help cleaning up from people who actually know what they're doing. Go on, you three. The adults have it from here."

Bennett's jaw muscle twitched, but he didn't rise to the bait and instead took Sam and Joana by the arms and steered them toward the museum exit. Joana threw Theo a single-fingered farewell before they stepped out into the brilliant sunlight. Sam was relieved to see that most of the buildings around them stood with little damage, their structures more solid and better able to withstand the earthquake than the small homes in Skotino village.

"I suppose we'd better do as Atchinson said and head down to the docks to purchase our tickets home," Bennett said glumly.

"But, Bennett—"

"No, Sam," Bennett said, his voice firm. "We've had our adventure, if that's what you want to call it. We've done enough damage. It's time to go home."

Sam started to protest again, but Joana put a hand on her arm. "He's like a clam. He needs time to steam, and then he'll be ready to open up. Let it rest."

Sam had to bite the inside of her lip to keep more arguments from spilling out. She knew Bennett well enough to know Joana was right, but she also knew how stubborn Bennett could be. They might be on a steamer halfway across the Atlantic before he decided to "open up," and she didn't have that kind of time.

And neither did the island, if the increased intensity of the second earthquake was any indication.

The air warmed considerably as they made their way down the streets of Heraklion back in the direction of their hotel, the cooling breezes of the ocean broken up by the collection of buildings around them. The stones baked under their feet, the brilliant white of many of the Venetian buildings causing Sam to squint against their light. She wouldn't have even known there had been an earthquake only a few moments before, based on the traffic of people and carts crowding the streets. Only the faint cracks in the ground gave any indication of trauma, along with the occasional broken roof tile littering the roads.

Sam had thought they were headed back toward the hotel, but she quickly lost her way in the twists and turns of the city streets. Sometimes they moved down, but the street would suddenly curve to the left or right, and they found themselves in a dead end or hiking up the steep streets instead. Several times they had to stop and ask for directions to get back on the downward track, and soon they were all sweating under the relentless heat.

"Forget the hotel, find me a taverna and a shot of raki," Joana grumbled after their fourth dead end.

"You know, Sir Arthur Evans has claimed the palace of Knossos is the site of the labyrinth of legend, but there are others who believe it refers not to the palace, but to the twisting and winding streets of Heraklion itself," Sam huffed, heading back out of a beautiful flowered courtyard.

"So long as we don't run into a man-bull," Joana said.

They headed down again, the hairline cracks in the ground growing slightly more pronounced on the street they entered. Several more cracks appeared as they walked, all of them pointed in the same direction. Without quite realizing she was doing it, Sam started walking alongside one of the lines, following its path.

"Sam, where are you going?" Joana murmured just behind her.

"I'm not sure," Sam whispered, glancing back at Bennett surreptitiously. "I think . . . Look at the ground."

Joana glanced down. "What about it?"

"Look at the cracks. They're all headed in the same direction."

"I see. What is it that I see?"

"After the earthquake in Skotino village, I noticed that all the fault lines seemed to radiate out from the inn where we were staying," Sam whispered. "I think the girdle itself is causing the quakes. So, if we follow the lines, it will lead us to the center of the quake."

"And therefore the girdle," Joana said, nodding in understanding.

"And hopefully the fraudulent Mr. Killeen," said Sam. "I have some choice words for him."

"I have some unsavory ones myself," Joana said.

"Sam," Bennett said from behind them, his tone a mixture of exasperation and warning. "What are you doing?"

Sam stopped abruptly, spinning to face him with what she hoped was an innocent expression. "Sightseeing. Why? What are you doing?"

Bennett crossed his arms. "Sam."

"I think you're busted," Joana whispered, pulling down one corner of her sun hat to protect her from the intensity of Bennett's gaze.

Sam did her best to continue looking innocent, which was difficult to do when an insistent trickle of sweat kept winding its way into her eye and making it sting. The grimace probably made her look guilty. "I'm just admiring this Roman architecture, Bennett. I'm not sure what you're trying to imply."

"First of all, that's Venetian. And second of all, I know you're following the cracks in the ground."

Sam gave a nervous little chuckle. "Why would I do that?"

He rolled his eyes heavenward. "Give me patience," he muttered. "Come on, then, out with it. Why are you following the cracks?"

Sam threw her hands out. "Fine! Yes, I was following the cracks. If the earthquakes are being caused by the wrong people handling the girdle, then it stands to reason the girdle will be at the epicenter of every quake. It certainly looked that way back in Skotino village. Really I was just . . . testing a hypothesis."

Bennett closed his eyes, pinching the bridge of his nose with two fingers. "You're going to follow these cracks whether or not I tell you to stop, aren't you?"

"No?"

Bennett's nostrils flared on an exhale. "We stay together, no one ventures out on their own for *any reason*. And if we find the imposter, you do *not* confront him. We call for the authorities and send for Mr. Killeen—the real Mr. Killeen. Under no circumstances are you to have any kind of contact with the false Mr. Killeen. Understood?"

"Amazing," Joana said in wonder. "A pitch-perfect rendition of a classic Daddy lecture. Now say 'And no drinking, smoking, or fraternizing, Joana Rose.'"

Bennett gave her a flat look. "I should think those go without saying."

Joana snapped her fingers. "There it is! That exact tone."

"This is a bad idea," Bennett started, but Sam held up her hands to stave him off.

"We'll stay together," she said, anxious to move on. "No confronting, call for the authorities. Cross all our hearts. Can we please continue?"

Bennett held up an arm tiredly. "Lead on."

"You know he was being a Bossy Betty," Joana murmured to Sam. "Just like Daddy when he gets his Irish up."

"Yes, and telling them so never gets *you* out of trouble, does it?" Sam countered.

Joana cocked her head to one side. "Hmm. I hadn't considered that."

Sam gave her an impatient smile. "You never do."

They traced the cracks through the streets, occasionally having to climb over fences or duck under laundry lines to follow their paths. All the fissures continued on in the same direction, growing wider in places and thinner in others, but more and more of them running together until it felt as if they were following an enormous geological arrow. It led them into a crowded business district, passing bakeries and olive oil stands and doctors' offices until the cracks all seemed to join in front of one tiny, dusty storefront.

Sam looked up at the carved wooden sign overhead, the letters jagged and sharp like Greek letters, but written out in English. "'Boivin's Cabinet of Curiosities,'" she read.

"Looks more like Grandmother Steeling's parlor in New York," Joana said, cupping her hands around her eyes and looking through the windows in sore need of a cleaning. "It's stuffed to the gills with junk."

"Not just junk," Bennett said, looking through the glass beside her. "Those are Minoan artifacts."

Sam sucked in a breath. "Do you think they're authentic? Could this be where the fake Mr. Killeen sold the girdle?"

Bennett's jaw twitched. "Only one way to find out."

He grabbed the exterior handle—which Sam distractedly noted was carved like a labrys—and jerked the door open, disappearing inside.

CHAPTER EIGHTEEN

"**S**o much for not confronting anyone," Joana muttered before following after him with Sam close on her heels.

It was hard to tell what had been damaged by the quake and what had always looked that way inside the shop, because within the cramped space, there were hundreds—possibly thousands—of artifacts. It was like a museum storehouse, if the museum was poorly organized and understaffed. Shelves and shelves bowed under the weight of so many pots, cups, plates, statues, bowls filled with beads, and clay tablets with crude markings etched into them.

"Do you suppose any of this is real?" Sam asked, sifting through a bowl of milk beads.

"Considering my current opinion of the man we followed here, I'd say no," Bennett said, bumping into a tall statue of a bull and catching it just before it crashed to the ground.

"They might be if they're stolen," Joana said, lifting a lid off a pot. She blinked at the contents, wrinkling up her nose before carefully replacing the lid. "Not what I was expecting in there."

"Hair?" Sam wondered.

"Teeth," Joana said succinctly.

"For once I sincerely hope these are fraudulent artifacts," Sam said, reluctantly letting the milk beads fall between her fingers and moving carefully through the overflowing store. Several items had been knocked off the displays, the aisles filled with shattered bits of pottery or glass or overturned shelves. "The loss of these treasures scattered on the floor would prove devastating. It doesn't seem like anyone is here, though."

"Maybe Mr. Not Killeen saw us coming and skedaddled," Joana mused, stepping over a wide amphora lying in the pathway.

"Hello?" Sam called, spotting a counter along the back wall. At least, she thought it was a counter. It was hard to tell through all the clutter. But there was a sign tacked to the wall, again in English letters with the sharp corners of Greek lettering. It read

BOIVIN'S CABINET OF CURIOSITIES
PRICELESS ARTIFACTS OF THE LEGENDARY
MINOAN CIVILIZATION
ALL PRICES NEGOTIABLE
HENRI BOIVIN, ARCHAEOLOGIST AND PROPRIETOR

"Mr. Boivin?" she called out, picking her way closer to the back counter. "Are you here?"

"Is someone there?" came a high-pitched voice in a French accent. "Oh, sacré bleu, thank you! Please, I'm back here, in the office space. A shelf fell over and part of the ceiling came in, and I am trapped!"

Sam looked to Bennett. "That doesn't sound like him."

"Maybe Mr. Not Killeen sold the poor idiot the girdle," Joana said with a shrug.

"It would explain the second earthquake," Sam said. "We have to help him. I'd bet no one even knows he's here."

They shoved the various stone figures and dumped-over pottery out of the way, making it to the door of the office where the voice had come from. Bennett turned the knob, but the door met resistance from something on the other side. Bennett put his shoulder to the door, shoving with a grunt, but it only gave half an inch more before getting stuck again.

"I can't budge it," Bennett said, leaning against the jamb with a huff.

"What if we all push?" Sam asked, giving it a shove. Whatever was on the other side was certainly not moving. She put her face to the crack in the door. "Mr. Boivin? Are you there? Can you hear me?"

"Yes, yes, I am still here!" came the voice. Something moved and scraped against the other side of the door, and then there was a sliver of a face peering back at her from under a fallen bookshelf. "Please get me out of here!"

But Sam was too busy experiencing a surreal and disjointed moment. The voice was certainly unfamiliar to her, but that sliver of face was not. She knew those ice-blue eyes, and as they set on her, they widened in surprise and the man gave a little humph of surprise.

"It *is* you!" Sam exclaimed. "Mr. Killeen! The fake Mr. Killeen, it's you!"

"What?" Bennett asked, wedging in beside her to get a better look. "Mr. Killeen? Is that you?"

"No, no, no," said the man on the other end of the door, disappearing from view. "I am not . . . that is not who I am. I am Henri Boivin, proprietor of this fine establishment and amateur archaeologist. I do not know this Mr. Killeen."

"Your place is chock-full of Minoan artifacts and you say you don't know the director of the Heraklion Archaeological Museum?" Joana said dryly. "Some con man you are."

"You'd better give us an explanation, and you'd better start right now," Sam declared, pushing on the door in her outrage and managing to gain them another inch. The door was now open wide enough for her to fit a hand in, and she reached through as if she could grab the man and drag him to justice. "Otherwise I'll finish what the earthquake started."

Joana raised both eyebrows at her incensed words. "Samantha Margaret Knox."

"I don't really mean it, of course," Sam whispered to her.

Joana gave a little pout. "Well, that's a disappointment."

Whether or not she meant it, Mr. Boivin seemed to take the threat seriously enough because he cried out in protest as Sam's arm swept the front of his vest. "Arrêtez! I relent, I will tell you everything. Please! Just do not damage my waistcoat. It is of the finest silk and the only one I have."

Joana snorted. "And men call me shallow."

"Answers, now," Sam demanded, removing her hand only to replace it with her glaring face.

Mr. Boivin's brilliant blue gaze looked back at her. "To begin, I suppose a small apology is in order."

"You suppose?" Bennett said at the same time that Sam said, "Small?"

"Oui, oui, very well. I owe you a large apology, for the necessary misdirections."

Joana leaned in. "The word is *lies*, and you're not off to a great start."

"Who are you?" Sam asked. "Really?"

Mr. Boivin huffed. "My name is Henri Boivin, and I am an archaeologist."

Bennett glanced around. "From the looks of your shop, you're more of a potter than an archaeologist."

"How dare you!" said Mr. Boivin. "What I sell is one hundred percent authenticated Minoan antiquities recovered from public sites by a locally renowned archaeologist and anthropologist."

"You mean you," Bennett said dryly.

"Of course I do," said Boivin, incensed. "I worked hard for every single piece displayed in my shop. I love the Minoan culture, so much so that I sold my ceramics shop in Paris and moved here twenty years ago to join Arthur Evans in his efforts to uncover the great palace of Knossos. But I had none of the fancy degrees or deep pockets they wanted, and I was treated as nothing more than a pair of hands to hold a shovel. My knowledge on the culture was no less accurate, but because it was self-collected—a far more difficult endeavor, I assure you!—I was dismissed outright as any kind of authority."

"I'm sure it has nothing to do with you conducting unauthorized digs and trying to sell your findings for profit," said Bennett, unmoved.

But Sam felt she could understand Mr. Boivin, even if she could not condone his methods. How many times had she been dismissed by professors or academics because of her gender and lack of family influence? She had written to so many Linear B enthusiasts and experts, even Sir Arthur himself, without reply. And the sting of Professor Atchinson's most recent dismissal still scathed her ego. She knew what it was to be rejected because of outward appearances.

"I do what I must for my survival," said Mr. Boivin with a sniff. "When it was clear I would make no headway with Sir Arthur's camp, I forged my own path. Began my own excavations, with obviously successful results."

"Who were those men after you?" Sam demanded. "The ones at Skotino cave. Who were they really?"

Mr. Boivin sighed, his gaze skittering to the side.

"Mr. Boivin!" Sam snapped, in no mood for any further delays.

"Creditors," Mr. Boivin said glumly.

"I told you," Joana crowed. "Why does anybody run? It's always money."

"What were they doing at the cave?" Sam pressed. "How did they even know to search there?"

"It was that confounded symbol!" Mr. Boivin said, frustrated. "I found it months ago, on a survey of Skotino cave. My local sources claimed—rightfully, you now know—that it was used as a place of worship from Neolithic times."

Bennett snorted at the use of *sources*, but Sam quieted him.

"I knew I had found something momentous, but I needed excavation equipment, men to dig. I needed resources. And because of Sir Arthur and his stranglehold on Minoan artifacts here, I was short on the funds necessary to secure them."

"So you told a bunch of crooks where they might find a treasure," Joana said, shaking her head and sighing to the cracked rooftop. "I swear, I ought to become a criminal mastermind myself. Everyone else is butchering it."

"I didn't know they were crooks at the time," Mr. Boivin sniffed. "They came to me through trusted contacts. But after several weeks of explorations with limited results, they became more . . . insistent."

"That's why you wrote to Professor Wallstone, isn't it?" Sam asked. "Because you were stuck."

"I could not risk Sir Arthur catching wind of the symbol and swooping in to steal the find for himself," Boivin said. "I thought an outside expert might provide the breakthrough I desperately needed."

"Well, Professor Wallstone is about as outside an expert as you can get," Bennett muttered.

"Exactly!" Boivin exclaimed. "I wrote to him several times over the weeks, but when I received no reply, I began to fear all was lost. I had been hiding in that rented room where you found me for three weeks, trying to find a way off the island before Nikolai and his men tracked me down."

"But why the ruse?" Sam asked. "Why pretend to be someone you're not?"

"Would you have listened if I presented myself as I am?"

Sam had to sit with the uncomfortable realization that, no, she probably would not have listened if he had not presented such distinguished—if false—credentials. She certainly wouldn't have upended her life and dragged Joana and Bennett halfway across the world on this exploration. Apparently Professor Atchinson was not the only one capable of elitism.

"You could have trusted us," she said softly, battling the discomfort of truth. "You could have given us a chance, but instead you chose lies and deceptions at every turn."

"I have been betrayed by those I trusted before," said Boivin. "Had my discoveries stolen from under my very gaze. The only thing I trust in my fellow man is the capacity to betray. Any further trust I place only in myself and my exquisite finds."

He said the last so proudly it dumbfounded Sam. "But . . . you're selling them. Why? These artifacts belong in a museum, if they are authentic as you say. They belong to the people, to history. Not to someone's bric-a-brac display."

Boivin sniffed defensively. "The stomach still requires filling, does it not? The head needs protection from the rain. However lofty our intellectual pursuits, our bodies are always of a base nature. What I sell, I sell only to fund my further explorations. I will not apologize for the means I pursued in order to build my shop and carve out my own corner of Minoan expertise. But I assure you my finds are of the highest quality, and I would be willing to subject them to any manner of testing to confirm."

"We're not here to authenticate your finds, Mr. Boivin," said Sam, suppressing the desire to strangle him. "We're here for the girdle."

CHAPTER NINETEEN

There was a long, heavy pause from the other side of the book-case before Mr. Boivin responded in a pathetic excuse for a casual tone. "What girdle?"

"Oh hell," Joana muttered, throwing up her hands.

"Listen here, Boivin," said Bennett, shouldering in beside Sam and taking charge. "We know you took the girdle, and we know it's here. We've already told Mr. Killeen—the true Hector Killeen—and our professor what happened, and they have alerted every one of their contacts to be on the lookout for the girdle. Whatever your intentions for it, you won't be able to sell it. And if you try, they'll have you locked up before you can name your price. If you give it over now for us to take to the museum, we will speak to them on your behalf. They might reduce your jail time."

Bennett was obviously bluffing, and the three of them knew it, but once again, the blow landed squarely on Boivin's more self-preserving instincts.

"Jail time?" Mr. Boivin echoed incredulously. "You would threaten me, in my own shop? You are but three children, really. It would be your word against mine, and I am a valued member of the community here. I will not be cowed by your attempts at black-mail. For all I know, you want the girdle for yourselves!"

"We weren't the ones who snuck out in the dead of night and stole it while abandoning you in Skotino to hightail it back here to Heraklion," Sam pointed out.

"I do not know that you would not have, given the opportunity," Mr. Boivin said from the other side of the door. "Only that the idea occurred to me first."

"I have another idea," Joana said idly, winking at Sam. "We leave him in there to starve and die, and then we take the girdle for ourselves."

"Jo!" Sam exclaimed at the same time that Mr. Boivin gave a shout of horror.

"Or," Joana continued, inexorable, "we just wait for the next earthquake to finish the job this one started. Or hadn't you noticed, Mr. Whatever-your-real-name-is, that they seem to follow you around since you stole that thing from our room in the dead of night like a petty thief?"

Mr. Boivin scoffed. "It is Crete. We have three earthquakes before breakfast some days."

"Yes, but how many of those earthquakes start right under your feet?" said Joana. "How do you think we found you? Random luck?"

Mr. Boivin regarded them skeptically. "How did you find me?"

"We followed the cracks," Sam said. "Caused by the earthquake. And they all led here, to you. You don't know what you have there, Mr. Kill—er, Mr. Boivin. You don't know what that girdle is capable of, and what damage it will cause if we don't properly handle it."

"Now I know you think me a fool," said Mr. Boivin. "You expect to scare me with talk of magic. Now who is the man who sells flimflam?"

"And we're back to my original suggestion—let him starve,"

said Joana. "The first two quakes were what? A day apart? Less than that? I say we leave him here, hit the beach for a round of mezedhes, wait for the next one to finish him off, and come back for the girdle."

"Jo!" Sam hissed.

"I don't mean it, of course," Joana whispered back. "Not entirely, at least."

"Mr. Boivin, you must realize you're not in a position to negotiate," said Bennett finally. "You're trapped here, and without our help, you'll remain that way until something worse happens. Your only option to save yourself is to give us the girdle and let us fetch someone to get you out of here. Or we can return later, when you are feeling more cooperative."

"Non, non, non!" the Frenchman shouted, snaking out a hand in the narrow gap as Sam had done only minutes before. "Please, do not leave me! I do not want to die back here."

"Then give us the girdle," Sam said forcefully.

"I . . . I will," Boivin hedged. "As soon as you free me."

Joana snorted. "Try again, Boivin."

The man gave a huffy little sigh. "You will help me, will you not, nice one?"

Sam shook her head, even though he couldn't see it now that she had stood up. "My belief in you is as cracked as the earth upon which you stand, Mr. Boivin. Give us the girdle, or we'll leave right now."

The man muttered several things to himself in French, the few snatches that Sam caught very unflattering to all their characters and anatomies. But when he made no move to produce the girdle, Sam's patience ran out.

"Fine, Mr. Boivin, we shall play it your way," Sam said, striding away from the door purposefully. Well, as purposefully as she could while still having to sidestep several broken pieces of clay scattered over the floor. "We will return tomorrow and see how amenable you are then."

Bennett and Joana trailed after her, exchanging a look of surprise but saying nothing. Sam had reached the door, the small bell above giving a little jangle as Mr. Boivin cried out again.

"Arrêtez! Please, stop! The girdle is not here! Please, don't leave me to starve."

Sam paused, pivoting to the back of the store. "If it's not here, where is it?"

"They took it!" Boivin cried. "Nikolai and his men. I swear it! I returned here only to clean the girdle and prepare it, but they must have had a man watching the store. He found me, and they took the girdle. And then there was the earthquake, and they escaped to leave me trapped here. It's the truth, I swear it."

"It would explain the earthquake," Sam whispered, chewing at one corner of her lip as she considered the evidence. "If the wrong someone else touched it, this Nikolai person, it would certainly have caused another disturbance."

"Now you will free me?" Boivin called hopefully from the back of the shop.

"We'll send the proper authorities to do so," Bennett said sternly. "We need to find this Nikolai before he tries to hand off the girdle to someone else and sinks the whole island."

"Wait!" Boivin cried. "I can help you! I know where Nikolai will take it. I can take you to him, but only if you free me and do not report me to the magistrate."

"Absolutely not," Bennett said. "We've been fooled by you long enough, Mr. Boivin."

"He has a point," Sam whispered, drawing closer to Bennett so Boivin couldn't see them. "If Nikolai is an artifacts thief, he'll have his black-market contacts, right? We could lose any chance of finding the girdle before more people get hurt. If Mr. Boivin can lead us to him, we need to take that chance."

"We have absolutely no proof that anything he is saying is accurate," Bennett said, exasperated.

"True, we don't. But we do know what he wants more than anything."

"The girdle," Bennett and Joana said simultaneously.

"He might not want to lead us to the girdle, but he's willing to take the chance to find it himself," Sam reasoned. "I'm sure of it. At least this time we'll know he's trying to dupe us and we can be on the lookout for any suspicious activity."

"It's too risky," Bennett said. "We don't know anything about Nikolai, except that Mr. Boivin is afraid of him. And if he is afraid, we should be as well."

"Oh, don't be a drag, Bennett," Joana said, shoving him with her elbow. "This is more fun than giving the feds the slip in the tunnels under the Green Mill."

Bennett frowned. "Don't tell me you've done that."

"Well, sure, I wouldn't tell *you*," Joana said, rolling her eyes. "Where do we think this Nikolai fella will try to fence the piece?"

"I don't know," Sam said, glancing toward the back of the shop. "But I do believe Mr. Boivin will. It's a risk we'll have to take, if we want to get the girdle back."

Bennett's frown only deepened. "I still don't like it."

"Of course you don't, brother," said Joana. "You never like anything fun."

Bennett pinned her with a look. "You could at least have the decency to stop grinning about it."

"Why *are* you grinning?" Sam asked.

"Because I know enough about these kinds of rendezvous to

know there's always a code word and a dress code," Joana said, linking her arm through Sam's. "Which means you and I get to go shopping."

Bennett sighed. "This is already a bad idea."

"But the best kind of bad idea," Joana said, pulling Sam toward the back of the room and raising her voice. "It's your lucky day, Bamboozle. We're going to dig you out, and you're going to get us in."

CHAPTER TWENTY

I t took a day and a half, several sizable bribes, two trips to a local tailor, and a great deal of grumbling from Bennett about the outsize cost of it all to secure them an invitation to the private event where Mr. Boivin swore Nikolai would display the girdle in an effort to interest buyers. Joana had sworn just as fervently that such an event would be attended by the elite of art appreciators, and the three of them would require appropriate garb to blend in. Bennett had fought that battle bravely, but they all knew he was no real match for Joana when it came to couture.

Sam was only interested in recovering the girdle; several times throughout that day and a half, in the quiet moments between fittings and arguments with Bennett, she thought she could hear it singing to her. Faintly, distantly, like catching a song on the radio through a neighbor's window before they turned the dial. Once she even tried chasing it down a street, out of the tailor's shop with half a dress stitched around her, but it faded with a strong gust of the wind.

She didn't ask herself why it was so important to recover the girdle because she didn't care for any of the answers. She only knew that once she had it back, she could correct the mistakes of the past few days and salvage their purpose for embarking on this trip. She could still fix everything; she was sure of it. Professor Atchinson could attempt to sabotage her reputation, but whatever accusations he leveled would be far overshadowed by the magnitude of the find they had made. She would have to figure out a way to stop the earthquakes, of course, but she would have plenty of time to do that once they had the girdle back.

"If you take any longer to get ready, we'll be reading about the girdle in the papers," Bennett called through the door to Sam and Joana's shared room at the little inn where they were staying in Heraklion.

"For someone who studies so much art, you hardly appreciate the time it takes to make it," Joana called back, pushing another hairpin carefully into her wavy hair.

"Those artists weren't facing down a vengeful goddess and an impending earthquake," Bennett replied. "We need to go. The car is waiting downstairs, and I don't trust Mr. Boivin to let it idle much longer."

Joana sighed, hastily shoving another three pins into her hair before jerking open the door. "You really are the wettest of blankets, brother."

Bennett gave her a flat smile. "It's my singular charm according to you two. Where is Sam?"

"I'm here," Sam said from the far corner of the room, where she had been sitting on her bed for the last half hour with her notebook open in her lap, waiting for Joana to finish. "I was looking over the patterns I copied from the girdle, trying to figure out what they might mean. I'm almost positive these are numbers, from the Minoan system of counting. There's a circle. That represents the number one hundred. And the lines each represent the number one. So it's three, three, one hundred, ten, and so on. But I can't figure out what these little directional arrows might mean . . . possibly a shift cipher? And there's still the symbol here on the head, the one I think represents the Snake Goddess. But the numbers . . . I've translated them all, and they don't seem to mean anything. There's no clear pattern or repeating motif. As far as I can tell, they're just random numbers."

"Perhaps whoever created the girdle had a different idea of what a motif should be," Bennett surmised. "There are other examples of broken motifs in Minoan art, like the Bull-Leaping fresco. Even Sir Arthur himself noted that there were patterns he couldn't reconcile within the painting."

"But that could have been a case of missing materials," Sam said, frowning at her list of symbols and their translated numbers. "The frescoes were mostly reconstructed from paint chips on the palace floor. And according to Professor Wallstone, their reconstructions were heavily influenced by the Émiles. Who is to say what the original fresco might have looked like?"

"Regardless of the liberties Émile Gilliéron, père and fils took with the restorations, there could be a precedent for it. Or maybe these marks are from the girdle's use. It's impossible for us to say."

Sam knew he was right, but there was still something about the marks and their lack of a pattern that tugged at her. She really never could leave a puzzle unsolved. And this one was greater than any treasure hunt Mr. Steeling had ever concocted for them.

"You'll have to save the homework for later, Sam," said Joana, nudging her foot with a brand-new pump. "We've got a party to crash and a belt to steal."

Sam set her book aside and stood up, brushing self-consciously at the skirts of the dress Joana had magically produced from some shop. It was made of a deep red velvet, the arms bare and the skirts reaching the floor, the folds artfully tucked and pinned. It dipped low in the back, which made Sam extremely self-conscious but did allow for a cooling breeze to relieve the heavy drape of the material. The only decoration on the whole piece was a golden strip of fabric studded with sequins that circled her waist several times. Joana had warned her, only half-jokingly, not to let any fashionable goddesses possess her as she helped wrap it around Sam's hips. Joana's dress complemented hers, a black velvet affair that stopped midcalf and showed off her collarbones under a thin veil of wispy black material. Joana had also procured a few pieces of glittering costume jewelry that looked awfully authentic to Sam.

"You look incredible," Bennett said, his voice uncharacteristically hushed. It had been so many days since Sam had heard that tone from him that it immediately caused her skin to flush a color alarmingly close to the dress she wore.

"You do, too," she said quietly, fidgeting with one end of the golden belt.

Of course, Bennett always looked perfect in Sam's estimation. But Joana had worked her costume magic for him as well, procuring an evening suit made up of a fitted black jacket with long tails and a pair of pants with a silk stripe down the side. Beneath the jacket he wore a white vest, along with a white bow tie. Joana had declared it charmingly outdated and therefore perfect for Bennett.

"Should I leave the room?" Joana asked, arching a brow suggestively.

Bennett cleared his throat, shaking his head. "I don't suppose I can make one last desperate attempt to convince either of you to give up this ridiculous charade and contact the proper authorities instead?"

"Not a chance, brother," Joana said breezily, grabbing her small clutch. "Tonight is exactly my kind of trouble, and you won't rob me of the opportunity."

Bennett sighed, stepping out of the doorway to allow her to pass. "Let's get it over with, then."

Sam thought he might wait for her, but he was halfway down the stairs after Joana by the time she locked up their door. She chewed at one corner of her lip in worry, knowing she was mangling Joana's careful job with her makeup. But she couldn't help it. Every step Bennett descended felt like one he was putting between the two of them. He'd barely spoken to her since the earthquake in Skotino village, and when he did, it was usually to express his displeasure with the whole situation. It seemed like ages, not weeks, since they had danced at the Green Mill and he'd run his hands down her spine and brought shivers to her skin. Now he barely looked at her, much less touched her with any kind of affection. Was he losing interest in her? Had she pushed him too far?

"Sam?" he called from the bottom of the stairs, none of the softness in his voice from a few moments before. "We'll be late."

"Right, of course," Sam said, gathering the drapes of her skirt and her confidence and carrying them both along with her. "I'm coming."

Mr. Boivin had insisted on hiring a car to drive them to the event, a move he claimed was to keep up appearances, but which Sam privately thought was meant to keep them in the dark about their final destination so they couldn't cut him out before they got there. Whatever the reason, the four of them piled into the hired car and Mr. Boivin spoke in rapid Greek to the driver, too fast for Sam to make out more than a few street names.

"Did you catch any of that?" Joana whispered to the two of them as the car lurched into drive, carrying them toward their mysterious destination.

"It's somewhere down by the harbor, from what I could tell of the street names I recognized," Bennett said in a low voice.

"I hope this party doesn't end with us dancing with the fishes," Joana said, leaning back with a sigh. "Makes me miss my little derringer."

Sam gave her a surprised look. "You have a gun?"

Joana returned the look. "You don't? Sam, we live in *Chicago*."

The car bumped and revved along the narrow streets, knocking them all about like cubes of ice in a tumbler. The feeling was rather like the one rumbling Sam's tummy, a nauseating mix of excitement and fear and shame and worry that had been curbing her appetite and stealing her sleep the past couple of days. If she let herself think about it too much, she was inclined to agree with Bennett that what they were doing was ludicrous. They couldn't really hope to infiltrate some kind of white-tie party for high-end art buyers and get away with it, could they? More likely they would end up in a trench under several feet of dirt. Or, if they didn't succeed in finding the girdle, at the bottom of the ocean after the next earthquake.

"I think we're getting close," Bennett murmured several minutes later, his voice low and tight.

Sam leaned forward, catching glimpses of the endless black of the ocean beyond the city. She could just make out the bobbing lights of the ships still in the harbor, casting their halos on the choppy waters crashing against the rocks. But there was another source of light far out at the very end of the island, where the white stone fortress that Bennett had pointed out when they first arrived stood guard against the sea.

"That's Koules Fortress," Sam whispered. "They couldn't possibly mean to . . ."

But the car bumped down to the harbor, stopping short as the driver said something to Mr. Boivin about not being able to go any farther. Boivin handed over the cost of the fare, and the four of them piled out, taking advantage of their distance to right their dresses and tailcoats. Sam's pulse pounded in her ears, louder than the surf crashing against the rocks of the dock. She had been to enough Steeling soirees to know the general expectations of a fancy party, but this was beyond an event in the garden of Steeling Manor.

"We've been spotted," Joana murmured, throwing back her head and swaying her hips as she marched toward the fortress. "Act like you already bought the place."

Sam was positive she could never achieve that same sashay without breaking an ankle in the shoes she wore. But then Bennett was there, the portrait of genteel refinement, putting out one elbow like he was tossing her a life preserver.

"I'm not sure I can do this," Sam whispered to him, even though she took his elbow and began the unsteady walk along the path.

"It seems a good time to remind you, then, that this was your idea," Bennett murmured back. "I wanted to go to the proper authorities."

"And risk another stranger touching the girdle and sinking us all?" Sam asked. She huffed out a small breath. "Just once in this whole business, Bennett, I do wish you'd understand what I'm trying to do. I wish you'd understand *me*."

Bennett looked down in surprise. "Why do you think I don't understand you?"

"Because if you did, you'd help me, instead of constantly trying to stop me."

Bennett looked as if he wanted to say more, but the wind had picked up as they made their way down the long stretch of cobble-stones, making casual conversation impossible. The high wall that had protected them from the sea came to an end as they reached the looming fortress and the gathered crowd of party attendees. During the day, the fortress had been brilliant and white—but at night, with little more than the bobbing lights of the ships in the harbor for illumination, it lurked like a predator, blocking out the horizon.

The entrance itself was rather plain, just a wide arch with two large wooden doors. Overhead, Sam could just see a faint outline of a marble relief in a whiter stone, the shape of an animal with wings. She thought it might be a lion, or some kind of mythical creature, but the sea wind had worn away so much of it that the details had long been lost.

There were half a dozen men in plain black clothes with grim faces stopping everyone who approached the doors leading into the fortress. Some of them carried Gatling guns, casually strung over one shoulder or held at their hips. Sam's grip on Bennett's arm tightened, and he returned the squeeze with one of his own.

"There's no turning back now," he said, leaning down to whisper in her ear above the howl of the wind. "Not without raising the wrong kinds of questions."

Sam nodded. "I know. I'm not."

But she did have to remind her feet how to take another step forward as they approached the fierce-looking men. She braced herself for an interrogation—or worse, an abduction—but once again, Henri Boivin proved a surprise.

"Alexander! Yiannis! Yiorgos! Long time no see!" the small Frenchman exclaimed in a perfect Athenian accent. "How are the wives? The little ones?"

"Growing too fast," grunted one of the men holding a Gatling gun. But the creases in his face turned upward in what Sam assumed was the heavy's version of a smile. "How are you, Nico?"

"As swell as the ocean in a storm," Boivin said, slapping the man on the back good-naturedly. "If I'd have known you would be on the door tonight, I would have brought some Turkish delight for those scamps of yours. Ah, perhaps next time."

"What in hell?" Joana murmured, drawing close to Sam and Bennett. "All those bribes and backstories we had to invent, and he knew the fellas on the door this whole time. And who is this Nico fella they're talking about?"

"I'm starting to think there were no bribes," Bennett murmured, looking down at the brand-new shine on Boivin's shoes. "I believe Boivin is the Nico in question. Seems we're not the only ones he's fed a false identity to."

Boivin drew closer to the man, dropping his head and his voice conspiratorially. "Listen, Yiorgos, I have with me some very promising new shoppers. Americans, and young. Long on dollars and short on sense, if you catch my meaning."

Bennett stiffened, but Joana gave him a discreet pinch, smiling and nodding dumbly along.

"How is the spread faring tonight, my good friend?" Boivin continued, looking for all the world like he was simply discussing a picnic meal and not a collection of ancient artifacts. "Pretty fresh? Any new meat for the hungry Americans?"

"We've got some choice pieces," said the man, but he frowned as he said it. "Does Nikolai know you're coming? I heard you two were on the outs."

"Rumors of our dissolution have always been circulated by those looking to put their own foot in the door, you know that," said

Boivin. He raised his brows suggestively. "You also know I always feed you and the family, don't you? Look at these kids. You know how the Americans spend. Up and over."

The man looked them up and down, and Sam did her best to appear both rich and dumb, the very antithesis of her personality. Whatever expression she made must have convinced the man because he gave a nod and stepped to the side, indicating that they could pass.

"You're a diamond among paste, Yiorgos," said Boivin, slipping the man a handful of cash.

"Watch your back, Nico" was the man's only reply as they passed through the low arches of the entrance into the fortress itself.

CHAPTER TWENTY-ONE

The entrance might have been plain, but the people passing through it were certainly not. Their evening finery put
the three of them to shame, which was no small feat considering
Joana's impeccable sense of style. Sam sucked in a breath as an
older gentleman passed by them with the most beautiful woman
she'd ever seen on his arm.

"Is that—" she started, and Joana nodded.

"They're always shorter in real life than they are on the screen,"
Joana said, tilting her head to the side. "He's taller than Buster
Keaton is, though. Oh hell."

"What?" Sam asked, on alert.

Joana rolled her eyes, turning her back to an older couple survey-
ing a tall painted vase. "The Jeffersons. They're friends of Auntie
Neem. I should have figured their type would be here. Their apart-
ments back in New York are always chock-full of knock-off junk.
Talk about long on dollars and short on sense. Just look at her hat,
I'm surprised that thing didn't take flight out on the seawall."

"Let's focus on why we're here, shall we?" Bennett interrupted,
steering them deeper into the fortress. "Mr. Boivin—or should we
call you Nico here?"

"Ah, Nico would be best," Boivin said hastily, smoothing down the edges of his mustache.

"Of course it would be," Bennett muttered. "Where can we find the girdle, Nico?"

Boivin gave a small shrug. "I could not say for sure, but it will certainly be the prize of the night. Nikolai often keeps the most precious pieces for display only to the highest bidders of the evening. We'll have to be discreet, though. Many of these are Nikolai's men."

Sam could have spent the entire evening wandering the fortress, admiring the thick metal bars set into the small windows and the collection of old military equipment on display, but the architecture paled in comparison to the pieces set up throughout the space. They were as impressive as the artifacts she had briefly glimpsed during her time in the Heraklion Archaeological Museum. There were Kamares wares, fruit bowls, vases, frescoes, statues, and pieces of jewelry that had been polished to a shine. For a moment, Sam thought perhaps they had been mistaken and this truly was an exhibit, until the woman in the ridiculous hat picked up a necklace made of thin strips of gold and draped it over her neck, making a cooing noise.

"What is she doing?" Sam said, the words choked. "She can't just . . . touch that! It's a priceless Minoan artifact!"

"It looks Mycenean to me, actually," Bennett said.

"But . . . these pieces belong in a museum!" Sam whispered, harshly enough that she drew the attention of a nearby couple perusing a set of amphorae. Bennett gave them a genteel smile and pivoted away, drawing Sam along with him. Mr. Boivin lurked among the artifacts, muttering comments to himself at the state of each piece. Joana trailed along behind him, giving Sam a hard look for abandoning her with the duplicitous Frenchman.

"Bennett, we can't just let them . . . sell all of this," Sam said, lowering her voice as she threw an apologetic look to Joana. "These pieces need to be authenticated, studied, and placed in the proper museum under appropriate conditions."

"You're contending with a practice that has been the bane of archaeology's existence since it's very inception," Bennett murmured, stopping to examine a small brass labrys. Despite her protestations, Sam had to physically stop herself from reaching out and removing it from the pedestal just to feel the history in her hands.

"The ancient Egyptians built their tombs with thick doors that required several laborers to move," Bennett continued, "as well as long shafts buried deep in the sands with false chambers to try and thwart ancient grave robbers. Time may have progressed, but human morality has not."

"But these people are just . . . art collectors," Sam said, looking about them at the attendees in despair. There again was the American movie actor and his lovely guest, no doubt looking to fill his Hollywood mansion with a bit of stolen history. "They don't understand the significance of these items. They'll just stick them on a pedestal somewhere and only trot them out when they've got someone to impress. These pieces belong to the world. They belong in a museum."

Bennett gave her an amused look. "And how do you think the British Museum comes by so many of their artifacts? Or the Oriental Institute back at the university, for that matter? Or have you not noticed that their offerings more than doubled after the Great War?"

Sam sucked in a breath, a horrible thought suddenly occurring to her. "Is this . . . is this how your father came by all the antiquities he owns? By illegally purchasing them from excavation site robbers?"

She thought of those pieces on display in Steeling Manor, antiquities she had admired and envied all her childhood. Pieces she had imagined proudly displaying in her own home one day. Was Mr. Steeling any better than the actor admiring a goddess statue on the far side of the room? Was she any better for envying them both?

"My father is not a thief, if that is your implication," Bennett said stiffly. "I may not agree with all his methods, but he comes by his finds honestly."

Sam drew her attention back to Bennett, noticing the sharp set of his jaw. It felt as if she had entered a minefield with him lately, every step the wrong one, always blowing them apart. His arm beneath her hand had been like a lifeline when they first approached the fortress, but now it felt like a manacle.

"Oh, Bennett, I didn't mean it that way," Sam said, twisting her lips in a frown. "I'm sorry. It's only . . . Shouldn't these pieces stay where they are, where we can learn the most from them? If they disappear into someone's private collection, they'll take their answers about the past with them."

Bennett looked down at her, his golden eyes swirling with complex emotions. "And what were you doing with the girdle, when you took it from the chamber?"

Sam drew back sharply. "That's not . . . Of course I wasn't . . ."

But . . . wasn't she?

Bennett cleared his throat, pulling his arm from under her hand. "We should continue circulating. We won't find the girdle standing here in the corner arguing."

"Bennett, please," Sam said, reaching for him. But Joana was there first, stepping between the two of them and linking their arms together tightly.

"We have a problem," she said in a low, singsong voice.

"What problem?" Bennett asked, alarmed.

"That problem," she said, nodding toward the other side of the room, where Boivin was now surrounded by several of the men in black suits with their guns gripped firmly in their hands.

"We need to get closer," Sam said. "They might be talking about the girdle!"

The three of them made their way across the room as casually as they could, ducking behind several ostentatious hats along the way to avoid detection. They found shelter behind a large stone relief with a winged lion cut into it, an obvious reproduction of the relief over the entrance of the fortress.

"At least we all bathed this afternoon," Joana muttered. Sam waved her quiet.

"—only trying to help, Nikolai" came Boivin's voice, back in its natural accent. "You will need papers of authentication and provenance, as well as a certified expert to—"

"All of which I have," said the man called Nikolai, his voice surprisingly melodic. In Sam's experience, men like him sounded like flint scraping against steel, but he sounded as if he could break out into an opera at any moment. It would be almost soothing, if it weren't for all the guns.

"The men from the cave," Sam whispered, nodding to the one holding Boivin in a grip that made the Frenchman wince. "That must be Nikolai."

"You have . . . How could you have an expert?" Boivin said sharply. "I am the one who found the girdle in the first place, you will recall."

"Only after I brought the symbol to your attention," said Nikolai. "And after you wrote to that professor in America to try and cut me out of the deal. I got tired of your story changing every time you told it, Henri."

Boivin pulled himself up in outrage, wincing as one of the men shoved the tip of a gun in his back. "I was simply expanding our resources! We were getting nowhere with the locals. If you took that to mean I was attempting to cut you out, then perhaps you would do best to work on your issues of trust."

Nikolai snorted. "If there's anything I trust, it's that the knife in my back will always be yours. I told you not to come tonight. And I told you what would happen if you did."

Boivin shrank down into his coat. "You are upset, and that's understandable. But, Nikolai, we're partners. We have done business peaceably for years, until this minor misunderstanding. Surely you don't mean to . . . to throw that all away now?"

Nikolai stepped forward, his voice dropping to a silken register. "I plan to throw away more than that."

He jerked his head to the side, and suddenly the whole group of them were on the move, headed toward a set of stairs presumably leading to the second floor of the fortress. Sam, Joana, and Bennett followed at a good distance, weaving through the growing crowd to ascend the stairs to the second level. Several of the guests watched the passage of Boivin and the armed men with avid interest, murmuring their gossip behind hand fans and beneath heavily feathered headbands. But no one stepped in to stop them.

There were even more goods on the second level, crowding all the free space of the narrow hallways with their high vaulted ceilings, and set up proudly in every alcove. To Sam's credit, she hardly lagged trying to take it all in and read the small descriptive cards explaining what the pieces were and where they had been found. She had to remind herself that this was not, in fact, a museum, and they were not, in fact, on a sightseeing tour. Still, the *quality* of some of these finds was exceptional.

"Samantha Margaret," Joana growled, jerking her forward. "Get the lead out, would you? You can gawk over old stuff when we're not trying to steal an enchanted artifact from a bunch of heavies with gats."

"Right, sorry," Sam whispered, hurrying past an exquisitely restored fruit bowl painted with thorns and decorated with white flowers.

She had expected the men would take Mr. Boivin to a more secluded section of the second floor, but they continued on through the displays toward a set of stairs that rose and twisted and rose again until they emerged on the roof of the fortress, the sky black and littered with stars above. There were far fewer guests up here, the sea wind too damaging to their carefully arranged coifs. Only a few lingered in the darker corners, conducting whatever manner of business people got up to in dark corners.

"Where are they going?" Sam asked, leaning in close to Bennett so he could hear without her shouting and giving them all away.

Bennett shook his head. "I don't know. There's nothing but the protective wall up here. Maybe they have a boat waiting somewhere?"

The men ascended a short flight of stairs that took them along the perimeter of the wall surrounding the roof, their silhouettes appearing and disappearing against the faint lights of the harbor. Sam, Bennett, and Joana hurried after, staying to the part of the roof below the walkway to avoid being spotted by Nikolai and his men. They hauled Boivin to a point on the far end of the fortress where there was nothing but the crashing waters of the port beneath them.

"This is highly unnecessary!" came Boivin's voice from a few feet above them, shrill over the whipping wind. Someone had hauled him up to one of the openings in the wall where he swayed dangerously in the strong gusts. "We can all share in the wealth, can we not?"

"I told you, I already have a new expert to certify the find," said Nikolai, arms crossed. "What use do I have for you?"

"Bennett," Sam said, her voice strangled. "I don't think they mean for him to leave here."

"We shouldn't be here," Bennett said, his frown severe. "We need to leave before they catch sight of us."

"But what about Mr. Boivin?" Sam protested. "And the girdle?"

"We'll have to find the girdle another way," Bennett said, already tugging her toward the stairs leading back to the second floor. "If we don't move, we'll end up taking the dive just after Mr. Boivin."

"I vote for the move that doesn't land me in the harbor," Joana said. "This dress is velvet. That salt water would eat it up in seconds."

"Wait—" Sam said, but she got no further in her protestations because both Steeling siblings had come up short, blocking her path. Except they weren't the only ones blocking the path. The man who had let them in the fortress—Yiorgos, Sam remembered in that distant part of her brain that was still functioning—stood before them, gun pointed directly at Joana.

"American investors, are you?" the man said in heavily accented English. "I think Nikolai will want very much to meet you."

"Oh, I don't think we'll want to meet him, though," Joana said, giving a bright smile and attempting to move past him. The attempt was hampered by the nose of his gun nudging them insistently toward the stairs leading up to where Nikolai and his men held Boivin.

"Walk," he said, tilting his chin toward the stairs up to the wall. "Now."

CHAPTER TWENTY-TWO

"**F**ound these three lurking," said Yiorgos in Greek as they approached the group of men on the wall. He nodded at Boivin. "Came in with Nico. He said they were rich, dumb Americans looking to buy some art."

"And so they are!" Boivin exclaimed. "It's what I've been trying to tell you all along, Nikolai. I've already secured buyers for the piece you sto—er, the piece I—we—found at the cave. No need for new experts! These Americans are ready to purchase, no questions asked."

Nikolai crossed his arms, looking the three of them up and down suspiciously. "They're children, Henri. You bring me children and expect me to believe they could be serious purchasers? You have always had the scent of desperation on you, but now you truly reek of it."

"These are not just any children!" Boivin said, misstepping in his enthusiasm and slipping one heel off the edge of the wall. He waved his arms wildly for a moment, trying to regain his balance. Sam lurched forward to grab at him, but the men with guns closed ranks and blocked her from helping. Boivin regained his balance, reaching down for Nikolai in desperation and snatching at his sleeve.

"These children are the Steelings," Boivin said, like he was casting a spell.

The magic took hold, because Nikolai's gaze sharpened. "You lie."

"I would never," Boivin said, affronted. "That one is Bennett Steeling, the eldest son of John Waltham Steeling, the textile magnate. The tall girl is his sister, Joana Steeling."

"And what about that one?" Nikolai asked, nodding his head at Sam.

Boivin prevaricated. "She . . . is . . . well, she is . . ."

"I am Mr. Steeling's antiquities advisor, I make all his purchases," Sam said in Greek, infusing her voice with as much authority as she could muster under the circumstances.

Which apparently wasn't enough, given the laughs from the men and the snort of derision from Nikolai. "You would do better to convince me you were his bastard child than his antiquities advisor."

"Well, I am," Sam said, smarting at the insult. When would men stop underestimating her? "His antiquities advisor, that is. Not what . . . not that other thing you said. And I am not sure that this is the best place to do our procuring, based on the samples downstairs."

"Sam," Bennett murmured in warning as Nikolai's eyes went hard.

"What would you know about our goods?" he asked, that melodic voice of his taking on a low growl.

Sam cleared her throat, hoping the thundering of her heart was only embarrassingly loud to her own ears. "Well, for starters, I know that stone relief of the winged lion downstairs is a complete fraud, and not a particularly skilled one at that."

Her proclamation earned quite the reaction from the men, and even Boivin seemed to be choking back a protest. Their grips on their guns tightened, and so did Bennett's grip on Sam's arm. But Sam soldiered on, committed to the part.

"Ancient stone workers would have used copper tools," she said, doing her best not to let her voice quaver. "Copper leaves softer cuts in the stone than our modern tools. And the wings are all wrong. They're too long and sharp, where they should be softer and more rounded. You'd better hope that American actor down there takes a shine to it because any collector worth their salt would spot that fake from a dozen yards away."

The silence between crashing waves tightened like a harp string, threatening to snap and lash out at them. Sam was positive she was right about the stone relief, and just as positive that these men didn't care for her pointing it out. It only occurred to her after she spoke that they might get rid of her just to keep her from blabbing to any of the other party guests.

"I knew we should have gone with Yiannis for the relief," Nikolai finally said, blowing out a breath in annoyance. "Ian cuts too many corners."

"You see," Boivin said with a shaky laugh. "The girl is who she says she is."

"And Mr. Boivin here promised us you had a treasure worth our time, and Mr. Steeling's money," Sam said, trying to sound professionally bored. "Something far better than fruit bowls and trinkets."

Nikolai's gaze narrowed once again. "And what is it our chatty Henri promised you?"

"A girdle fashioned of pure gold," Sam said, figuring it was best to not mince words. The effect on the men was instant; their spines straightened, their shoulders lifted, their mouths grew hard, and their formation closed in around the small group.

Only Nikolai remained relaxed, his gaze drifting over the harbor to the ships bobbing below. "Sounds like the find of a generation. What would Henri know of such a thing? He traffics in milk beads and pottery."

"How dare you—" Boivin started, incensed.

"Money would be no object for such a find, if it were to be real," Bennett said, sweeping in to keep Boivin from derailing the conversation. "My father has paid far more for far less. But I would expect men like you already know that, considering how often my father travels to Greece."

"Yes, but your father is not known to procure his goods from professionals such as us," Nikolai countered. "And why send his children in his stead, if this find is so attractive to him?"

"He's busy," Joana said, hitting the bored-socialite tone perfectly. "Daddy's always busy with something. Building a new mill here, acquiring a failing company there. Every childhood memory I have of him is half a face, already out the door on some long trip."

Sam frowned at the turn in Joana's voice, far too casual for her offhand comment to be a lie. But Nikolai was still staring out at the harbor, presumably musing over their offer. She couldn't lose the advantage now.

"We would have to see the piece before we could begin negotiations, of course," she said. "After the items I saw downstairs, I would insist."

One corner of Nikolai's mouth quirked up. "You would insist? What about your current position makes you think you have the luxury of insistence?"

Sam hesitated, the wind whipping up to remind her of their very precarious position. But as her mother always said, once the water is hot you might as well start scrubbing.

"Would *you* not insist, Mr. Nikolai? If it were your purchase? Surely you would not expect us to exchange any significant amount of money based on the word of a smuggler."

Nikolai's gaze traced over the harbor once again, before one corner of his mouth curled up in an amused grin. "I see why Mr. Steeling would keep someone like you around. Unfortunately for you, we already have a buyer."

"What?" all four of them exclaimed simultaneously.

"You can't do that!" Sam protested. "You don't know what you've done. Please!"

"I found that piece," cried Mr. Boivin. "You have no right to try and sell it without me!"

"We'll double whatever they're offering," Joana said, slipping in beside Nikolai and tucking her arm into his. "We're more than good for it, you know."

He gave her an appraising glance but extracted his arm with a regretful look. "The deal's already made, and the buyer is on their way to pick it up this very night, though I'd be happy to show you some pieces downstairs that would complement that soft throat of yours."

"Please, Nikolai, you can't do this," Sam said, hugging herself as much to protect against the turn in events as against the wind. "You can't let someone else have it. You have to understand, that girdle, it's special. More than special! It has the power to—"

"Enough, it's done," Nikolai said, waving away her cries.

But as Sam's voice faded, others from below filtered up. Not the tinkling chatter of party guests, but the sharp shouts of men used to being obeyed. The men around Sam were instantly moving, pushing her and the others down the walkway toward the stairs leading back into the fortress. One of the guards came running up the stairs from the second floor, panting from the effort.

"The magistrate," he huffed, jerking his head below. "They're raiding the place."

"And that's our cue," Joana murmured, taking Sam's and Bennett's hands and dragging them down the stairs as the men rushed past to secure their goods and scramble before the magistrate's officers could apprehend them.

"We need the girdle!" Sam cried.

"We need to get out of here first," Joana said as they hit the thick of panicked party guests. The luxurious gathering had quickly unraveled into a snarl of screaming women and blustering men, all of them shocked at the blatant challenge to their privilege.

Still, Sam resisted Joana's pull. "But if the magistrate's men touch the girdle—"

"The girdle isn't here!" Joana said, using her elbows with vicious intent as they reached the stairs leading down to the main floor. Uniformed officers flooded the space, seizing antiquities and party guests.

"What do you mean, it isn't here?" Bennett asked, moving ahead of both of them to use his height and weight advantage to clear a path. They had to dodge around several clusters of officers, the fake stone relief coming to their aid again as it made a small corridor to slip through in their pursuit of the front door and freedom.

"I'll explain once we're out," Joana said.

"All of this will be for nothing if we don't get the girdle," Sam insisted.

"Oh, we'll get it," Joana said, her long legs eating up the distance as they reached the docks. A figure detached from the crowd of party guests to dart into the streets leading up to the city, the lamplight catching one side of his face and illuminating an icy-blue eye. Sam grabbed for Joana's arm, stilling her.

"Mr. Boivin," she whispered. But by the time Joana looked where she pointed, the man was gone, disappeared in the direction of the main streets of Heraklion.

"Of course he's well versed in giving these kinds of situations the slip," Joana said. "I'd admire the talent if it wasn't proving so damn inconvenient to us. Come on, quick like."

But rather than following Boivin up into the city, she turned left toward the ships bobbing in the harbor.

"Where are you going?" Bennett asked. "The magistrate will search all of these ships now."

"Exactly why we need to get to them first," Joana said, stalking down the length of one dock and back. "Not that one."

"Not that one what?" Sam asked, bewildered.

"Come on, don't just stand there gawking. It's got to be on one of these ships. We just need to figure out which one."

"What makes you think it's on a ship?" Sam asked, still confused but hurrying after her.

"Because Nikolai kept looking down here every time you said the word *girdle*," Joana said, checking the length of the next boat in the dock. "All those pieces they had back there were just the appetizer course, but somewhere on one of these ships is the main meal."

"That one," Bennett said, pointing to a ship at the far end of the dock. "It's sitting lower in the water than all the others, which means its hull must be full. It's small and fast, and they've got all the lights off. They didn't want to be noticed."

They hurried down the docks, the commotion from the raid at the party fading in the harbor wind. Bennett was right; the ship practically blended into the black waters of the night. Sam wouldn't have spotted it from anywhere else but down here. As they approached, though, a clicking sound coming from the deck of the small ship brought them up short.

"Stop there," said a gruff voice in Greek. "Go back to the party."

"What do we do?" Sam whispered.

"Hey, do you know some fella . . . wasshis name?" Joana called out loudly, weaving toward the boat. "You know the fella! The one . . . he's got the hair, like this. And the voice, he's always singing or something. You know the fella!"

"You need to leave," the man tried in English. "Private property."

"Nick! Thass the one, Nick . . . nick . . . Nicko . . . rye? Whiskey? That doesn't sound right. Niko . . . lai! That's the one. Nikolai. Handsome fella, isn't he?"

"What about Nikolai?" said the man on the boat, suspicious.

"Lessee, what did he say?" Joana tapped one finger against her lip, stumbling toward the edge of the dock. Bennett lurched forward, grabbing her and steadying her.

"Sister, I think you're drunk," he said loudly.

"Of course I am," Joana declared. "That's how come the coppers let me off."

"What is coppers?" asked the man on the boat, his voice sharp with alarm.

"Thasss what he said!" Joana said brightly. "He said there's a raid. They need help moving the pieces. Does that sound right? Pieces of what?"

The man on the ship swore harshly in Greek and climbed down a side ladder, leaping to the dock and sprinting toward the fortress, which was now swarming with people. Joana straightened up, shaking out her skirt and stamping her feet.

"Shall we?" she asked, moving toward the ladder the man had just descended.

"Sometimes her mind worries me," Bennett said.

"It did work in our favor this time," Sam contended as they both followed Joana up the ship's ladder. It took some maneuvering in the dark, but they eventually found the door leading down to the hull of the ship. Sam pulled on it, but it held fast.

"Locked," she said, stepping back with a frown.

"Not for long," Joana said, reaching down the front of her dress and extracting a set of keys. She held them up with a grin, giving them a little jangle.

"Where in the world did you get those?" Bennett asked, baffled.

"Lifted them off that Nikolai fella back on the roof," said Joana, sorting through the keys until she found one that fit. "What, did you think I was actually flirting with him?"

"I don't know what to think anymore," Bennett said, shaking his head.

Joana flashed him a smirk. "Good. Come on, they'll be searching the dock soon enough. Let's get the girdle and get out."

CHAPTER TWENTY-THREE

Sam had never been on a ship this small, but both Joana and Bennett moved with a confidence that reminded her of all the summers they had abandoned Clement for their Mediterranean tours. All those summers she had huddled away in their father's antique bookshop, cataloging and repairing and dreaming. She didn't always like to be reminded of the vast economic divide that separated her from her best friend and her boyfriend, but sometimes it served to keep her grounded, and to hold their feet in the process.

The experience was, however, working in their favor just now as Joana managed to locate a flashlight and guide them down to the hull. It was a tight space, considering that it was packed with wooden crates of all sizes as far as Sam could see in her limited view.

"Are these all . . . ? Do you think these are all stolen goods?" she asked, her stomach churning.

"Most likely," Bennett said grimly. He glanced at her, catching her uncomfortable expression. "The good news is, Joana is right. The magistrate will surely find this ship in their search, and these antiquities will be turned over to the museum."

"All but one," Joana said, setting her hands on her hips with a frown. "Assuming we can actually locate it in this mess. We don't have time to search all these crates, so how do we find the girdle?"

"If Nikolai considered it a prize piece, it's possible he would have kept it somewhere more secure," Bennett reasoned. "Maybe in a separate safe in the captain's quarters?"

"Or if he was smart, he wouldn't have called attention to it like that," Joana said. "He'd have stuck it down there with the rest of the haul so somebody like us wouldn't come poking our noses in the wrong place."

They fell silent, weighing their options. But rather than the usual cacophony of her rapid-fire thoughts, Sam heard a distant singing in her mind. A singing that tugged at her consciousness, drawing her into the crush of wooden crates.

"Sam, what are you doing?" Bennett asked as she crawled over a short crate to reach deeper into the hull.

"I'm listening," she murmured, closing her eyes and letting the singing guide her. The wooden slats of each crate were rough beneath her hands as she clambered over them, little splinters biting into her palms. She had to scale several of the larger crates when the space got too tight, which was no small feat in her evening gown, but this time at least she managed to keep from snagging the hem on any wayward porthole bolts. The singing grew in volume and intensity, filling her chest and emptying her mind of any other thoughts as she reached a small, nondescript crate in the far reaches of the hull.

"Point goes to Joana," she murmured as she grabbed the crate and scuttled back out to where the others stood waiting. Bennett located a crowbar, and they pried off the lid, a small metal box nestled into a padding of straw within. Sam sucked in a breath as she unlocked the lid and opened the case, her heart hammering as the singing exploded in her mind.

"Sam," Bennett said, his voice like water on the fire. "Don't touch it."

"I won't cause an earthquake," Sam said, her voice reverent.

"That's not what I'm worried about," Bennett said flatly.

"Come on, box the thing up and let's skedaddle," Joana said, stepping anxiously from one foot to the other. "I've already bailed you two out at least two times this evening. Let's not go for the triple play."

"Right," Sam said, shaking herself and closing the lid on the girdle firmly. But when Bennett reached to take the case from her, she jerked it back from him. "I should hold on to it, just to be safe. We don't know how . . . sensitive it is."

Bennett's nostrils flared, an argument etched in the frown lines forming on his forehead. But he said nothing, only giving a short nod and sweeping his hand to let her pass. She wanted to believe it was a chivalrous move, but she was pretty sure it had more to do with Bennett needing to keep an eye on her.

"Hurry up, you two," Joana muttered as they climbed out onto the deck. "The G-men are practically breathing down our necks. They're already checking the ships at the far end of the docks."

"They're looking for Nikolai and his men, not drunk partygoers," Sam reasoned as they descended the ladder back to the dock.

"Drunk partygoers with a gold girdle in their possession probably don't pass muster," Joana countered.

They did their best to stick to pockets of shadow as they hurried down the docks, hiding behind one ship's bow as the magistrate's men boarded the ship beside it. When the way was clear, they practically sprinted toward the road leading up into the city. They'd made it past the bulk of the magistrate's men and to the first row of buildings on the road before Joana barreled directly into someone coming down the cobblestone path. Bennett and Sam were close on her heels, all of them piling together and falling over on the sidewalk with a collective whoosh of breath.

"We're so sorry," Sam gasped, the edge of the metal box digging into her midsection. Another gorgeous dress, ruined by circumstance. "We were just trying to . . ."

"Oh, what in the fresh hell," Joana spat as their obstruction came into full view of the nearest streetlamp. "Theo Chapin, what are you doing here?"

Before Theo could answer, Bennett moved forward with surprising aggression, pushing past him as he shielded Sam and the girdle from knocking into the other boy. "We don't have time for you, Theo."

"Hang on," Theo said, sticking out an arm. "What's that Sam's got there?"

"It's nothing," Bennett said tightly. "Let us pass."

"Master Chapin, do not block the way" came an unwelcomingly familiar voice from behind Theo. "The magistrate is expecting us. We must get there before— Oh, of course. You three."

Professor Atchinson said the last two words like he had just discovered rats in the wall of his office, which Sam considered entirely unfair since he shouldn't have even been there at the moment.

"Professor Atchinson, what are you doing here?" Sam asked.

Professor Atchinson sniffed, straightening the lapels of his jacket as he pulled himself up with importance. "I do not care for your tone or the implications of it. Hector Killeen and the magistrate require all hands on deck to inspect and collect a cache of stolen antiquities seized down at the docks this evening. Though judging by your ridiculous outfits and the timing of your appearance, I assume you already know that."

"Probably looking to pick up a few new pieces for Daddy's collection," Theo sneered.

"Why are *you* here, Chapin?" Joana shot back. "Couldn't unstick your lips from the professor's boots before he hopped at the chance to be in the papers?"

"How dare you, you insolent product of nepotism," the professor hissed. "Master Chapin is here along with the rest of the field school to help in the initial cataloging. He was invited, unlike the three of you. I shall take great pleasure in seeing all of you—"

"Expelled and blacklisted, we know," Sam said, impatient to get the girdle out of there. "Good night, Professor."

"She's got something with her, Professor," Theo said, blocking Sam's path. "Probably something the little beggar stole to try and claim it as her own."

"Miss Knox," Professor Atchinson said, his tone a nauseating mix of reprimand and glee. He spotted the box, his eyes going hawkish. "Give me that."

"No!" Sam said, jerking her arms back. "You don't understand what you are dealing with, Professor Atchinson."

"I do not under—I do not . . . You are the most *vile* of females," he said, all venom. "Ignorant, impertinent, always reaching above your station. Your kind is exactly why I lobbied against allowing your gender in the school."

Sam's eyes went wide. "You voted to deny entrance to women at the university?"

She didn't know why she was shocked. A good part of her was not, but the part of her that still held to the purity of opportunity and ideals was shaken down to its core. It was no wonder he had shamed her and expelled her from his class; no wonder he looked through Evelyn like she was made of glass.

"I did," he said viciously. "And I will do it again, as soon as I am made head of the department under the new university president."

"That confident, are you?" Joana challenged.

The professor sniffed. "There is no doubt that they will appoint me head when I return with a cache of antiquities recovered from these smugglers to fill the new museum of Minoan artifacts to rival the Oriental Institute. The Atchinson Center of Minoan Artifacts."

"Oh lord," Joana muttered, rolling her eyes.

"I have been working with the trustees for years to establish such a collection, and you three have unwittingly provided it. A collection that will finally bring the university into the international spotlight and make us a foremost authority on Minoan civilization to prove out all my years of hard work. And children like you, Miss Knox, will have absolutely no place in it."

"Professor Atchinson," Bennett said, shell-shocked. "You can't really mean that. To deny women access to higher education . . . You can't . . . You can't really hate Sam that much."

"I do not hate her, Master Steeling," said the professor. "I *despise* her. And her kind. They are nothing more than an annoyance and a distraction. They bring no true value to the field, they require special accommodations for their female weaknesses, and they are prone to bouts of hysteria. You cannot possibly think a girl like this could survive in the deserts of Egypt or the snake-infested plains of Mexico."

It was nothing Sam hadn't heard muttered by other male students when she surpassed them on yet another exam, but it still brought tears to her eyes. This was a professor, an educator. If he thought this about her, simply for being a woman, what hope was there for her anywhere else? With anyone else?

"Professor Atchinson," Bennett said gravely, speaking as if every word pained him. "Sir, you . . . are a pompous ass."

The professor's jaw unhinged, hanging slack. "I beg your pardon, Master Steeling?"

"Your ideals are unacceptably antiquated, your lectures are too long, your morals are reprehensible, and your fieldwork is, frankly, sloppy."

Everyone sucked in a sharp breath at the last, even Joana. Professor Atchinson looked as if he could commit murder there on the spot, and Theo looked only too happy to cover it up for him. But Bennett did not budge, his spine rigid and his champagne eyes gone dark with fury.

"If you think my work is so . . . *sloppy*, why is it you informed me of this event in the first place?" the professor said hotly.

Now it was Sam's jaw that came loose. "You did *what*?"

"Bennett, you absolute moron," Joana said, sounding more disappointed than she ever had in her life.

Bennett could not—or would not—look at the two of them, directing his anger at the professor. "I told you about the stolen antiquities auction for our safety. Which I now realize was a mistake, since you care only about yourself and your reputation."

The professor snorted indelicately. "You stand here trying to smuggle out a piece of history for your own glory and you think to lecture me on reputations? Give over that box now, Miss Knox, or I will have the magistrate's men take it from you."

"Allow me, Professor," said Theo, stepping forward and grabbing Sam by the shoulders. Bennett shoved into him, sending Theo one way and Sam the other. She cried out, the box flying from her grip and landing in the center of the cobblestone street. The impact knocked the latch loose, spilling the glowing, glorious contents onto the common rock of the road. Sam cringed, afraid of the goddess's wrath at the insult.

"Exquisite," the professor said, his eyes going wide. "It truly is real. How extraordinary."

"Professor? Theo?" Evelyn Hamilton emerged out of the dark,

her delicate brows drawn down. "Sam? Bennett? Jo? What are you doing here?"

"Get that girdle, Miss Hamilton," the professor hissed.

"No!" Sam cried, Bennett and Joana echoing her.

Evelyn looked to the piece lying on the cobblestones, her mouth opening in a soft O. "What is this?" she asked, her face taking on the glow of the girdle in the soft evening light as she reached for it.

"Evelyn, don't touch it!" Sam cried, trying to scramble up from the cobblestones to retrieve it first. Her skirt tangled in her heels, dropping her back to her knees.

"Pick it up, you daft girl!" the professor said.

"Evelyn, no!" Bennett shouted.

Evelyn stooped over, sliding her thin fingers under the heavy metal of the girdle and lifting it like an injured animal from the street. Sam cried out again as Bennett took her and Joana under his arms, dragging them to the center of the road and shielding them as best he could. They crouched there, waiting for the inevitable rumbles of the earth, until their thighs burned and their heads pounded.

But nothing came.

"What a bunch of nattering idiots," said Theo.

Sam peeked out from under the edge of Bennett's coat. "I don't understand. It should have—"

"Now, if you three are quite done with your dramatics, we will be returning the girdle to its rightful place among our future collection," said the professor. "And I will be reporting your intended actions to Hector to decide how he wants to prosecute you."

"Professor, you can't take that girdle," Sam huffed, pulling loose from Bennett's protective grip. "We have to return it to the chamber and undo what we've done. Take all the other pieces here, but let us return this one. Please, I am begging you."

"Return it?" the professor said, aghast. "You ignorant woman, I will make it the pièce de résistance of my collection! People will flock from all around the world to glimpse such an incredible artifact. Perfectly preserved. What a find."

"Give rats enough time in the dark, Professor, and even the dumbest among them can find a hunk of cheese," Theo said arrogantly. "They got lucky, that's all."

"Yes, of course they did," the professor said. "And probably made a great many errors along the way that we shall have to do our best to correct. We'll need to visit the cave and locate the chamber for ourselves to confirm its state. We certainly cannot trust a word from them."

"Evelyn?" Joana asked, her tone unusually subdued. "Are you all right?"

Evelyn had been staring at the girdle in wonder, the soft light it emanated bathing her face. "Do you not hear it?" she asked, her voice so quiet she might not have spoken at all.

But it was only then, when Evelyn asked, that Sam realized what she heard. Nothing at all.

"This space is off-limits to the public!" called a stern voice in Greek from the docks below. "We are conducting an investigation. You'll have to leave."

"It's fine!" Professor Atchinson announced loudly, withdrawing his identification papers from his coat pocket. "I am here by the invitation of Hector Killeen, director of the archaeological museum. These two are my students. The other three should be escorted from the scene immediately."

"Professor, please don't do this," Sam whispered. "You can't possibly understand."

"All I understand is that I *stand* on the threshold of making the greatest discovery of Minoan culture in our times, and I will not let you three ruin that for me," the professor said in a low voice. He glanced back at Evelyn. "Stop gawking, would you, girl? Put that back in the box and keep it with you. The last thing we need is a greedy magistrate looking to line his own pockets with such a find."

"Yes, Professor," said Evelyn, almost as an afterthought.

"Evelyn, don't let anyone touch the girdle," Sam said desperately. "It's enchanted. If the wrong people touch it, it will cause another earthquake like the one that nearly trapped us at the museum."

Theo gave a loud snort. "You're as mad as your professor."

"Evelyn, do you understand?" Sam asked, ignoring him.

Evelyn raised her gaze from the lid of the box and met Sam's. "Of course I do. No one else will touch it."

"Come on, then, Mr. Atchinson," said the magistrate's man, approaching their small group. He gave Sam and the others a circumspect look. "What should I do with these three? They look like they might have been at the party down there; we could hold them for questioning."

"Let them go," the professor said dismissively. "They are no one."

The professor paraded down the street, Theo trotting in his wake and Evelyn trailing after, cradling the box like a newborn. As it receded, the silence echoing through Sam's mind only seemed to grow louder, until it was all she could hear or think.

The singing was gone.

CHAPTER TWENTY-FOUR

"**W**ell, wasn't that a complete bust," Joana groused, eschewing her heels to walk barefoot over the cobblestones. "There are far too many uniforms around for us to steal the thing back. And thanks to Bennett the snitch over here, the professor knows about the hidden chamber. Even if we try to return the girdle to the altar, he'll only steal it again. His own museum, what an overinflated windbag. What are we going to do now?"

"We're going to go back to our hotel and go to sleep," Bennett said, his voice as heavy as his step while he followed after her. "There's nothing more we can do tonight except exhaust ourselves waiting around. We'll figure everything else out in the morning. At least we know the girdle will be well protected."

Joana snorted. "You're only lucky Evelyn didn't sink the whole place when she picked it up. What do you think that was all about, Sam?" Joana paused, looking around and only then realizing that Sam still stood several paces behind them, looking at the empty spot in the road where the girdle had tumbled out. "Sam, you loon, what are you doing back there? We need to hightail it before Atchinson decides to make the uniforms give us the old wrist bracelets."

But Sam couldn't yet move. There was too much filling up her mind, too much emotion coursing through her body, to do such a complicated thing as *walk*.

"I had it," she said softly, accusingly, the three small words making her hands shake.

"Sam?" Bennett called, hesitant.

The timbre of his voice drew her attention, and she snapped her head up to lock eyes with him. "I had it, Bennett. We had everything we needed. We were *right there*. How could you do this to us?"

"I was trying to protect us," Bennett said defensively, though he seemed uncomfortable as he shifted his shoulders within his jacket. "I had no idea what we were walking into with Boivin, and I couldn't have the three of us going in with no backup plan. I didn't know Atchinson was planning a museum in his name, or that he would take the girdle for himself."

"You should have trusted me!" Sam said. "We would already be on our way to Skotino cave with the girdle by now. I had everything under control!"

"Did you?" Bennett countered, his posture stiffening. "Because I saw your face when you found the girdle. That thing has a hold on you, and you keep pretending that it doesn't. It's like you learned nothing from what happened in Dublin."

Sam's mouth fell open in outrage. "That's entirely unfair."

"You forget I was there with you in Ireland. I saw what it did to you." Bennett sighed, pinching the bridge of his nose. "I'm just worried about you, Sam. I'm worried *for* you, and Jo, and our futures. I'm worried about what will happen if we don't stop these earthquakes. I'm worried about what Atchinson will do to us if we do manage to get the girdle back. I was only trying to do the right thing. Atchinson wasn't the ideal choice, I know, but at least he convinced the magistrate and his men to come down to the fortress for the raid. If they hadn't shown up, who knows what that Nikolai fellow might have done."

"But look where we are now!" Sam cried, throwing her hands out toward the docks down below. She caught the attention of a uniformed officer standing there, presumably to keep people from trying to get to the docks while the raid was ongoing. He frowned at her, which was finally the motivation she needed to start walking. She hiked up the steep incline of the road, blowing past Bennett and Joana.

"Sam, wait!" Bennett called. "I know you're upset—"

"I'm not just upset, Bennett," Sam said, huffing as the grade of the road increased. She wondered how the locals managed this. They must have fantastic haunches. "I'm hurt. I'm angry. I feel betrayed. And I feel like a fool. This was all my fault, and I was trying to fix it, and now it's worse than ever. I know the girdle was affecting me, but it wasn't like the bowl at the Hellfire Club. This was something else entirely. But you didn't trust me enough to assume I'd know the difference."

"If you hadn't been so reckless—"

"Reckless?" Sam echoed incredulously. "I suppose you would see it that way, wouldn't you? You've never made a mistake in your life."

"I never said that," Bennett said, trotting to keep up with her. She took an undue amount of pleasure in the way his breath puffed out from the exertion. She wasn't the only one who had suffered from a semester hunched over library books. Joana trailed several feet behind them, the gap growing with every angry stride Sam took. Joana gave a wave of one heeled shoe.

"I'll just be back here, not getting in the middle," she called. "Don't mind me."

"Sam, please," Bennett said. "I was only trying to do what I thought was best for everyone."

"Yes, by once again letting me be humiliated in front of Professor Atchinson."

Bennett snorted. "You shouldn't give a fig for what he says, not after the way he just spoke to you."

"That's an easy thing for you to say," Sam shot back. "You've got wealth, and connections, and your family name to take you anywhere you want to go. Professor Atchinson might have pull with the university board, but your father has friends the world over. You'd have no trouble landing on your feet. But if I were to be expelled from the university with prejudice, there's not a single school or worksite that would consider taking me on. My reputation is all I have in this world."

"I . . . I didn't consider that," Bennett said, frowning to himself.

"No, you never do," Sam said. "None of you ever do. Your family has always been kind and welcoming. But the rest of the world doesn't operate that way, and there's only so much your father can do for someone like me. I've got to do the rest, and I was trying my best to do it. And now it's all shot to hell."

"It's not shot to hell," Bennett said. He reached for her hand, forcing her to draw to a stop beneath the terra-cotta overhang of a shuttered café. "There has to be a way to get the girdle back and return it to the chamber without causing any more earthquakes. Maybe if we ask to speak with Mr. Killeen—the real Mr. Killeen— he'll listen to us now that he knows the girdle is authentic."

"Are you kidding?" Joana snorted as she caught up to them. "He runs a *museum*, Bennett. He's no better than Atchinson. They're probably both crowing over the thing now, wondering how it will bring them more wealth and fame."

"We still have to ask," Bennett said.

But Sam shook her head. "No, Jo is right. We don't have time to convince him, or risk him denying us completely. He'll have his hands full for months trying to manage the items that will come in from tonight's raid. He'll need to transport all of them back to the museum for authentication, including the girdle. We need to get access to the museum workroom without alerting him to our presence."

"I'm going to assume you're not talking about breaking into a museum," Bennett said, his tone making it clear what he thought of such a suggestion. "Aside from the fact that it will be nearly impossible, I should point out that doing such a thing would make us no better than men like Boivin and Nikolai, sneaking into caves and stealing invaluable relics."

"But we're not stealing anything," Sam said. "Not really. We're putting it back where it belongs."

"And if we get caught?" Bennett countered. "Atchinson nearly had us arrested tonight. What do you think he'll do if he catches us anywhere near that museum?"

"We won't get caught," Sam said confidently. "Because we have Jo. She once snuck into your father's office and stole his cigarette case out of his jacket pocket while he was wearing it, without your father ever being the wiser."

"She did what?" Bennett asked, frowning in his sister's direction.

Joana gave him a wide smile. "I also put it back without him noticing either. Sam's right; we'll be fine."

"I don't like it," Bennett said, shaking his head.

"That's because you never like anything," Joana said. "Which means I'm obviously in. Anything that annoys you is bound to be a gas."

"It's a bad idea," Bennett insisted.

"And you haven't got any better ones yourself," Sam said, knowing as soon as she said it that it sounded mean and petty. But her feelings still smarted from his betrayal, and it was a twisted comfort to see the hurt in Bennett's gaze. He squared off with her for several long moments, the feeling of being at odds with Bennett sitting in her stomach like curdled milk, spoiling her appetite.

"Fine." He sighed, turning away from her. "Since neither of you would listen if I had a better idea anyway."

"Perfect, now let's get back to our rooms," Joana said. "If I'm going to lurk criminally, I'll need my beauty rest. Can't break and enter with puffy eyes."

CHAPTER TWENTY-FIVE

The street out front of the Heraklion Archaeological Museum was quiet in the early morning, the sky not yet bleached of its midnight blues and the fresh smell of the sea blowing in from the harbor brimming with potential. Sam had slept poorly and risen earlier than the others to wander the streets of the city like a drunken sailor, straining to hear one snatch of that ancient song from the goddess's girdle until her head ached. Whatever had happened the previous evening—however she had failed—the song eluded her.

"What's our best bet here?" Joana asked as they stood before the unimposing entrance. One wouldn't know the modest building at the intersection of two streets could hold all the treasures of a once forgotten civilization. She tugged the door handle with a shrug. "I suppose all the windows are sealed up tight, too."

"There's a loading bay in the back," Sam said, rubbing at gritty eyes. "Where they bring in the larger pieces for storage and conservation before putting them on display. They're often open earlier than the rest of the museum. We could check back there."

They crept around to the back of the museum, careful to stick to the shortening shadows cast by the building as they approached the loading bay. There were, indeed, several museum workers moving around, far more than anticipated. There were a few large pieces propped up, workers swarming around them with an excitement that felt like a personal insult to Sam's fatigue in that moment, but Joana tugged her and Bennett aside.

"That's a lot of people to just slip past," she said, nodding at the door leading into the museum. "I'm back to looking for a loose windowpane."

"Why are there so many people?" Sam asked. "Do you think it could be because of the raid last night?"

Bennett shrugged. "Having never been party to an antiquities raid before yesterday evening, I couldn't say."

"What are you doing here?" someone asked in a gruff voice.

Sam nearly jumped out of her skin as she whirled around. A man in a simple blue uniform stood behind them, the official-looking patch on his sleeve identifying him as museum security.

"Busted," Joana muttered.

"The museum is closed presently," he said in Greek, repeating the phrase in English. "Come back tomorrow."

"Oh no," Sam said in English, pressing both hands to her cheeks as much to hide the blush creeping up there as to give a dramatic performance. "But we leave tomorrow! Oh, I was hoping to see the stone rhyton shaped like a bull's head. Is it true the Minoans used to drink from them? Oh, and the larnax! I've heard the birds and patterns are exquisite. Please, don't say the museum is closed!"

She gave Joana and Bennett a look, jerking her head in the direction of the security guard. Joana cleared her throat, making her voice slightly louder than necessary.

"Oh, yes, yes, of course, the . . . I want to say it was a rider?"

"Rhyton," Sam prompted in a whisper.

"Yes, that, the rhyton," Joana said, giving a dramatic pout. "I wanted to see that drinking thing. You're breaking our hearts here. Isn't there a way we could, you know, just sneak a quick look? We'll be on our best behavior, promise. Don't we look like trustworthy girls?"

The man crossed his arms. "Museum is closed today. Very important visit from the man who discovered Knossos. He's bringing many important visitors. Come back tomorrow morning."

"Can't we work something out?" Joana asked, raising her brows suggestively. "You give us twenty minutes for our own personal tour, and we give you—"

"A hundred dollars," Sam blurted out.

Bennett made a strangled noise. "A hundred what?"

But the man dropped his arms, his eyes darting to one side and the other. "Let me see it."

"See what?" Bennett asked.

Joana elbowed him. "Go on, Bennett, give the man a hundred dollars."

"I don't have a hundred dollars to give," Bennett said through his teeth.

"Sure you do, you've got three hundred in your front jacket pocket there," Joana said, patting his chest for emphasis.

He narrowed his gaze on her. "It used to be four hundred."

"Yes, that's how I know there's only three hundred there now. Do you want to find the girdle or not?"

"For a hundred dollars, I'm not so sure," he muttered.

"Oh, go on, you cheapskate, pay the man," Sam hissed.

Bennett lifted his brows in surprise at her, but he extracted the bill and held it up. When the man reached for it, Bennett held it just out of reach. "After you get us inside without trouble."

"Oh, sure," the man said amiably, the wheels now properly greased. He led them around to the front of the street, fitting a key to the lock and pushing the door open. "You've only got thirty minutes before the delegation arrives, though. You'll have to be out by then."

"We'll take the whirlwind tour," Joana said, dragging Sam and Bennett inside.

There were more workers inside, dozens of them, clustered around displays where the antiquities had sustained the most damage from the recent quake. Thankfully, their attention was fixed on the displays as they made plans for their restoration, and not on the spaces between, making it easier for the three of them to slip past.

"Where to now?" Joana asked, ducking behind the glass case with the stone rhyton she had claimed to be so enthusiastic about, hardly giving it a second glance.

"Any new arrivals will most likely be put in the workroom at the back," Bennett said. "That would be the best place to start searching."

They dodged around heavily laden shelves and edged past large stone reliefs, making a direct line for the back of the museum. They had just reached the last display case of stirrup jars before the workroom when a door opened and Mr. Killeen—the real Mr. Killeen—appeared from within. They ducked behind the glass as he walked by, with Professor Atchinson of all people trailing after him.

"Arthur will have his hands full here with the board members from the British School at Athens, you understand," Mr. Killeen was saying, passing so close that Sam only had time to scuttle back before he was level with her hiding place. "As well as the preparations for the gala this evening. I hardly think he'll have time to discuss your plans for this museum you are so keen on opening in America."

"He will certainly want to make time when I share what we discovered during the raid last night," said Professor Atchinson smugly. Sam's fists curled involuntarily at the tenor of his voice.

"Examining and authenticating those pieces will take months," said Mr. Killeen, his voice growing faint as they passed deeper into the museum. "Whatever was discovered, if any of it was authentic, will certainly have to wait until after the gala."

"Or perhaps the gala will be the perfect place to discuss my findings. We shall see," Professor Atchinson said, following after him. Their conversation continued, too faint to be heard as they moved toward a group of museum workers examining a cracked pithos jar.

Joana let out a gusty sigh. "That was close enough to get the old ticker dancing, wasn't it?"

"Let's just find the girdle and get out of here," Bennett said.

They crept up to the workroom door, Joana keeping one eye on the nearest group of workers as Sam reached for the workroom door. But her heart rate doubled when she tried to twist the knob and it held fast. She tried to twist it harder, but it wouldn't budge.

"It's locked," she whispered harshly. "What do we do now?"

"We really should have thought of that," Joana said, ever practical in the face of potential disaster.

"We need to pick the lock," Sam said, unable to keep the frustration out of her voice.

"Well, sure," Joana said, as if it were the most natural thing in the world. "How do you propose we do that?"

"I thought you with your infinite skills might be able to," Sam said.

"Ahhh," Joana breathed, the light of clarity in her eyes. Sam sighed in relief, but then Joana shook her head. "I don't know how to do that."

"What?" Sam and Bennett said simultaneously, loud enough that the three of them cringed.

"What do you mean you don't know how to do that?" Sam continued, glancing nervously toward the museum floor.

Joana shrugged. "My skill is convincing other people to open locked things for me. I never could get the hang of the bobby-pin trick like the other girls at the academy. Trust me, I'm as disappointed in myself as you are right now. But if that door is locked, we're obviously not getting through."

Sam hesitated, turning her gaze up to Bennett imploringly. "Maybe not," she said, giving him a suggestive head tilt.

"No, Sam," Bennett said, a deep furrow forming between his brows. "Absolutely not."

"Bennett, it's an *emergency*," she reasoned. "I wouldn't ask otherwise. But we need to get in that room, and apparently Jo can't help us."

"Now I'm insulted," Joana muttered. "What is it you expect Bennett to do? Boss his way through the door? Lecture it until the hinges rust off?"

Sam shook her head. "Bennett knows how to pick locks."

"What?" Joana screeched silently, her eyes so wide they defied their anatomical limitations. Her mouth drew into a small, tight circle, and she raised an accusing finger in Bennett's direction.

"This is why I didn't want to tell her," Bennett said to Sam, holding out a hand to Joana.

"I know, and I'm sorry, but we really do need to get in that room. So please? Don't you have your kit on you?"

"You have a *kit*?" Joana hissed. "This really is the end of times."

"Professor Wallstone gave it to me," Bennett said defensively. "As I told Sam the last time I had to use it, I am a seeker of knowledge, not a treasure hunter. But sometimes a treasure hunter's methods are necessary to gain that knowledge."

"Exactly," Sam agreed. "Like right now."

Bennett huffed out a breath. "Fine. But turn your backs. I don't want Jo getting any ideas."

"And miss my horribly responsible older brother picking a lock in a museum?" Joana countered. "Not on your life. Let's see that kit of yours."

Bennett grumbled a warning, but he withdrew a small leather pouch from his coat pocket. He knelt before the door, fitting his tools into the lock. Joana watched him work in fascination, not taking her eyes off him even as she reached to give Sam a sharp pinch on the soft flesh just inside her elbow.

"Ouch!" Sam whispered, drawing back to rub at the offending spot. "What was that for?"

"That was for knowing my sanctimonious brother was actually a criminal and not saying anything to me," Joana said, crossing her arms to continue watching him work. "I could have been hanging this over his head for months. What a waste."

"He made me promise not to tell you! And he's right, it *was* for a good cause. We had to break into a crypt in Dublin, and it was only Bennett picking the lock that got us in there. He did it to save you."

"Oh," Joana said, her mouth twisting to one side in a frown. "Well, that sucks the fun right out of it."

"Got it," Bennett said softly as the doorknob turned and clicked open.

They slipped inside as quickly and quietly as they could, the room within dark and cool and smelling of dirt and the peculiar mustiness of ancient things. The door clicked again as Bennett closed it, dropping them into total darkness.

"If you were planning on doing this in the dark, I should warn you this is the least successful of my parlor game skills," Joana said. "I once thought a fur stole was someone's house cat."

"Hang on," Bennett said, grunting as he bumped into something. But a moment later, a light flicked on, bathing the workroom in a pristine bluish white light. A wide wooden table took up the center of the space, precious artifacts laid out on its surface with neat paper labels propped up before them. Someone had left a ceramic vase on the work top, partially reconstructed.

The rest of the room was packed floor to ceiling with wooden crates, straw littering the floor around them. There were hundreds of them in varying sizes, ranging from the size of a bread box to a case as tall as Sam herself. A few had their lids pried open, giving a tantalizing glimpse of the cargo within. But the majority of them were nailed shut. Even if they had the rest of the day, they'd never make it through all the boxes.

"Well, damn," Joana muttered, craning her neck back to take them all in. "What do we do now?"

CHAPTER TWENTY-SIX

"Impossible," Sam breathed. "There must be at least two hundred crates here, maybe more. It's like trying to find a golden needle in a bunch of crate haystacks."

"Can't you do what you did last night to find it?" Bennett asked. "You seemed to know where it was right away."

"That was just luck," Sam said, far more peevishly than she intended.

"I don't think that luck is going to hold," Joana said, cracking the workroom door to peek outside. "We've got thirty minutes by the guard's count, two hundred boxes, and whoever left this satchel here on the floor will most likely be back for it in less time than that."

"What do we do?" Sam asked, shaking out her hands as if that might shake off some of her panic. "Bennett, what do we do?"

"We search as many as we can and hope that luck returns," Bennett said. "Jo, watch the door for anyone coming. Sam and I will do our best."

But it was quickly apparent that Sam's so-called luck was so far run out that it had turned bad because the first few crates they searched didn't turn up anything they recognized from the raid, much less the girdle. Straw littered the floor, catching on Sam's shirt and poking into her skin as she moved from crate to crate, not caring whether she packed the items back neatly as desperation drove her on to the next box. She could hardly appreciate the exquisite history she held in her hands when none of it was the particular bit of history she wanted. Still, there were a few pieces she mentally cataloged to gush over later, after they'd saved the island.

"Anything?" she asked Bennett after uncovering just such a piece, a beautiful gold amulet featuring bees and a lotus flower. She lowered it regretfully back into the straw.

He shook his head from across the room, examining a ceramic statue of a woman with arms held high. "Nothing. This is hopeless."

"Wait!" Sam exclaimed, holding out a hand to stop him. "I recognize that statue."

"This one?" he asked. "It's the goddess with upraised arms."

"Yes, except she's missing part of her hand, isn't she?" Sam moved across the room, tapping the chip in the hand on the left side. "This statue is from the bench shrine, I'm sure of it. Boivin must have gone back to the cave and taken it after he stole the girdle in Skotino village."

"Which means that Nikolai fella must have taken it from *him* when he stole the girdle from Boivin's shop," Joana said, keeping her careful watch on the workroom door.

"Look through the rest of the crate," Sam said, her energy returning at the prospect of having discovered something worthwhile. "See if there is anything else we recognize here."

"But none of them are the girdle," Bennett said.

"I know, but maybe there was something else in the shrine that could give us a clue how to find the girdle or how to stop the ceremony," Sam said. "Aha, see there! That tablet was in the shrine as well."

Bennett held up the unassuming-looking tablet, the decoration along the edges minimal with traces of paint in abstract patterns and a slightly raised border. The surface itself was flat and plain, like a handheld mirror that had lost its glass. "It's blank."

Sam frowned, leaning in closer to examine the bottom corner of the tablet. "I'm not sure it is. There's a little chip of clay missing here, see? It must have been layered on at a later time. And it looks like there's something underneath. There are lines, but I can't make out what they mean."

"So we do what?" Joana asked, momentarily abandoning her post to consider the tablet. "Smash it?"

Sam looked at her in horror. "I can't smash it."

"You want me to smash it?"

"No one is smashing it, Jo," Bennett said, exasperated.

Joana spread her hands wide. "How else are we supposed to see what's underneath, then?"

"This is delicate work that requires the attention of professionals, not a smash-and-grab approach," Bennett said, laying the tablet on the table. "Even with these tools, Sam and I certainly don't have the skill set to attempt such a—"

"Oh, for Pete's sake," Joana muttered, stalking away from the door to pick up a hammer and chisel.

"Jo, what are you—" Sam started, but she choked back the rest as Joana set the tip of the chisel to one edge of the blank tablet, giving the handle end a firm, swift tap from the hammer.

"Jo, no!" Sam and Bennett breathed together.

A small chunk of clay jumped out of the corner of the tablet and landed on the tabletop with a *thunk*. Sam lurched forward, reaching out one hand.

"Jo, what have you done?"

"Oh please, we would have been here debating the merits of

conservation versus restoration all day if I hadn't stepped in." She leaned over the tablet, jabbing a finger into the now-vacant corner triumphantly. "Ha, see? There is something there. Saved you the rest of our precious time arguing about it."

"I see it," Bennett said, wincing as Joana took another chunk out. "Jo's right, there's something there under this layer of clay."

Joana stopped her work, shoving the chisel and hammer into Bennett's hands before collapsing into the nearby chair. "I've done my part, now you do yours. I'm exhausted."

"From chiseling two small chunks?" Bennett said dryly as he went to work clearing the rest of the surface.

"Oh please, brother, don't act like this isn't the stuff you two live for," Joana said, stretching her arms up and linking her fingers behind her head. "You've probably been criticizing my form in your head the whole time."

"You were a little overenthusiastic with the chisel," Bennett muttered, taking far more care with how and where he aimed his blows.

Joana grinned. "See? Point proven."

Sam watched as he cleared more and more of the clay covering the etching underneath, grabbing a small brush and sweeping away the dust left over to better see what had been hidden on the tablet. "I see lines that seem to be in a repeating pattern, though it doesn't appear to be Linear A or Linear B. I can see a corner, and parallel lines. It almost looks like . . ."

Bennett reached for a brush, quickly swiping away the remaining dust and stepping back to allow the soft light of the workroom to illuminate the carefully etched grooves on the tablet. "A labyrinth," he said. "It's the labyrinth."

"Wait, you mean like *the* labyrinth?" Joana asked, leaning forward on the chair to get a better look. "The one with the bull-man?"

"The Minotaur," Sam said absently, the gears in her mind whirring too fast for even her to keep up. "Why a labyrinth?"

"The connection is not unprecedented," Bennett mused. "There have been many interpretations of the Snake Goddess's existence, in shrines like the one we found. There is the goddess with upraised arms, like this statue. And the cave in Skotino was allegedly dedicated to the goddess Britomartis, but we found the bench shrine to the Snake Goddess there. And there was also King Minos's daughter, Ariadne."

Sam sucked in a breath. "She was the keeper of the labyrinth."

"Exactly," Bennett said. "She was the one who told Theseus the secret to the labyrinth so he could defeat the Minotaur."

"Which he repaid by abandoning her sleeping on an island on his way back to Athens," Sam said.

Joana clucked her tongue. "Typical man."

"The isle of Naxos," Bennett said, nodding. "But she came out all right in the end, since myth says the god Dionysus found her sleeping there and fell in love with her, making her his wife. There are even those who believe Ariadne was a goddess in her own right. Including as—"

"The Snake Goddess," Sam finished. "Which could explain the link between the goddess and the labyrinth. So Ariadne is the Snake Goddess, and they're both the keeper of the labyrinth. But what has the labyrinth got to do with the girdle and the renewal-of-power ceremony?"

"What does every ceremony to the gods require?" Bennett asked grimly.

Sam let out a breath that completely deflated her. "Sacrifice."

"Well, now I regret chiseling off the clay covering," Joana said.

Sam looked up at Bennett. "We can still stop this, can't we? The goddess isn't fully risen yet, since no one has put on the girdle and completed the epiphany. If we just—"

A rattling interrupted Sam as the knob of the workroom door turned loudly. Sam dove behind the closest stack of crates as Bennett dropped with surprising speed beneath the worktable, leaving Joana to fold herself into a nearby cabinet and pull the door nearly closed. Sam's heart hammered, making it hard for her to hear the footsteps of whoever entered the room.

"See if Arthur continues to ignore my ideas after this evening," a familiar voice muttered, making Sam's heart beat twice as hard.

Her vision was going black at the edges, her lungs begging for fresh air, but she was afraid to so much as flare her nostrils out of fear that Professor Atchinson might hear them move from a few feet away. She couldn't see him from behind her stack of crates, but she could tell from the proximity of his voice that he must be somewhere near the worktable. If he chose to walk around the back of it Bennett would be instantly exposed, but Sam could hardly warn him from where she was hiding.

"Take all the time you want with your cohorts from Athens," Professor Atchinson continued. There was a muted shuffling, as if the professor had picked something up or put something down. "After the gala, they'll be asking my opinions on Minoan culture before yours."

His footsteps were short and fast as he crossed the room, and for a moment, Sam feared he was coming toward her. But then the overhead light flicked off and the workroom door shut, dropping them into darkness. Sam waited until she was truly afraid she might pass out before granting her lungs more air.

"Sam? Jo?" came Bennett's voice. "Are you both all right?"

"Define *all right*," Joana said after the slight creak of a metal door. "There was a *skull* in there, Bennett. A whole human skull. Just sightless sockets boring into my soul."

"Sam?" Bennett said, moving past his sister's distress. "Are you there?"

"I think so," Sam said, feeling her way around the crate cautiously. "What was Atchinson doing in here?"

Joana flipped the lights back on. "That was his satchel on the floor. He came back for it."

Sam sighed. "At least he didn't find us. I don't think we'd survive another run-in with him."

"That's the least of our worries," Joana said. "I saw what he tucked into his satchel when he came to get it, and I can tell you pretty confidently that the girdle isn't here."

"What do you mean it's not here?" Sam asked. "Where else could it be?"

"I think that dirty snake Atchinson stashed it for himself," Joana said. "He had a drawing of a costume that looked suspiciously like the mural of the Snake Goddess we found in Skotino cave, from the massive headpiece down to our shiny missing girdle."

Bennett frowned. "Why would he want a costume of the Snake Goddess?"

But Sam was already ahead of him, right with Joana. "Oh, that idiot," she said, startling even herself with her vehemence. "That's what he meant when he said they'd all be coming to him after the gala. He's planning on dressing somebody up as the goddess and parading her around in the girdle at the gala Sir Arthur is hosting at the Villa Ariadne tonight to celebrate the twenty-fifth anniversary of the finding of Knossos. He must think if he does it publicly, Sir Arthur won't try to claim the credit of discovering the girdle for himself."

"Sir Arthur would have no need to steal anyone else's discovery,"

Bennett countered. "The world already knows him as the foremost expert on Minoan civilization."

"Yeah, but stealing credit for someone else's discovery is exactly the kind of thing Atchinson would do, and well we know it," Joana said. "That's why he's so paranoid about someone else doing it to him. It's awfully soon to crash another party, and you know my feelings on wearing a dress in public more than once. But I suppose emergency situations call for emergency measures."

Sam shook her head. "We can't risk waiting until tonight, or having Atchinson discover us at the villa."

"Well, how in hell are we supposed to get the thing back, then?" Joana asked, spreading her hands wide.

"I have an idea," Sam said, blowing out a breath. "But you're not going to like it."

CHAPTER TWENTY-SEVEN

"Caterers?" Joana said, spitting venom as they approached the stone gate of the Villa Ariadne in borrowed clothes with crates of fresh fruit loaded on their shoulders. "First steerage class, and now you want me to play a caterer? The disrespect you two perpetrate upon my person, I swear."

"It was necessary, Jo," Sam whispered, moving under the arch into a lush, Victorian-style garden. The cool pebble path and the large palm trees—imported from the mainland—lent a bit of relief from the relentless heat and swarming mosquitoes of midday. Wide stone stairs led up to the main house, but Sam, Joana, and Bennett followed the other workers hauling in the food for the party toward the back of the complex, where the kitchens were located.

"This way we get access to the villa before the event," Bennett said from behind them, following in the line. "And we avoid the possibility of Atchinson spotting us."

"Because there is no way he'd be caught dead fraternizing with the help," Sam muttered.

"But caterers?" Joana insisted as they passed into the spacious interior. "Couldn't we have been visiting foreign dignitaries or something? Rich donors?"

Sam suppressed the urge to roll her eyes. "A little honest work never hurt anyone, Jo."

"I am allergic to honest work and you know it," Joana retorted.

The villa grounds were quite luxurious, in Sam's estimation, the dense gardens giving way to the yellowed stone of the main house with large potted plants and sweeping staircases. They passed a life-size bronze statue of a warrior with the head missing. Sam guessed he was some kind of soldier or important official, possibly Roman based on his garments.

"Emperor Hadrian," Bennett whispered, catching her looking.

"Look at the railings on the stairways, too," Sam whispered back, nodding toward the stone steps they passed along with the other catering employees. "Sir Arthur has had horns of consecration put into the metalwork."

"I've heard the drains are marked with the labrys as well," Bennett said.

"I officially renounce both of you," Joana said. "Unbelievable."

"We're focused, Jo," Sam said, skirting through a crowd of servants putting up tables and chairs and covering them in linen out in the garden. "We just need to get in the house and look for our opportunity to break away and search the grounds for the girdle. Atchinson has to be holding it somewhere close but secure, since he'll be wanting to keep it secret until the very last moment. We just need to wait for our chance to disappear."

A chance they got as soon as they climbed the stairs into the pandemonium of the kitchens. There were cooks everywhere—chopping up fruit, stirring fragrant bowls of sauce, roasting heavenly legs of lamb or goat, pulling delicately fluffed pieces of bread from steaming ovens. It was hot, and delicious-smelling, and overrun with people shouting orders across the room in a mixture of Greek, Italian, English, and Spanish. The entire continent was represented, which Sam should have expected based on what she knew about the guest list. It would be an event for the papers—and possibly one for the history books, if they didn't find that girdle soon enough.

"Over there! Are you listening? Put them over there!" someone shouted at them in French, a blustery man with a red face and deep brown hair stuffed up under a chef's hat. He took a wooden spoon and prodded at them, pointing to where the other catering staff had set their boxes.

"Right, sorry," Sam replied in French, grateful for Madame Iris and the special attention she had always paid to the language of her homeland.

They crossed the chaotic scene and set their boxes among the others, lingering even as the rest of the catering staff trooped back out of the kitchens to retrieve more supplies. Sam took Bennett and Joana by the sleeve, drawing them instead toward a side door that appeared to lead back into the house.

"This way," she murmured, not that she needed to. The kitchen was so loud they barely even heard her. But the three of them were able to take advantage of the harried distraction of the kitchen staff to slip quietly out the door and into the halls of the villa itself.

Sam wasn't sure what she had expected, but the interior was rather more comfortably furnished than she'd thought. She had imagined something along the lines of Steeling Manor, ornate fixtures and soaring ceilings and expensive pieces of decoration everywhere you looked. But the villa had been built for a working man during a busy season and had been constructed in such a way as to maximize airflow in the heat of summer and trap warm air in the dead of winter. The ceilings were low; the doors and windows wide and open to allow a breeze to pass through and cool the interiors. The furniture was dated—no doubt brought in when the house was constructed in 1906—but of high quality and well-maintained.

"So where do we start?" Joana asked after they had passed a few rooms and checked the interiors unsuccessfully.

"Professor Atchinson and the graduate students must be staying at the Taverna," Bennett said, checking another room down the corridor. "It's a smaller building on the estate. Maybe we should check there?"

Sam shook her head. "He wouldn't want it where just anyone might find it. Where would you hide something vitally important in someone else's home, where you want it to be kept safe from anyone accidentally discovering it, but still have it readily accessible to you when you need it?"

"The tank of the toilet," Joana said, so fast that both Sam and Bennett gave her a surprised look. "Oh, what, neither of you has had to stash your jewelry at a party with a bunch of sticky fingers?"

"You have to know the answer to that is no," Bennett said.

"There is a private bathroom in the basement," Sam said helpfully. "The quarters belong to Sir Arthur, I think, but maybe Jo has a point. We could check down there."

They rounded a corner, only to come up short as an older gentleman coming from the opposite direction nearly collided with them. He wore a three-piece suit in a lightweight linen, a bright spot of red flashing from a pocket square tucked into the front. His hair lay in waves from a center part, gray and feathery, his mustache neatly trimmed.

"Oh, hello there," the man said, tugging at the lapels of his linen jacket and giving them a patient smile. "You gave me a small fright. Everything all right with the preparations?"

Sam was completely, utterly frozen. She recognized this man— of *course* she recognized him, anyone would be a fool not to. Her mind registered that he had spoken, and that what he said required some sort of response, but she could not for all the discoveries of the ancient world make her mouth form one. Bennett seemed to have a similar affliction, for he stood stock-still, his mouth hanging slightly open.

Joana suffered no such compunctions, however, glaring at the two of them like they'd lost their minds. "All good," she said to the man with a smile. "Just checking for some spare linens for the tables outside. You wouldn't happen to know where they keep them around here, would you?"

The man gave her an indulgent smile. "I believe I would. Just down that hall there's a linen closet. Take whatever you need."

"Thank you, we will," Joana said, taking Bennett and Sam by the arm and forcing them out of sight of the older man. "What in hell is wrong with the two of you?"

"Jo, do you have any idea who that was?" Sam said in a strangled voice, digging her fingers into her friend's arm.

"An old British man, don't they all look the same?" Joana countered.

"That was Sir Arthur Evans," Sam wheezed. "Sir Arthur . . . That was the man who excavated Knossos. Who named the Minoan civilization, who holds the key to the Linear B tablets."

Joana tossed a look over her shoulder. "Hmm. They're never as tall as you think they'll be. If you two are done losing your minds over another small British man, can we remember what we came here to do?"

"Right, right, Jo is right," Bennett murmured. But Sam could have sworn she heard him mutter to himself, "That was Sir Arthur Evans. *The* Sir Arthur Evans."

They crept through the remaining expanse of the ground level of the villa, occasionally darting into nearby rooms or alcoves when someone passed by. It seemed mostly to be house servants, preparing for the party that evening. But as they reached the stairs leading to the basement level of the house, they heard a familiar set of voices ascending the steps. They dodged behind a cluster of enormous pots with frondlike plants sweeping out.

"This does not go beyond us, do you understand?" came Professor Atchinson's voice, unusually tight and urgent. "Everything must go off without a hitch this evening if I am to achieve my goals."

"Of course, Professor," said Theo Chapin. "Nobody knows we're here, anyhow. All the other lads are at the hostel getting ready. Tonight is going to be your night."

"Long overdue," said Professor Atchinson, coming into view at the top of the stairs. He straightened the lapels of his coat with a sniff. "The trustees will have to grant me my museum when they read of my discovery in the international papers. A stamp of approval from Sir Arthur Evans himself."

"Will he approve, do you think?" Theo asked. "Can't imagine he'll like being upstaged at his own party."

"I am not upstaging him," Atchinson snapped. "I am simply expanding his legacy. Once we find that hidden chamber the girl was on about, we will have so much more information to grow our knowledge of Minoan culture. He'll be down on his knees weeping and thanking me."

"Sure, of course," Theo said, sounding not at all sure.

"I need to get ready for this evening," Atchinson said irritably. "Did you have the laundry woman return my suit?"

"I did, sir. Hung it up in your rooms myself."

"Good, I couldn't very well make such a prodigious announcement in wrinkled attire."

Their voices drifted away as they continued down the corridor and disappeared from view, leaving the stairs leading to the basement free and clear. Sam, Bennett, and Joana emerged from behind the potted plants and hurried down, checking their surroundings once to be sure they were alone. The basement was cool, a limited amount of light coming from the windows looking up at the courtyard. Heavy curtains had been partially drawn over the glass to keep the heat out, leaving them in muted shadows.

"The girdle must be here somewhere," Bennett said. "Why else would Professor Atchinson and Theo have come down here?"

"But where did the old blowhard stash it?" Joana asked. She turned to Sam. "I don't suppose your magic trick with the girdle is working now?"

Sam closed her eyes, listening hard. But it was the same as it had been since the previous evening. Silence.

"Guess we're doing this the old-fashioned way," Sam said, trying to keep the disappointment from her tone.

They did a cursory search of the bedroom, Sam cringing every time she opened a drawer and found personal effects. She had read that the villa was in the process of being turned over to the British School at Athens, to serve as a post for their students and instructors who would be doing research on Crete. But the transition wasn't meant to happen until the following year, 1926, and Sir Arthur must have made use of the bedroom down here while he was staying for the twenty-fifth anniversary. She froze, a drawer of shirts open before her, when the thought of being discovered going through the personal effects of one of the greatest archaeologists of their time by the archaeologist himself occurred to her.

"Sam, what is it?" Bennett asked, catching sight of her from his examination of a bedside table across the room. "Did you find it? The girdle?"

"No, I . . . What if Sir Arthur . . . ?" she said. "What if he comes down here to get dressed for the party and finds the three of us snooping in his things?"

She slammed the drawer before her, suddenly and forcefully. Joana gave a snort from where she was digging through the dirt in a potted plant near the window.

"Should have thought of that before we started the snooping," she said. She sat back on her heels. "This is a waste of time. If the girdle were here, we'd have noticed it, wouldn't we? I mean, the thing practically glows."

"But Professor Atchinson probably left it in the box," Sam reasoned, getting down on all fours to check in the narrow space beneath the chest of drawers. "Thankfully. He wouldn't want anyone to find a golden belt lying around, stuffed between rolls of socks."

"Why don't we check the bathroom?" Bennett offered, moving toward the attached room. "Ah, the famous bathtub and copper heater."

"Famous to who?" Joana muttered, but she followed after. "I'm not seeing where he could stuff a box down here either. Where in the hell is that girdle?"

"I think I can help" came a voice from behind them.

CHAPTER TWENTY-EIGHT

Sam yelped in surprise and jumped back from the ghostly figure who had appeared in the bedroom doorway. Joana produced a pocketknife from somewhere on her person, flashing it at the intruder. But whoever they expected to have caught them in their snooping, it wasn't Evelyn Hamilton. She raised her hands at the sight of Joana's knife, her eyes going wide and round.

"I'm not . . . I don't have any weapon," Evelyn said, pausing just out of stabbing reach. "I'm sorry, I didn't mean to scare you. I only thought I might be able to help."

"Help with what?" Bennett asked. "Evelyn, what are you doing here? Is Professor Atchinson with you?"

"Or that jerk you inexplicably call your boyfriend?" Joana added.

"I'm alone," Evelyn said. "Theo and Professor Atchinson are down at the Taverna, getting ready for the party tonight. I was looking . . ."

She trailed off, her eyes going glassy. Sam sucked in a breath. Was that what she had looked like, every time she touched the girdle? No wonder Bennett had worried so much over her. Evelyn looked . . . lost. Or possessed. Or transported to another plane of existence. She didn't look herself.

"You want the girdle," Sam said softly. "It called to you, didn't it?"

"You know?" Evelyn said in surprise, her eyes coming back into focus as she looked at Sam. Her face lit up with a smile. "I see it in your eyes. You know, too. You heard the goddess calling. Isn't it the most extraordinary thing you've ever experienced?"

Sam glanced uncomfortably at Bennett and Joana, quickly returning her attention to Evelyn. "Evelyn, I know you're Professor Atchinson's student. And I can't imagine what kinds of things he's said about us. Well, I suppose I can, given that he's said a good deal of them to our faces. But you have to understand, that girdle . . . We can't let Professor Atchinson do what he's planning. We can't let him put that girdle on anyone."

"Oh, I agree," Evelyn said, nodding enthusiastically.

"The consequences would be dis—" Sam paused. "Wait, you agree?"

"Of course," Evelyn said, slightly horrified. "The girdle has incredible power. We cannot trust that to just anyone. Certainly not anyone the goddess would not approve of."

"Right," Sam said slowly, frowning. "But . . . we can't let *anyone* wear the girdle. Regardless of goddess . . . approval. The results would be disastrous. If someone dons that girdle, it will raise the Snake Goddess and initiate the renewal-of-power ceremony. These earthquakes the island has been experiencing have been a result of the wrong people touching the girdle. We have no idea what might happen if someone actually fully awakens the goddess. We need to return the girdle to the bench shrine where we found it."

"Return the girdle," Evelyn echoed faintly, her eyes gone glassy again.

"And we lost her," Joana muttered.

"Evelyn!" Sam said sharply, reaching out for the girl and taking her by the wrist. The physical contact seemed to help bring her back to their earthly plane. "Evelyn, do you understand? Can you help us?"

Evelyn nodded. "Yes, of course. You're right. Of course."

"Do you . . . ?" Sam hesitated. "Do you . . . hear it?"

Evelyn closed her eyes in an expression of pure bliss. "Oh, yes, I do."

"Good," Bennett cut in, clearly relieved. "Can you point us to where it is?"

Evelyn took a deep breath, opening her eyes and piercing him with a stare. "Yes. But it's not here. Quickly, come with me."

They followed her out of the bathroom and through the bedroom toward the stairs, pausing at the top of the short flight to check that the hallways were clear.

"But we just saw Professor Atchinson coming from down there," Sam whispered in confusion as they retraced their steps through the villa. Evelyn led them past what looked like a sitting room to an open veranda beyond. The intoxicating drift of jasmine drew them outside, where the party preparation continued like a machine.

"Yes, but only because he was retrieving a key to Sir Arthur's private storage," said Evelyn. "Where he once kept any of the more precious or finer pieces he found at Knossos before sending them down to the museum in Heraklion. That's where he's been keeping the girdle ever since we found . . . well, since last night."

"And he actually told you where the private storage is?" Bennett asked, sounding surprised. When Sam gave him a chastising look, his eyes widened slightly. "What did I say?"

But Evelyn smiled as they wove through the gravel pathways of the garden, farther from the main villa. "No one ever sees me," she said softly. "Even Theo, when he talks to me, it's like he . . . like he looks right through me. Like I'm transparent."

"Oh, Evelyn, I'm sure that's not true," Sam said, even as Joana gave her a look as if it were the most obvious thing in the world.

Evelyn turned her smile on Sam. "You're kind to say so, but I'm not like you, Sam. I don't make a big splash whenever I enter a room. I don't get anyone talking in hushed whispers about how I must have cheated to beat the record in finishing Professor Charles's final exam, or how someone heard from someone else that I discovered a Neolithic passage tomb in Dublin. I don't inspire that kind of interest."

"I don't . . . Is that what people say about me?" Sam asked, startled.

"You're quite a topic of conversation on campus," said Evelyn. "Sure, there are some people who aren't very nice, but really they're just envious. Even Theo, he's only afraid that you'll make him look like a fool if you really decided to challenge him."

"A healthy fear for him to have," Joana muttered.

"But most people don't even know I attend the university, much less as a graduate student," Evelyn continued, turning down a narrow path leading through palm fronds and lush greenery into a secluded section of the grounds. "Most of the professors assume I'm only Theo's girlfriend, not a student in my own right. And the men often talk about me like I'm not there, even when I'm standing right beside them."

"Give 'em a punch in the gut," Joana said critically. "Then I bet they'll look you in the eye."

Evelyn lifted her gaze skyward. "But she sees me. As soon as I touched it, I knew. You know it, too, don't you, Sam?"

Sam thought back to the last time she'd heard the singing in her mind, just before Evelyn touched the girdle. It had felt . . . accepting. Welcoming. Beckoning, even. She felt a sharp pang of envy that Evelyn now had that hymn thrumming through her own mind.

"I do know," Sam said softly, not wanting Bennett or Joana to hear.

Evelyn smiled, nodding. "She sees us, Sam. For what we are. For what we can be. She *sees* us. Even when no one else does."

"Sees you right down to the bottom of the ocean," Joana countered. "Is this the place?"

They had reached a small outbuilding, simple in construction and a little dilapidated. There was a gate set where the door would be, a lock hanging open on it.

"It doesn't look that secure," Joana said doubtfully, pulling at the gate that screeched on rusted hinges. "What did you say he kept in here?"

"Originally Sir Arthur built it as a secure place to store his more important finds from Knossos," said Evelyn, waiting patiently as the three of them entered the dim little shelter. "But since excavations on the palace have long been completed, he mostly uses it for storage of odds and ends."

Sam looked around at the walls, mounted with hooks and shovels, hoes, and rakes. "It looks like garden tool storage now. Are you sure Professor Atchinson would keep the girdle in here?"

But when Sam turned back around, she was met with the metal gate clanging shut in her face. Evelyn stood on the other side, clicking the lock into place.

"Evelyn?" Sam asked, more confused than worried. "What are you doing?"

Evelyn gave her an apologetic smile. "I'm sorry, Sam, really I am. But I can't let you put the girdle back, not when I've just found her."

"What?" Sam asked, eyes going wide. She gave the gate a pan-icked shake, but despite the derelict appearance of what she now realized must have always been a gardening shed, the gate held firm. "Evelyn, no! You can't do this. You don't understand!"

"I understand far better than you do," Evelyn said kindly. "It was why she chose me instead of you. You could have been her earthly vessel, Sam, but you chose . . . what? To try and save a world that would throw you away in an instant? Men like Professor Atchinson will never ever see you. Not for who you truly are. Not for what you could truly be. She could have given you so much more, but you weren't ready. I am. I will do what she requires. I will wear her girdle, become her earthly vessel, and raise the Snake Goddess."

"Evelyn, please, you can't do this," Bennett said, stepping up beside Sam and giving the gate another shake. Still, it held firm. "If you go through with the epiphany, people will die."

"No, no, she's not like that," Evelyn said, clutching her hands to her heart. "She is light, and purity, and justice. She only punishes the unworthy. I know that now. Sam has touched the girdle. She has seen what the goddess will do for us. Professor Atchinson and Sir Arthur and their like, they believe that a patriarchy is the ulti-mate utopia. She will show them the error of their thinking. She will put the world to rights."

"Evelyn, I understand," Sam said desperately. "I did touch the girdle, I do know her light. Please, let me out and I can help you."

Evelyn gave a disappointed shake of her head. "Don't turn away from her light, Sam. That's what they want. They want to keep you small, and quiet, and invisible. Same as me. But if we step into her light, she will set the balance right. She will punish those who have wronged her. Who have wronged us. You'll see."

"Evelyn, you batty loon, let us out!" Joana shouted, kicking at the gate.

But Evelyn backed down the path, the fronds already obscuring her from view. "You'll see, Joana. She will show you all. She will bring the light and reset the balance."

"Evelyn!" Sam called, but a movement in the garden off to the side caught her eye. She thought it might be a worker, come to rescue them, but the shape moved all wrong. She hopped back from the gate as the first snake slithered out of the greenery, dropping onto the rocky path and moving in idle undulations toward the shack. Another one slithered down a tree, and more and more emerged from the garden as the three of them retreated into the safety of the shack.

Except Sam heard a hissing behind her in the supposed safety of the interior. She felt her soul momentarily depart her body as a snake came down the tine of a rake to drop on her shoulder. She flailed, knocking the creature to the ground, but there were more and more emerging from every crack in the dilapidated shed.

"Evelyn!" she screeched. "Make them stop!"

"You'll see, Sam," came Evelyn's voice like a ghost from the far beyond. "She will bring the light."

And then she was gone.

CHAPTER TWENTY-NINE

The snakes seemed to come from everywhere. Down the bars of the gate locking them in, up through invisible gaps between the storage shed wall and the ground, even curling along the bare beams of the narrow roof overhead. They slithered over Sam's boots, hissed across the collar of Bennett's shirt, and wove between their feet like braids of sweetgrass. The three of them huddled together in the middle of the shack as the serpents gathered in sentry.

"What do we do now?" Sam whispered, tears choking her voice. She wasn't quite afraid of snakes—they were a common enough occurrence when you lived on a farm—but such a prolific gathering was fraying even her hardy nerves.

"Burn this shack down with us in it," Joana said, her voice bleached of emotion.

"Mr. Killeen—I mean, Boivin—said that none of the snakes on the island were poisonous," Bennett reasoned, his own voice strained. "It's entirely possible for us to escape here without serious threat to our health."

"That's not a bet I'm willing to take," Joana said. "Boivin lied about plenty."

"Bennett, do you think you could pick the lock?" Sam asked, scrunching under his arm as a particularly large snake played footsie with her right boot.

"Maybe?" Bennett said. But as soon as he shifted toward the gate, the snakes took up hissing in one voice. He quickly shrank back, wrapping one arm around Sam and the other around Joana. "I don't think they want me to."

"Sam, can you work your weird hypnosis on them?" Joana asked, eyes wide and electric. "Like you did with the snakes back in the bench shrine. They let you take the girdle. Maybe they'll let you slip the noose here."

"I don't think so," Sam said, agonized. "I think they let me take the girdle because I made a sacrifice. But now that Evelyn has touched the girdle, I think . . . I think their loyalty is to her. She must have been the one to call them here."

"Great, so I'm going to die in a shack, dressed as a damn caterer, surrounded by snakes," Joana said, tugging at the collar of her starched shirt to pluck a loose cigarette from her bra. "Might as well go out in style."

"Wait, Jo, that's it!" Sam said, clinging to a new idea.

"What's it?" Joana asked, pointing the tip of the cigarette at Bennett. "Don't you dare give me a peep."

"No, the smoke," Sam said, visually searching through the accumulated tools in the shed. "Snakes have very sensitive noses, and they hate the smell of smoke. If we can create enough of it, maybe they'll retreat and Bennett can pick the lock so we can catch Evelyn before it's too late."

"I'm all for a good lung poisoning, but won't too much smoke also knock us out?" Joana asked.

"They've got masks here," Bennett said, nodding to the far wall. "Gas masks, looks like they're left over from the Great War. They should be good enough to keep us breathing through the smoke, if we can reach them."

"That's a big if, brother," Joana said, but she let the cigarette hang unlit from her lips. "So, what are the odds the slither squad will let us pass?"

"Only one way to know," Sam said, carefully sliding a foot toward the far wall where the gas masks hung. The snakes hissed, several of them raising their heads, but none made to strike at her. She took another careful step forward, Bennett's whispered warnings at her back, but the snakes let her pass.

"I think they're only guarding the gate," Sam whispered, moving with more confidence toward the wall. She lifted the gas masks from their hooks, swallowing a scream when a baby snake fell out of the mouthpiece of one of them. She checked the other two before sliding back toward Bennett and Joana and handing them over.

"Great, we've got the masks, but how do we make enough smoke?" Joana asked, peering into the eyeholes on the mask and wrinkling her nose. "This will wreak havoc on my finger curls."

"You'll survive, Jo," Bennett said flatly, fitting the mask over his own face. His voice emerged muted and oddly tinny from the long nose of the mask. "There are several tarps over there, I'd guess from painting and renovations. If we light them, they should make plenty of smoke."

Sam put her mask over her face, the smell within musty and strangely intimate. She briefly wondered who the last person might have been who had been forced to wear it, and under what conditions. She wondered if her father had ever donned such a mask, before his own death in the war. But there was no time for speculating, not with a den of serpents keeping her from saving the island.

"Bennett, are you ready?" she asked, her voice loud and echoing within the confines of the mask.

Bennett gave her a nod. "Ready when the two of you are."

Joana heaved a loud sigh. "Here's hoping we don't all go up in smoke."

She set her lighter to the pile of tarps, running the small flame back and forth until the fabric began to blacken and smolder. Sam was afraid it might not catch at all—she hadn't checked whether it was coated in wax or made of some fabric impervious to flame—but then the whole pile seemed to catch all at once, flooding their small confines with billows of smoke and waves of heat.

The snakes immediately uncurled and retreated from the flames, hissing and spitting as they gathered at the gate of the shack. They might have been under Evelyn's command, but they were still wild creatures at heart and reacted to negative stimuli in the way of all animals concerned with survival. The greater the smoke and the higher the flames, the farther they retreated, until they had dissipated into the greenery of the garden beyond.

"It's working!" Sam cried. "The snakes are gone."

"And now we're on fire," Joana reminded her. "Brother, put those larcenous digits to good use and get us out of here."

Bennett went to work on the lock, his vision hampered by the mask and his neck drenched in sweat from the rising flames. And the flames were, unfortunately, rising. Sam and Joana edged closer to the gate, away from the cloths that had now started a tidy blaze in the corner. Only then did it occur to Sam to wonder what material the rest of the shack was made of, and how flammable it was.

"Come on, Bennett, it's a garden gate lock, not a safe at the bank!" Joana shouted through the mouthpiece of her gas mask, crouching down beside him.

"It's not exactly easy, Jo," Bennett retorted, turning his head at an awkward angle to try and press closer and get a better view of the lock. "I can barely see through the eyepieces on this, I'm having to do everything backward, and I don't think I want to turn around and see how this smoke idea of Sam's is going."

"It's going slightly less according to plan," Sam said, pressing into the front corner of the shack beside the gate. She couldn't stop watching the flames as they crept higher, teasing at the exposed beams of the shack roof overhead. Her heart pounded, her skin tightening unbearably as if she could already feel it blistering and withering away in the flames. It wasn't the first time she had been trapped in a closed space with a roaring fire, and the memory of the bookshop fire had a scream crawling up the back of her throat. The mask was too tight, too close, the smoke everywhere now. She almost wished for the snakes to return, if only to put something between her and the growing blaze.

"I've got it!" Bennett shouted, pulling down on the lock and unlooping it from the catch on the gate.

The three of them tumbled out of the shack, tripping down the pebbled path and ripping off their gas masks with heaving breaths. Joana chucked hers into the nearest stand of palm fronds, scratching at her neck and wriggling around violently.

"There's one on me!" she said, halfway to a screech. "It's down my shirt! It's on my back. Get it off!"

"Jo, wait!" Sam said, grabbing her by the shoulders to try and still her. "Let me check."

"Sam, get it off!" Joana screamed.

Sam pulled at the bottom of Joana's shirt where she'd tucked it into her skirt, a long green item snaking out from the hem. Sam cried out and jumped back, but the thing fell harmless to the ground, soft and feathery.

"Jo, it's a plant!" she said, her heart beating so hard she thought she might vomit. "It's only a leaf. It's not a snake. You're all right."

"Do I look all right to you? I nearly stripped naked in the middle of a garden party." But she hastily tucked the hem of her shirt back in, smoothing back the frazzled and crushed finger curls framing her face. "If I so much as spot a lizard, I'll burn the rest of this place down."

Sam looked back to the little garden hut, relieved to see that their accidental bonfire seemed to be contained within the shelter. Plumes of smoke still billowed out, but the structure wasn't burning down.

"I think the snakes are gone," Sam said, looking around. "The smoke worked."

"Some Snake Goddess Evelyn turned out to be," Joana said. "I'm starting to think she's not the quietest little mouse in the church anymore."

"Where did she go?" Sam asked, looking around the empty stretch of garden. She turned to Bennett. "Where would she go? To complete the epiphany?"

Bennett shook his head. "I'm not sure. Sir Arthur theorized that the throne room at the palace might have been used for religious ceremonies, including epiphanies. There was a lustral basin, for bathing and preparing the body of the priestesses. And griffins, painted in murals on the walls. They would have indicated someone important, royalty perhaps."

"Or a goddess," Sam said. "Isn't Knossos close by?"

Bennett nodded. "Maybe three hundred meters from here."

"Then we need to hurry," Sam said.

They started up the path at a brisk walk, not wanting to bring attention to themselves the closer they got to the main house and the party preparations. Some of the workers gave them strange looks as they emerged from the side path with smoke-stained clothes and wild hair from the gas masks. But Bennett squared his shoulders, putting on his best air of Steeling authority and moving through the crowd as if he were Sir Arthur Evans himself.

They had nearly made it to the wide arch leading out of the villa and onto the road to Knossos when someone raised a shout from the main house.

"What the hell are you three doing here?" Theo Chapin bellowed, rushing down the stairs toward them. "Professor Atchinson, it's them!"

"Theo, wait!" Sam called, holding up her hands. "You don't understand! Evelyn is—"

"What did you do to my girl?" Theo said, his face turning red in his fury.

"We didn't do anything, she's got the—"

But Sam didn't have a chance to say what Evelyn had got because that was when the first earthquake hit.

CHAPTER THIRTY

It threw them down, filling the garden with the cries of the workers and the shattering of broken glass and the clattering of fallen
tables. For as long as she lived, Sam didn't think she would ever
get used to the surprise of the ground heaving under her. It was
one of the few things she relied on so completely—the ground
staying where it was meant to be—that it came as a shock when it
suddenly bucked the rules. Even as the quake subsided, the rocks
still felt like they vibrated beneath her boots, keeping her heart
clipping at an unsustainable pace.

"Sam, Jo, are you both all right?" Bennett asked, getting to his
feet unsteadily.

"I'm all right," Sam said, taking his hand and scrambling up. The
trees still swayed, an unnerving sight. "What do you suppose could
have caused that earthquake, though? Do you think someone took
the girdle from Evelyn?"

"Or she's just having a little lark," Joana said, hauling herself
up. "Tossing us around like popcorn for the fun of it. I'm going to
throttle that girl when we find her."

"I'm not sure she'll still be a girl when we do," Sam said.

"I'm not above throttling a goddess either," Joana said darkly.

"You did this!" came Theo's voice. He rose from the bottom of the stairs, where the earthquake had thrown him, weaving on his feet but with venom in his voice. "I don't know what you did, but you did this. Professor! Professor Atchinson!"

"You picked a hell of a time to start believing us, Chapin," Joana groused.

"What the bloody—" Professor Atchinson emerged from within the main house, holding fast to the frame of the doorway like he might tip over if he didn't. "What the bloody hell are you three doing here? I've had enough. Just enough! I'm calling the magistrate myself to detain you. This charade has gone on too long!"

"We should run," Sam murmured, though she didn't trust the ground to stay where it belonged. She raised her voice, giving a wave and a hasty smile. "Sorry, Professor, but we've got somewhere else to be!"

"Somewhere else—" the professor huffed in outrage, but the three of them were already through the arch. "Stop them, Master Chapin!"

"What are the odds he catches us?" Sam panted as they reached the road and turned north to the main thoroughfare that would connect them to the palace of Knossos.

"Atchinson?" Joana scoffed. "I doubt that mule has ever been above a trot."

"That's the entrance there," Bennett said, pointing to a narrow walkway tucked into the side of the street. It was lined with trees and a trellis had been built to let the branches grow over the stones and provide shade from the high heat of the day.

They followed the walkway, the trees eventually opening up to the blaze of the sun on bleached white ruins, the excavated remains of buildings in the distance, small half walls winding across the open plain, some of them appearing in striations from previous excavations. Sam looked around in wonder at her first real excavation site. But the earth rolled and bucked in another quake, sending her stumbling to the side. Bennett had to grab her by the arm to keep her from falling down a giant hole in the ground.

"Careful, Sam," he said, his voice sharp with worry. "You nearly fell in the kouloura."

"The kouloura," Sam said, studying the deep pit lined with stones beneath her feet that was thought to be used for either dumping waste or grain storage. There were two more beside it in a line, the opening wide and deep. "We must be in the west court, then."

"And that must be the west facade of the palace," Bennett said, pointing to a section of wall looming before them. The wall was surprisingly complete, the edges sharply squared off. The surface was yellowed in comparison to the rough, natural rock under their feet. "I suppose the rumors are true, then."

"What rumors?" Joana asked.

"That Sir Arthur used concrete blocks to make extensive restorations," Sam said, approaching the newly constructed wall. It stood out in stark contrast to the large, naturally hewn blocks that supported the base of the wall. She walked around it, gasping at the brilliant red column that held up the small chunk of ceiling above, the only corner of the room left standing. The column, too, had been restored by Sir Arthur, the original cypress tree that would have been used for support having long since rotted away. She walked through it, marveling at the fact that she stood in a structure that had been erected so long ago. Had some palace clerk stood in this very spot, three thousand years ago? She laid a hand on the wall, wondering at the lives that had passed by it.

Bennett came to stand beside her, frowning at the red column. "He certainly has taken his liberties, hasn't he? Professor Wallstone was right to have his reservations about this excavation. It's as if

Sir Arthur is constructing the ruins to match his vision of Minoan society."

"Maybe he was just trying to better preserve what was already here," Sam reasoned, though she had to admit the reconstructions seemed extensive.

"Would the two of you focus?" Joana said, exasperated. "You can go full Wallstone later, when we've stopped an ancient goddess from rising."

"Right," Sam said, shaking her head. "Let's find the throne room."

They continued through the ruins, careful to keep clear of the more perilously stacked columns and rock walls as the earth continued to surge and buck, the intervals between the quakes shortening each time. The palace took shape the deeper they went. Sir Arthur had indeed taken extensive liberties—much of the structure had been replaced with concrete blocks made of modern materials. The pathways twisted and turned, the low rock walls cutting off in all directions and rising up into stairs only to end in small chambers or drop off to other smaller pathways. Some of the rooms seemed to have no entrance or exit, and more than once they trekked up a set of stairs only to find themselves stranded on an unfinished platform.

"I'm starting to see where Sir Arthur came up with the idea that the palace itself was the labyrinth of myth," said Sam as they hit their third dead end. "It's massive and confusing."

"The throne room is just off the central court," Bennett said, climbing up a short stone wall to get a better look around. "We entered in the west court, so we just need to go directly east. Most likely."

"This was all much more orderly when it was drawn out on a map," Sam muttered to herself.

They eventually found their way through the confusion of the ruins to the massive central court, a wide space framed on all sides by the leftovers of the former palace. The hills of Crete embraced the palace at its heart, the sky behind them a relentless blue, broken up only by a few smears of white clouds. Sam paused in the open court, turning slowly to take in the glory of the palace even three thousand years after the height of its existence.

"Bennett, it's the grand staircase," Sam said excitedly. She crossed to the massive opening, leaning over a stone wall to gasp at the two levels of the palace exposed below, the staircase descending at right angles all the way down. It had been difficult to tell the extent of Sir Arthur's excavations from the western exterior, but here, from the central court, the full scope of what he had uncovered was readily apparent. On the western side, more segments of wall rose up another level, showing evidence of a palace that was several stories tall and sprawled over hundreds of chambers and storage spaces.

"It's the Prince of the Lilies fresco," Bennett called to her from the opposite side of the central court, standing beneath a section of a hallway that had been covered by concrete to protect the mural. "You can certainly see the influence of Piet de Jong here."

"And I've lost them," Joana said, throwing her arms out and speaking to the sky.

"There you are," wheezed a voice from the far end of the central court. Professor Atchinson stood with Theo Chapin, both of them heaving from the exertion of chasing Sam and Bennett and Joana through the ruins. In the splendor of the excavation site, Sam had momentarily forgotten they were even a threat. But now, here, with the imminent rise of an ancient goddess, Sam could finally see Professor Atchinson for what he was. An outmoded, misogynistic relic of a past era. He fit right in with the old stones, stubborn against the wear of time. What a trick he had pulled the past semester, convincing her that she needed his approval for *anything*.

"You three," he began, his breath lost to anger as much as exercise. "You three are—"

"Here to stop Evelyn from putting on that girdle and sinking us all," Sam said, loudly and firmly. "And you can either help or get out of the way. We're not—*I'm* not appeasing you any longer. You, sir, are no Barnaby Wallstone."

"Wallstone?" the professor sputtered. "Of all the . . . the *insulting* things to say to someone like me. You impertinent . . . wretched . . . ignorant . . . *female*."

"I'm beginning to see why you never married, Professor," Joana said dryly.

"Master Chapin, detain these fools," spat the professor. "I have already sent for the magistrate, who should be arriving shortly."

Theo gave them a wicked grin. "With absolute pleasure, Professor."

"Chapin, don't think about it," Bennett said, stepping in front of Sam and Joana.

But Joana was just as gleeful, hopping out from behind Bennett. "Come on, Chapin, you've been hurting for this since that drunken stunt you pulled at the Green Mill back in March. They'll be studying your bloodstains a thousand years from now."

"Jo," Sam said, reaching from behind Bennett's back to try and drag her best friend out of the line of attack. "We've got more pressing issues, right?"

"Hey, you had your little sidetrack with the stairs, let me have mine," Joana said, cracking her knuckles as if she were about to step into the ring.

Theo took another menacing step forward before Bennett moved in front of her. "Come on, Steeling, your sister's had it coming since the day she was born. She needs to be put in her place."

"I don't care what position you played on the field, I'll lay you out if you put a finger on my sister," Bennett said. And though he didn't have the advantage of bulk, his threat landed just as heavily.

"Fine, two Steelings, one stone," Theo said, raising a fist.

"Stop!" Sam cried out.

But it wasn't her interjection that broke the two of them apart. It was the sudden, violent roll of the central court ground. It sent all of them sprawling, Bennett falling back on Sam and Joana as Theo staggered to the side. Even Professor Atchinson gave a yelp of surprise as the unsteady movement threatened to send him off the edge of the south entrance where he stood.

"Nothing to worry about," called the professor, though his voice was higher-pitched and warbling. "Just an aftershock from the earthquake earlier."

"That's not an aftershock," Sam said, scrambling out from under Bennett to peer at the opening behind the professor. "It's Evelyn."

Evelyn walked into the sunlight, standing at the edge of the central court with her head high, the light gleaming from the golden girdle wrapped three times around her waist, the ends secured with a sacral knot.

CHAPTER THIRTY-ONE

"The epiphany," Sam whispered as Theo went clomping toward Evelyn with a dark expression.

"Where the hell have you been?" he demanded, grabbing her by the arm roughly. "And what are you doing with the girdle? You were supposed to wait until the gala this evening. Take it off now, and hand it over to the professor before you damage it."

Evelyn looked down at his thick hand on the thin expanse of her upper arm, her expression unchanging as she wrapped her delicate fingers around his wrist and tore free of his grasp as if he were a small child. Theo only had time for his mouth to gape open in surprise before she used her grip on his wrist to throw him across the central court.

"Look out!" Sam exclaimed as Theo landed in a heap before them with an impact that shook the rock deep below. The columns of the palace swayed and the trees shivered, little cracks appearing beneath Evelyn's feet. She didn't even look, her gaze fixed forward toward the throne room.

"Did she kill you, Chapin?" Joana asked, toeing the groaning pile of person at their feet.

"What . . . ? How the hell did she do that?" Theo wheezed as he rolled over and sat up, swaying along with the columns.

"Oh good," Joana deadpanned. "You're alive."

Professor Atchinson backed away from Evelyn, clutching his own arms as if she might do the same thing to him. "What . . . what is going on here?"

"We tried to tell you," Bennett said, his voice uncharacteristically rough. "Now we're too late."

"Maybe not too late," Sam said as Evelyn began to walk across the court toward the throne room. The girl's expression was blank, her eyes distant and unmoving. If Evelyn was still in there—and Sam prayed she was—she was no longer the one in charge. "If we can undo the sacral knot, maybe we can get the girdle off her and still stop the ceremony."

"Did you miss the part where she tossed Chapin here like a moldy banana peel?" Joana asked. "If we try to lay a finger on her, she'll give us the old heave-ho, too."

"Then we need to distract her somehow," Sam said, edging carefully across the rumbling central court to follow in Evelyn's wake.

"Wait!" Theo called, his voice surprisingly uneven. "Don't just leave me here!"

"You're a big boy, Chapin, get yourself up," Joana called back, following after Sam as Bennett joined her.

"So how do we do this?" Joana asked. "Maybe we *should* recruit Chapin. He knows all those ridiculous football plays."

"She seems to be in some kind of trance," Sam said. "Maybe if we, I don't know, interfere with the—"

Sam lost whatever suggestion she was going to make when something off to their right caught her attention, causing the words to lodge in her throat. It slithered into the light at her feet, making her jump back as it navigated the uneven terrain with unpredictable undulations, its body dipping into every crevice and reappearing in surprising places. Sam reached for Bennett's hand on instinct, her other hand finding its way into Joana's.

"Not again," Joana whispered in despair.

Evelyn lifted her sightless eyes upward, taking a breath that opened up her chest and drew her shoulders back. The snake found its way to her, caressing its golden head against her shoe before climbing up her ankle and encircling her calf. Another snake came from the wall above her, dropping onto her shoulder. Sam chewed on the scream that climbed up the back of her throat and stuck in her teeth as another snake appeared from a set of broken columns overhead, its scales gleaming in the harsh afternoon light.

"Are those snakes?" Professor Atchinson cried, his voice gone shrill and hysterical. "Where are they coming from? Someone fetch the magistrate!"

"Stay where you are!" Sam shouted, her voice ringing out with the authority the professor's now lacked. After all, only one of them had faced down an ancient goddess before. "We'll handle Evelyn. The snakes won't bother you if you stay put, you and Theo both."

She wasn't exactly sure that was true, but it sounded right enough. There were more of them now, of ordinary striping and color, climbing the stairs of the grand staircase and descending from the rocks of the palace ruins overhead, wrapping around the wide red columns and entering from the various doorways leading to the court. There were dozens, then hundreds, all of them crawling their way toward Evelyn. Chapin shouted a curse, scrabbling up off the ground and huddling close to Professor Atchinson as he shook off a snake trying to climb his sleeve.

"So many snakes," Joana breathed.

"Well, she *is* the Snake Goddess," Sam whispered back.

"Thank you for the reminder," Joana said icily.

"We need to untie the sacral knot," Sam said in a low voice as they moved forward, a half dozen snakes slithering past across the court. "I think I can get close enough to do it, if we move quickly."

"I'm not sure this is a good idea," Bennett said, sidestepping a particularly long serpent.

"Where is she even going?" Joana asked.

"That's the central palace sanctuary there," Bennett said, pointing to a restored structure with partially finished columns on the left side of the court. "And just beyond is the throne room. Sir Arthur hypothesized that the throne was a seat of power and critical to their religious ceremonies. If she sits on the throne, it could trigger the epiphany."

The three of them followed carefully after her procession to avoid stepping on any of the snakes. There were so many of them now, they covered the ground of the central court, the walls of the ruins coming alive with their writhing forms. Sam, Bennett, and Joana were just catching up to Evelyn outside the throne room when a dissonant humming filled Sam's ears like bees trapped in a metal pot. She thought it might be the girdle calling to her once again, but a quick glance at Bennett and Joana told her they heard it as well.

"What is that?" Bennett asked, pausing to try and locate the source of the sound. "Is that the goddess? Where is it coming from?"

"It sounds like . . . everywhere," Sam said, also spinning around trying to locate the sound. It was growing louder, and closer, descending on them from all angles. Sam was afraid it really was a hive of bees—perhaps the Snake Goddess was also in charge of the bees—when a shadow fell over them. Sam shielded her eyes against the sun, squinting to make out the figures cresting the wall overhead.

"Are those . . . people?" she asked.

"Better than snakes," Joana muttered.

"What are they doing here?" Bennett asked, his grip on Sam's hand tightening.

More and more people arrived, climbing the walls and scaling the ruins to converge on the central court. They flowed past Professor Atchinson and Theo, still huddled at the entrance, their terrified expressions lost among the growing throng. The new arrivals raised their faces to the sky as one, their eyes filmed over and their song reaching a deep resonance that touched off a memory in Sam. They were singing the song of the girdle.

"I think they're here for her," Sam whispered.

"Why aren't we affected?" Joana asked. She held up her hands when Sam looked at her. "Not that I'm complaining. But last time a bunch of people were in thrall to an ancient goddess, you ruined a tube of my favorite lipstick. What gives?"

"I think . . . I think because we're not *her* people," Sam said, pointing at where Evelyn stood beside a wide staircase at the northwest end of the central court, a set of doors beside it and the levels above it nearly completely restored.

"That's the stepped portico," Bennett said. "And the polythyron. Also known as the pier-and-door partition. She's almost to the throne room."

"We've got to stop her," Sam said, starting forward even as more people spilled onto the central court, processing toward Evelyn and blocking their way. "Excuse me!"

"Sam, I don't think it's manners they're concerned with," Joana said, elbowing the crowd aside like a Chicago professional. "Come on, if we're going to make it to Evelyn before she sits on the throne, we've got to dispense with the pleasantries."

Sam followed after, feeling bad for every foot she stepped on or rib cage she elbowed, but if anyone she passed noticed, they didn't respond. They were in thrall, their song rising and falling and intertwining so that Sam felt as if she were inside a tuba being blown at full volume. Several times she lost sight of Evelyn leading the charge, only the general flow of the crowd keeping her on the right path. At some point the throng parted enough that she could glimpse Evelyn disappearing through the first of the four doorways to the throne room suite, her entourage of serpents following after, and her entranced worshippers not far behind.

"She's gone inside," Sam called to Bennett and Joana over the thrum of their song. "We need to hurry!"

"Sam, wait!" Bennett called, tugging on her hand.

"Bennett, if we don't stop her before she sits on the throne, we won't be able to stop her at all."

But someone beat them both to it as a shadow darted out from the cover of the throne room entrance and headed straight for Evelyn and the girdle.

CHAPTER THIRTY-TWO

"**M**r. Boivin!" Sam shouted, lurching through the crowd and reaching out for the small Frenchman even though he was still several paces ahead of them. "Mr. Boivin, please stop!"

But the curio collector gave no credence to her pleas, as his attention was fully focused on the gleaming girdle wrapped around Evelyn's waist. He disappeared through the ceremonial doors after her, his step light and quick around the growing river of serpents gathering at his feet. Sam, Bennett, and Joana picked up their pace, shoving past the congregating worshippers and risking the displeasure of the surrounding snakes to try and catch up with him.

"Mr. Boivin, stop!" Bennett said, his tone slightly louder. "Don't touch her!"

"I have to have it," the Frenchman said, his eyes wide and round as they fixed on Evelyn's midsection. He seemed barely aware of his surroundings, stumbling down the four steps leading into the antechamber of the throne room and nearly falling into a large purple gypsum basin in the middle of the space. Evelyn glided around it, her steps as sure as if she had walked this path a thousand times.

"Mr. Boivin, you can't touch that girdle," Sam said, barely

pausing to admire the wooden throne in the antechamber and the surrounding gypsum benches and note their similarities to the bench shrine.

"Boivin, if you try to take that girdle, you'll kill us all," Bennett added.

"That girdle is mine by rights," said the man, enraptured by the slight sway of Evelyn's hips. Bennett had gotten close enough to grab one of his arms, but he barely seemed aware of it. He barely seemed aware of anything that was not that sacred garment. "I was the one who found it! I did all the work, and now they plan to just stuff it in some American museum? Non. It belongs to me."

"Mr. Boivin, it's not safe!" Sam called, taking his other arm. She worried that Bennett couldn't hold him if he decided to make a break for it. Evelyn paused at the entrance to the throne room, the interior blocked from their view by her small frame. She seemed to be waiting for something, something on a different plane from the one they currently occupied. Sam paused as well, almost reflexively, and the worshippers that gathered around her lowered their voices and dropped to their knees in anticipation.

"Mr. Boivin, I know it will sound mad, but Evelyn is currently possessed by the spirit of the Snake Goddess, and if we don't stop her, she will enact an epiphany that will awaken the goddess."

"I know, isn't it grand?" Boivin said, his eyes luminous.

"What?" Sam and Bennett intoned simultaneously.

"I knew it the moment I touched it, that it was different," Boivin said with a dreamy sigh. "Greater than any relic I had ever found. So much power held within its links. A girdle that truly belongs to an ancient goddess? A goddess who can be raised by any ordinary woman who dons it? Look at all of these people! Imagine the crowds of tourists such an attraction will bring!"

"Mr. Boivin, you can't possibly—" Sam shook her head. "You can't possibly think to make this a . . . a tourist attraction?"

He turned those enormous eyes on her, the icy blue of them nearly translucent. "Oh, but I do. Imagine seeing a true epiphany for yourself. People will come from all corners of the earth! They will speak of Boivin's goddess in the most elite circles. It won't be Sir Arthur's name in their mouths any longer."

"These idiots," Joana muttered. "Listen, Boivin, if we let Evelyn sit on that throne with that girdle on and raise the Snake Goddess, there's a good chance she'll open the labyrinth, wake up the Minotaur, and sacrifice us all."

Boivin cocked his head in surprise. "Truly? Well, this changes everything. Everything."

"Finally." Bennett sighed.

"Elite attendees can pay to test their mettle against the Minotaur!" Boivin exclaimed. "World-class pugilists, circus strongmen, Olympic sprinters. All of them can test their strength and skill against the great beast. Ah, sacré bleu, the tickets we will sell!"

"Oh hell," Joana spat. "We should have let you starve in that junk closet of yours."

Sam shook her head in shock. "Mr. Boivin, you can't—"

But the worshippers' song rose in volume then, reaching a crescendo and cutting off Sam's protest as Evelyn began to move once again into the throne room. The layout within was similar to the antechamber—gypsum benches surrounding a throne. But this throne was also carved of gypsum and set into the wall, the benches and seat surrounded by a restored fresco of brilliant reds and whites. Two griffins flanked the throne on either side, and a second set framed the door set in the back of the room.

Another purple gypsum basin sat in front of the alabaster throne. To the left a pair of columns held up the ceiling as a set of stairs descended into what Sir Arthur had called the lustral basin, a place where he claimed worshippers would ritually bathe before presenting themselves to the goddess. Evelyn swept around the room, her nose crinkling slightly as if she found the arrangement distasteful.

"We're running out of time," Sam said, letting go of Boivin in favor of pursuing Evelyn.

But Boivin was faster, using the distraction to wrestle free of Bennett's grip and leap forward, shoving Sam out of the way.

"I must have it!" he cried, latching on to the tail end of the golden belt.

"Mr. Boivin, no!" Sam exclaimed.

He tugged sharply, trying to release it from the sacral knot. But the metal held fast, not even shifting a scale at the interruption. Evelyn was less undisturbed, however, pausing in front of the throne to turn and face him, her brows creasing over her sightless eyes. Sam shuddered at the expression—or rather, the lack thereof—as Evelyn took firm hold of Boivin's coat lapel.

"Apologies, Your Excellency," said Boivin, holding up his hands with a sheepish grin. "I wish only to show the world the true majesty of your power. Please, let me be your great emissary to the uneducated masses. Together we can change the world, shape it into our own!"

Evelyn spoke a few words in an ancient, unfamiliar language, her voice deeper and more powerful than anything that had ever come out of her mouth before. From the edge of her shirt sleeve came a glimmer of gold, and Sam didn't even have time to shout a warning to Boivin before the snake struck. It sank its teeth into his neck, his scream of pain dissolving into a gurgle.

"Mr. Boivin!" Sam cried, but she could only watch in horror as the skin where the snake had struck turned red and angry, blistering and spreading out along his collarbone and up through his cheek as the snake worked its teeth in deeper, dispensing its venom into Boivin's bloodstream. The man's eyes rolled into the back of his head until only the whites were showing.

His fingers danced and twitched, his body writhing painfully as more blisters appeared, covering every bare inch of skin until Sam was sure he would burst. It turned her stomach in the most revolting way, the shape and form of him distending as the skin stretched and filled with poisoned blood. The boils on his neck popped first, exploding over his jacket and filling the room with the sharp tang of blood and other bodily fluids. Sam squeezed her eyes shut, but she couldn't close her ears to the sound of flesh bursting and dissolving. She was nearly sobbing by the time the worst of it faded away, and she was too afraid to open her eyes and find what was left of the Frenchman. She screamed when someone took her by the arm, lashing out on instinct with her fist.

"Oof, Sam, it's me," Bennett said. "Stop, it's me."

"Oh, Bennett!" Sam said, sinking into his arms. "Bennett, I can't . . . Mr. Boivin, he—"

"I know," Bennett said grimly.

"The girdle? How do we get the girdle now?"

"It's too late," Bennett said, his voice hollow. "We're too late."

Sam looked up just in time to see Evelyn take the throne. The song of the worshippers became unbearable then, pounding against Sam's eardrums like an echo of the rumbling earth as they pushed forward on their knees, several of them pressing their foreheads to the ground and scraping their skin raw as they moved. Sam cringed back from the sight of Boivin's remains spilled out on the ground before her, holding her hands over her ears.

The first swell of snakes lapped at the edge of Evelyn's shoes like a wave cresting against the beach, writhing and amassing until they had covered her up to her ankles. More and more snakes came slithering in, winding up her calves and over her thighs, climbing the legs of the throne to wrap around her arms. They piled in her lap and crossed over her chest, draping themselves around her neck like jewelry. They covered her one snake at a time, until there must have been hundreds all over her, interlocking with one another until Evelyn disappeared under their mass. Her eyes were the last to be seen, the blank slate terrifying in its trance.

"What the hell are they doing?" someone shouted behind Sam. Chapin's mouth hung open in shock as he stumbled into the throne room. "Evelyn! Snap out of it! Do something. Stop them!"

But even as he spoke, the snakes began to slither away, revealing first Evelyn's hands and feet, then gradually more of her. Except that as they withdrew, it wasn't Evelyn's face they revealed. Nor was it her diminutive body, or her soft brown hair or sensible clothes. The figure occupying the throne was taller by several feet, her impressive height crowned by a ceremonial headpiece, where two of her golden-headed snakes entwined. Her skirt was tiered and flounced, the layers of decorated wool alternating with layers of gold. The girdle gleamed the same, but instead of wrapping around Evelyn's button-down shirt, it wrapped around a highly decorated bodice that left her chest bare, her waist cinched in tight. The snakes gathered and coiled on the floor of the throne room as the figure rose to a height that touched the ceiling overhead.

The deep colors of the throne room walls rippled and shifted, the flakes of paint distending and bubbling as the patterns themselves seemed to come alive. The sheaves of wheat began to wave in an unseen breeze, the reds turning so deep they looked as if they had just spilled from an animal's throat. Sam gasped, Bennett drawing both her and Joana closer as the griffins flanking the throne shook their heads, the paint shifting and changing into flesh and fur and wickedly curved beaks. They stepped from the fresco, the fully formed beasts each as large as a horse as they sat back on their haunches beside the throne. Sam caught her breath at the energy and power emanating from the figures poised before her, the urge to fall to her knees among the worshippers nearly overwhelming her.

The Snake Goddess had risen.

CHAPTER THIRTY-THREE

This, Sam realized, was no simple mother goddess from Sir Arthur's rudimentary estimation of the past. She was no beacon of fertility or mundane household chores. She did not while away the hours knitting or stirring a pot, nor did she hold vigil for a husband off at sea or war. This goddess was power and strength and beauty; she was softness and light and the steel edge of a double-headed axe. She was not a precursor to the patriarchy; she obliterated the patriarchy. The goddess placed a hand on each of the griffins, stroking between their ears as if they were nothing more than hunting dogs. As she gazed down on them, her eyes deep and searching, Sam had one thought.

This was what it meant to be female, a totality that encompassed more than anatomy or physiology. More than societal expectations or limitations. More than Sir Arthur's narrow view. The Snake Goddess was no man's idol.

"She's incredible," Sam whispered.

The gathered crowd went wild at the sight of their goddess, tearing at their hair and beating at their breasts and clawing at the stone ground, singing her praises. The song they sang was excruciating now, like the thrum of a second heartbeat making Sam's own heart thump erratically. They pressed forward, knocking Sam into Bennett and squeezing Joana against his other side as they raised their arms in supplication to their mistress. Several of them even scraped through the remains of Mr. Boivin in their efforts to get closer, a sight that threatened to turn Sam's stomach inside out.

"What do we do now?" Sam cried, her words nothing more than a breath inside the maelstrom of the worshippers' song.

Bennett shook his head, having caught her expression if not her actual words. *I don't know,* he mouthed, looking helplessly to where Evelyn had stood only seconds before.

The goddess raised her arms, her deep red lips and coiling black hair like a mural come to life. And in that gesture, the crowd fell silent, the absence of their song so sharp it left a ringing in Sam's ears. They paused, their faces caught in expressions of ecstasy. Sam crowded against the throne room wall, dragging Bennett and Joana with her, the back of her knees bumping the carved benches there.

The goddess spoke again in that ancient language, the words like lines from a clay tablet come to life, at once familiar and strange to Sam after her intense study of Linear B this past semester. She couldn't have known their meaning, but she understood their shape and cadence somehow, and the expression of it left her breathless.

"What did she say?" Joana whispered.

"Nothing in our favor, I don't think," Bennett whispered back.

At the goddess's command—for surely, everything she spoke must be—the crowd began to move with purpose, pushing over and past one another. They pressed against Sam, jostling her hand free of Bennett's grip, and at first she thought they were only trying to better position themselves to receive the goddess's benediction. But then they were snatching at Bennett's coat sleeves, dragging him forward and holding her back.

"Bennett!" she gasped, fighting against their grip. "Bennett, no!"

"Let me go, you perverts!" Joana screeched beside her, held fast by four slack-jawed worshippers. "Hey, where are you taking my brother? Let him go!"

"Bennett!" Sam screamed.

But her cries fell on enraptured ears, and the worshippers held her down as the others dragged Bennett toward the Snake Goddess. The deity moved around the throne room, her griffins stalking in her path, and exited to the antechamber with Bennett in her wake. He fought against their grip, but there were simply too many of them, filled with too much purpose.

"Sam, what are they doing?" Joana asked, snapping her teeth at one of the men who held her. "Why are they taking Bennett?"

"I don't . . ." Sam huffed, still fighting her own battle. But she had a better view of the antechamber from her position than Joana had, so she was able to see clearly when the worshippers stopped before the wooden throne there. They shoved Bennett down, holding him fast as snakes slithered up the legs and arms of the chair, wrapping around him like coils of rope. Two golden snakes crawled down from above, resting their heads on his shoulders. His eyes caught hers across the short distance, a terrifying certainty within their champagne depths.

Sam went utterly still, like she'd been plunged into the swimming hole in Clement in the dead of winter.

"Sam," Joana said, her voice shrill. "I don't like that look, Sam. What is it? What's gone wrong?"

Sam could hardly breathe—hardly think—but she owed Joana the words. "I think the goddess has chosen her king-consort."

"I'll kill her," Joana snarled, practically feral. "I'll rip that girdle off her myself and strangle her with it, snakes be damned. You hear me, you overgrown statue? I've been called statuesque myself. You don't frighten me! Let my brother go now and let's settle this, statue to statue!"

"Jo," Sam said softly, her entire body trembling. "I don't think that will help."

"Well, it can't hurt, can it?" Joana said, glaring at the goddess as she continued her procession out to the central court. "Like hell I'll let her just . . . just take my brother. Where's Chapin? Isn't he the one you want instead? What good is a bad boyfriend if you don't use your new goddess powers on him? Make him your king. He's got the perfect insufferable disposition for it."

"I understand," Sam said, shivering in fear. "I'd choose Bennett as my king-consort over Theo Chapin any day."

The worshippers crowded after the goddess, blocking Sam's view of Bennett, but she could feel him even through their mass. She could always feel when Bennett was in a room, like someone turned on a lamp in the darkness. He was her light, and the Snake Goddess was going to snuff it out.

She couldn't let that happen.

But how to stop the ceremony now? The goddess was risen, and Sam didn't think simply removing her girdle would put her back to rest. After Mr. Boivin's demise, she wasn't sure she *could* remove the girdle. She needed another way to interrupt the ceremony, before the goddess claimed Bennett.

But before she could figure out *what* that way was, someone was shouting from outside the throne room. Someone decidedly not in thrall to the goddess, someone whose normally blustery tone was pitched high and tight in panic. Joana made a noise of disgust deep in the back of her throat.

"Is that Chapin?" she spat. "Sure, he shows up now. Where was he when she was picking out new playmates?"

"Jo!" Sam called as the worshippers' grips on her arms tightened, dragging her to her feet and toward the doors of the chamber.

"Hey!" Joana shouted from a similar disadvantage. "What are they doing now?"

"I don't know!" Sam cried. "But don't fight them. Whatever they're doing, I think it's part of the ceremony. Maybe we can find a way to help Bennett, to stop the goddess."

"Letting myself get dragged by a mob is not really my forte, Sam," Joana said, but she stopped actively fighting against them. She didn't exactly help them either, and they practically had to lift her and carry her out.

The crowd marched the two of them through the doors of the throne room into the antechamber, and Sam caught a glimpse of Bennett. He was completely still, his skin pale as he eyed the two golden-headed snakes still resting on his shoulders. But he caught her gaze as she was dragged past, his eyes wild.

"Bennett, we're going to get you out of this," Sam whispered. "We'll find a way, I swear it."

"Just get Jo out of here," Bennett said, swallowing hard and pressing his eyes closed as one of the snakes flicked out its tongue. "Both of you, get out of here now. Get somewhere safe. Don't worry about me."

"Don't be an idiot, brother," Joana said from behind Sam. "I can't be an only child. It'll make Mama unreasonable."

"Jo," Bennett started.

"Don't you dare, brother," Joana said, her voice thick. "I won't hear it, and I won't tolerate it. We're getting you free. That's all there is to it."

Sam might have said more, but the worshippers dragged them both out onto the central court. It was packed now, every spare stone covered in worshippers on their knees with their hands raised, just like the ceramic statues of the goddess with upraised arms. It was chilling to behold, their arms trembling with human fatigue even as their eyes were filled with divine inspiration.

But there was one among their ranks not so divinely inspired. Theodore Chapin had a small army of worshippers holding him down, his massive shoulders twisting under their grip as they forced him to kneel before the Snake Goddess. The goddess, for her part, seemed oblivious to him, her face raised to the sky, her profile exquisite.

"Let me go!" Theo shouted, managing to pull free of two of the worshippers only to have five more appear and press him down. "Evelyn, this is ridiculous. I demand you let me go right now!"

"That's not Evelyn anymore, you idiot," Joana snapped as the worshippers dragged her and Sam forward and forced them to kneel behind Theo.

The worshippers went still once again as the goddess raised her arms, speaking a few words in her ancient language. Five more worshippers stepped forward, all of them women, kneeling beside Sam and Joana. More worshippers knelt beside Theo, making another row of seven men. Sam hardly had time to consider the significance of that before she became aware of a great pressure in the base of her skull, her entire body going heavy. She could barely drag her eyes up—they felt like lead weights in her skull—but she managed to lift them to the towering figure standing before the crowd.

The Snake Goddess was looking at her. Dimly, Sam registered the mythical beasts at her sides, her hands resting lightly on their heads and stroking the feathers there. The goddess's eyes were like supernovas, the light and crush of them crumpling Sam into a singularity, their depths fathomless. Looking at the goddess was like standing in the middle of a rushing river, the water freezing and powerful enough to knock her back and sweep her away. All the air pressed out of Sam's lungs from the impact of it.

The goddess spoke again—or did she speak at all? It felt as if the words were projected directly into Sam's mind. Briefly she thought of that cache of tablets found at the palace here, their secrets as yet unrevealed. And in that moment, just for that moment as the goddess gazed upon her, she felt as if she could taste their answers in the sweetness of the goddess's short command.

End this.

And then the stones dropped out from under Sam's feet, plummeting her into darkness.

CHAPTER THIRTY-FOUR

She fell silently, the shock of sudden weightlessness robbing her of her voice. It wasn't until she hit the floor below that a cry tore out of her throat, the rough impact jarring her from her feet up through her teeth, rattling her thoughts like dice in a player's hand. She curled in a ball as dust and rocks rained down around her.

"Jo?" she wheezed once she was sure she wasn't going to be brained by a falling rock. "Jo, are you there? Are you all right?"

"All right is a luxury right now," Joana grunted from somewhere nearby. "But I'm in one piece. How about you, Sam?"

Sam rose to her feet gingerly. The descent hadn't been kind, but it didn't seem to have broken anything either.

"I think so," Sam said, peering up at the clouds of dust still sifting down.

There was just enough light to make out the vague shape of her surroundings, some kind of lower tunnel not yet excavated by Sir Arthur. The passage itself seemed rather mundane compared with the restored splendor of the palace overhead. It was large, certainly, towering a good ten feet over their heads and wide enough that Sam and Joana could stretch their arms out and still not touch each other. The blocks of stone were broad and thick, each piece at least three feet long and a foot tall. The walls might have been constructed for protection given how sturdy they were, built to keep out invaders. Perhaps the tunnel had been a passage for soldiers to mobilize without detection.

"Where are we?" came Theo's gravelly voice, considerably less arrogant than it had been topside. His golden hair had gone gray with dust, a look that suited the pallor of his face. There were others around him, the worshippers who had knelt beside the three of them before the floor fell away. They appeared dazed but without injury, climbing to their feet with slack expressions.

"Oh, Chapin, you're here as well," Joana said flatly, looking him over. "And you continue to survive. I suppose that's a good thing."

But if Theo heard her, he didn't respond in kind for once, instead looking into the darkness of the tunnel beyond the shaft of light that fell from the impromptu opening above. He looked a good ten years younger from the fear that made his eyes grow wide and softened his lips into a tremble.

"Theo?" Sam asked, reaching out softly to touch his arm.

"Don't touch me!" Theo snapped, batting at her hand like it was an invasive species. "Don't . . . don't touch me."

"You're afraid of the dark," Sam said suddenly, recognizing a fellow night-lighter.

"I'm not afraid of anything," Theo said harshly.

Joana snorted from behind him. "There's the Theodore we know and loathe."

The rest of the worshippers who had fallen in with them suddenly turned as one, lifting their rapt faces up toward the opening above where the goddess towered.

"What now?" Joana muttered.

The goddess raised her arms again, speaking like that rushing river, the words washing over Sam in a confusion of noise. The worshippers in the tunnel cried out in joy, their calls pinging off the surrounding stones and expanding the sound of their excitement until it felt as if there were a thousand of them down there instead of only the eleven that Sam could count in addition to the three of them. Or maybe that was the cheer of the crowd from above? It was hard for Sam to keep track down in the passage.

But then the goddess was looking directly at her again, and the cheering fell away. There was something almost . . . sad in her expression. A weariness, as if she had done this a thousand times and seen it to its conclusion a thousand more. But her arms cut down sharply, as if of their own volition, like her body and her essence were detached from each other.

"What the hell?" Theo said, bringing Sam's attention back to the passage. "Where are they going?"

Sam looked around in surprise, the worshippers suddenly disappeared. "Where did they go?"

"They just took off," Theo said, shaking his head. "Like it was some kind of race or something. No flashlights or anything. All they'll do is get themselves lost or break their necks."

"Get themselves lost," Sam whispered, several things clicking into place at once. Eleven worshippers, plus the three of them. Seven men, seven women. Fourteen in all. She looked up sharply, but the goddess was no longer visible from above. Instead, the hole was surrounded by worshippers, watching them intently.

These walls weren't built to keep something out; they were built to keep something *in*.

"Bull leaping and sacrifice," Sam rasped just as a beastly roar tore down the tunnel, the stones throwing the sound like aural knives and shredding her skin into goose bumps from the impact.

It was impossible to tell where it came from, it was so loud. It felt like it was coming from everywhere at once, like it was all around her and she lived inside the sound.

"What in hell was that?" Joana demanded, her voice pitched high and tight.

"We're in the labyrinth," Sam said, her limbs shaking. "She called the Minotaur. We need to run. Now!"

The walls of the labyrinth vibrated and quaked. Terrified, Sam clamped on to Joana's hand and stumbled along in what she hoped was the opposite direction from which the roar came. She kept one hand on the wall, stretching her eyes open so wide they burned, not that it helped her gain any more sight. Once they moved away from the opening beneath the central court, there was nothing but darkness.

"Sam," Joana gasped, grunting out a curse as she stumbled over some unseen impediment. "Where are we going?"

"I don't know," Sam huffed, squealing as they hit a break in the passage. "There's no more wall! The wall is gone! I can't see anything, and the wall is gone!"

The stones shook with another roar, followed faintly by a scream halfway between agony and ecstasy. Sam shivered at the tone.

"One down," Joana said grimly.

"Thirteen to go, if the myths are true," Sam huffed, swinging her arms around for anything to ground her. She met with something soft and yet solid, swallowing back a scream as she lashed out with a fist.

"Hey, quit it," groused a familiar voice. "I'm not that thing."

"Chapin," Joana said with a sigh. "Was it too much to hope you'd have fled in terror in the opposite direction?"

"Do you know where you're going?" Theo asked, his voice unnaturally subdued.

"I don't, no," Sam said. "Just . . . away."

She managed to find the wall again and realized that the corridor had split off to the left and right instead of disappearing altogether. She heaved a sigh that caught halfway in her throat as she realized she had no idea whether to go left or right.

"Sam?" Joana asked.

"There's a split," Sam said, trying to calm the galloping of her heart. "I don't . . . I don't know which direction to go. I don't know what to do."

"Right it is," Joana said, tugging her in that direction.

"But what if that's wrong?" Sam asked in a harsh whisper.

"We'll figure it out soon enough, won't we?" Joana said.

"Don't leave me here!" Theo protested in a strained voice, all pretense of his arrogance gone.

"What's the matter, Chapin, did the monster under your bed come at night?" Joana asked, her voice sharp with tension.

"My father used to put me in the cellar when I was small," Theo said, sounding all of seven years old. "There were rats and roaches, and . . . and other things."

"Oh hell, Chapin," Joana said. "Don't go making me feel sorry for you. How egregious."

"There's another split," Sam said, running her hands over the stone. Every time her hand met with air, her body lost another year of life. "I think . . . it feels like there are three tunnels leading off of this one. Which one this time?"

There was a pause, filled with another distant scream and roar. Sam reasoned this one at least felt farther away, but really it was impossible to tell anything in the darkness. When no one said anything or made any kind of move, Joana gave a frustrated snort.

"I suppose it's down to me again, isn't it?" she said. "Fine. We go through the center."

"We're never getting out of here alive, are we?" Theo said.

They continued like that for what felt like ages—lifetimes, eons—until Sam couldn't have said remotely where they were in relation to the central court. All she knew was that the air was stale, her chest hurt, and every noise made her want to crawl out of her skin. Even Joana seemed affected, gripping Sam's hand involuntarily whenever someone spoke.

"How do you think the others are faring?" Sam asked quietly, when she couldn't stand listening to their footsteps rasping against the dirt any longer.

"The other victims, you mean?" Joana asked flatly.

"The other sacrifices," Sam said quietly. "I think this is part of the renewal-of-power ceremony. Seven young men and seven young women, same as the myth of King Minos and the Minotaur."

"I thought you were working on finding a way out of this without us having to become bull feed," Joana said.

"I was," Sam said. "I am. I just . . . I don't know what to do down here. I don't understand why she would send me down here?"

"Who?" Joana asked.

"The Snake Goddess, she . . . she spoke to me. I think she put me down here for a reason. But I can't figure out why."

Nor could she figure out why the goddess had looked so . . . *sad*. Wasn't this what she wanted?

Sam was so distracted she ran right up against a wall, her nose smarting as her eyes filled with tears. Joana and Theo made similar noises beside her, the three of them pausing to nurse their various injuries. Sam ran her hands over the rock walls, looking for the next break, but there was nothing. Nothing but stone.

"What is it, Sam?" Joana asked. "I hear you panting. What's wrong?"

"We hit another dead end," Sam said.

"Oh hell," Joana said as Theo swore a far more colorful response. "That's the fourth one in a row."

"Great job, Jo," Theo muttered.

"I told you to take a different tunnel if you're so keen, Chapin," Joana snapped. "I don't know where I'm going any better than anybody else. I'm just the only one willing to pick."

"We'll have to retrace our steps," Sam said. "Try a different tunnel."

But another roar rattled the stones around them, and there was no ensuing shout of joyful terror. The Minotaur had caught their scent, and they were trapped.

CHAPTER THIRTY-FIVE

"**S**am, if you've got a great idea, now is the time to share it," Joana said in a harsh whisper.

Sam shook her head, not that anyone could see her. What great idea could she possibly have? Every decision she had made—had forced on the others—had led them down here. Had led Bennett to play king-consort to Evelyn's misguided epiphany. Sam hadn't made a single level-headed choice since she opened that letter from Mr. Not Killeen and let a grainy image of a symbol lure her out here. Just a bunch of dead ends.

"Dead ends," Sam whispered, putting her hands on the wall and running her fingers over the surface of the stones. Dead ends and symbols. The symbol of the Snake Goddess had guided her thus far, from the depths of Skotino cave to these dead ends in the labyrinth. The tablet had shown the same symbol in the center of the labyrinth. What if it wasn't just a symbol of the goddess but a direction? What if there was something at the center of the labyrinth? Something that could stop the Minotaur, or at least protect them from the beast. On the tablet, the symbol had been surrounded by dead ends.

"Sam? You haven't gone into a trance, have you?" Joana asked.

"No, I think . . . We need to feel the stones."

"Feel for what?" Joana asked wildly. "A loose one?"

"The symbol," Sam said. "The one from the cave. It was on the tablet, in the center of the labyrinth. If we're at the center, as I think we are, there might be something here. Feel for chisel marks."

They ran their fingers over each stone as fast as they could with shaking hands. Sam was starting to feel the panic crawling up her spine by the time they reached the lowest row of stones. Maybe she was wrong. Maybe this was just a dead end, no tricks or hidden chambers. Just another tick in the wrong column for—

"I think I found it," Joana announced, the triumph in her voice making Sam jump. "You were right, Sam. There's something here. Feel it."

Sam scooted over slightly, her heart thumping for a different reason as Joana took her hand and guided her to the spot on the stone, her fingers dipping into chisel marks so clean they could have been etched that morning. The rest of the stone felt plain and ordinary, but Sam knew better than to be thrown off. She put her hand flat over the symbol and pushed, rewarded with a groan as the stone sank back and the entire wall gave way, shuddering open.

"What did you do? What's that?" Theo pressed forward, knocking the two of them forward toward the narrow crack between the tunnel wall and the false wall.

Sam squinted against the sudden intrusion of light in the chamber after so many minutes spent in total darkness. Basins of alabaster burned with ethereal fire—though who had lit these, she couldn't imagine—staining the interior with a soft golden light that only served to enhance the paints of the murals covering the walls.

"Can we get inside, please?" Joana asked, nudging Sam forward. "Before that thing finds us?"

They slipped inside, having to tug Theo's arm to fit him through the tight gap before shoving the door closed again. Sam took a deep breath, resting her head momentarily against the stone wall. They hadn't solved anything yet, but they were safe from the Minotaur. At least, she hoped they were safe. Perhaps the beast knew the secret of the heart of the labyrinth as well.

"What is this place?" Joana asked.

Sam opened her eyes, steeling herself to face the next challenge. The chamber was circular, with an altar in the middle. The three of them exchanged a look before taking a careful step forward, peering over the lip of the altar.

"What the hell are we supposed to do with *that*?" Joana blurted out.

Sam took a soft breath. "The sword of Aegeus."

Sam had never seen a sword in real life before. Only wooden props in Madame Iris's schoolhouse, or on the stage at a few of the productions Bennett had taken her to in Chicago. Those had been for show, oversize and dramatic and cheap in their tinfoil coverings. This one lying on the table was nothing like those, the blade more delicate and finely wrought than she would have imagined from a broadsword. Or was this even a broadsword? She was admittedly rusty on her sword categories. This one looked both heavy and light, if that was such a possibility, as if it existed in two realms and could be used to sever the veil between them.

"That's ridiculous," Theo said almost reflexively. "You're talking about a mythological object from a mythological person. They're not real."

Joana gave him a flat look. "We're in the heart of a labyrinth fleeing a Minotaur after your girlfriend turned into the Snake Goddess. What about any of this makes you think it's not real?"

"The sword that slayed the Minotaur," Sam said, ignoring them. She wanted to touch it, to lift it and swing it and let it give her some measure of the courage that had seeped out of her pores the moment the goddess dropped her into the labyrinth. She also wanted to run screaming from it and take her chances with the beast instead.

"Well, if somebody's already beat us to the punch and slayed that thing, what are we doing here?" Joana asked incredulously.

"I think it must be part of the ceremony," Sam said, pointing at the mural. "Awaken the Snake Goddess, she awakens the Minotaur, the sacrifice is made, and the king-consort's power is renewed. Either you slay the Minotaur, or . . ."

"Or you and thirteen of your friends pay the price for a new king," Joana said grimly.

Sam studied the murals as if she might find a different answer within their pigments. But if she had turned to them for comfort, there was nothing comforting to find. The murals stretched around the circular chamber, same as the hidden room in Skotino cave. But where that mural had shown the progression of worship to the Snake Goddess, these murals played like a zoetrope, a cylindrical toy that would show moving pictures if you spun it fast enough. Sam even pivoted in a full circle several times trying to play them all together, making herself dizzy.

"Sam," Joana said, catching her when she staggered slightly to the side. "What are you doing?"

"It's the ceremony," Sam said, approaching the nearest image. "Look, there is the priestess, and the snakes, and the epiphany of the goddess. And there, the smaller man, that's the king-consort. And down here is the labyrinth, and the Minotaur. And now look at the king-consort; he's a deity now. And it just keeps repeating."

Look, here. The priestess again. But the buildings in the background are different. I think this has all happened before. Over and over. For thousands of years."

"So what changed?" Joana asked. "I mean, I'm admittedly out of date on my global affairs, but I haven't heard of any king-consorts or goddesses walking around."

"Theseus," Sam said, finding an abrupt change to the pattern on the chamber walls. "Look, here. Theseus killed the Minotaur, and Ariadne gave him the ball of waxed yarn to escape. And he stopped the cycle. Without a king, Knossos fell."

"So we just have to defeat a mythical beast that has killed thousands of poor saps before us," Joana said, her sarcasm hollow and pointed. "What should we do, flip for the honor? I haven't got a coin on me. How about a Trojan thumb war?"

But Sam shook her head, studying the mural of Theseus's victory as if it would suddenly paint a different picture. "The Snake Goddess, she . . . she spoke to me. She said, *End this*. I mean, it was in my head, as a sort of thought, but not my own thought. I don't . . . I can't believe she would send me down here just to be a sacrifice. I think there was something else she wanted me to see, something she wanted me to find. I don't know why yet, but I can't imagine it was because she thought I was her best chance at a champion. There's something I'm still missing. I just need time to figure it all out."

"Time is the one thing we don't have," Joana said. "I know you want to do your Sam thing, but if we're voting, I vote to try the thing that's already worked to stop this ceremony before. At least with a sword we'll go down swinging."

"I don't think the sword is the answer," Sam said, looking over her shoulder at the altar. Theo stood over the weapon, his gaze unfocused and distant. He'd been so quiet Sam had nearly forgotten he was there, but now her skin prickled with apprehension at the set of his jaw and his clenched fists.

"Theo?" she said tentatively.

He shook his head, his fingers flexing open. "This was supposed to be the summer that changed everything for me. That made Professor Atchinson realize I could be more than some kind of glorified bodyguard. But it didn't matter what I did. He couldn't see past his own genius. And then you came along, sucking up all the air in the room with your questions and your theories. And the professor would complain, but I saw him working out your suggestions later on. He thought you were onto something with Linear B, even if he'd never give you the credit for it. I couldn't get him to really consider my papers beyond a grade, but you piped up with one stray comment in office hours and he was off on a tangent. I couldn't crack it with him, but you did."

"Theo," Joana said in warning.

His gaze snapped up to hers, narrowing and hardening. "This was going to be the summer I changed all that. And then the three of you showed up on that boat and wrecked everything. You got under the professor's skin, distracted him from our field school with your ridiculous theories about a golden girdle. And then when he actually found the girdle—"

"You mean stole the girdle that *we* found," Sam said.

He snorted derisively at her. "What good would it have done you? A bunch of nobody undergrads? The professor was the only one who could give your claim any legitimacy. He did you a favor, taking that thing."

"Clearly not," Joana said, her voice bone-dry.

"Theo," Sam said, trying to bring them back to the task at hand.

"I know it's a lot to take in, what's happening right now. We've been in your shoes. But we need to—"

"I'm tired of hearing what *you* think we need to do," Theo said, cutting across her attempts at harmony. "I don't take orders from a girl. Especially not a nobody like you."

"Chapin, don't you dare—" Joana started, but Theo beat her to the punch.

He snatched the hilt of the sword, lifting it from the table and holding it out before him. The ground bucked and rolled, throwing Sam and Joana off balance and knocking them to the floor. Only Theo remained standing, braced against the side of the altar.

"Theo!" Sam exclaimed, trying and failing to gain some purchase as the ground continued to roil. She crawled toward the wall, using it to pull herself to a sitting position. "Please, you're not thinking straight. If you take that sword, you're only continuing the ceremony."

"I don't care about any damn ceremony," Theo spat. "I only care that I get a head start on the rest of the fools down here. Don't think about getting in my way or stopping me either. Now open that passage for me."

"Chapin, you dung heap of a human being, put that sword down," Joana said.

He swung the blade toward her, the firelight making it flash. "Look in my eyes right now, Joana, and see if I won't do it. Open that door, or I'll make you open it."

"Theo, please, consider what you're doing," Sam begged.

He pointed the tip of the sword at her. "Let me out, Sam. Now."

Sam edged toward the hidden door, finding the symbol and pressing it again. The door swung in, shoving her back as it cracked open. Theo shook his head as he moved toward the opening.

"This isn't how I want to leave things, but it's how they've got to be," he said, looking almost regretful for a moment.

"Theo, please don't leave us here like this," Sam begged, still braced against the wall. "Let us at least come with you."

"And give that creature more reason to come after me? I don't think so. Sorry, Sam, I can't have you weighing me down. If you're the genius you think you are, I'm sure you'll find your own way out. But this one's mine."

"Theo!" she called, but he was through the opening, taking their only hope of escape with him.

CHAPTER THIRTY-SIX

"**I**'m starting to think he and Evelyn were perfect for each other after all," Joana said as Sam shoved the door closed again and crawled her way across the rolling floor. "Neither one of them seemed to have any trouble abandoning us in a disaster."

"What do we do now?" Sam asked, huddling closer to Jo. "We've got no way to protect ourselves, and if we stay here much longer, I'm afraid the whole thing will come down on us. But if we go out there . . ."

Joana flipped out a hand in consideration. "Well, if my brother were here, this is about the time when the two of you would go full librarian on me and toss out some obscure bit of mythology that cracks the whole thing wide open."

Sam hugged her knees to her chest, looking up at the murals surrounding them. "Do you think Bennett is all right?" she asked in a small voice. "Do you think he's still . . . ?"

"Bennett?" Joana said, her tone subdued. But then her expression turned fierce. "Of course he is. You think Bennett would let somebody else be in control? If anybody can fend off the advances of a goddess, it's Bennett Steeling."

"If we fail, we'll be dead," Sam said. "But he'll be . . . *other*. We can't let that happen, Jo."

"We won't. Now come on, we're not just going to curl up and let Chapin and his girlfriend have the last laugh. Bennett may not be here, but we don't share the same parentage for nothing. For now, the role of Bennett Steeling will be played by yours truly, in a very limited production. Meaning this never leaves this room. So come on, get up and let's noodle this thing out."

Sam nodded, gathering the scraps of her courage from the chamber floor and draping them around herself like the goddess's tiered skirt. "Right."

She inspected the murals, doing as she always did when an answer did not readily present itself and turning inward. She had so many pieces but no way to connect them all together yet. She laid them out mentally, like little islands on the map of the paintings before her.

"The goddess said, *End this*. She dropped me down here in the labyrinth. She could have meant 'end this by being a sacrifice for my pet bull-man and completing the renewal-of-power ceremony.'"

"But . . ." Joana prompted. "You don't really believe that, do you?"

Sam took in a breath, letting her gaze skate over the paintings. "Why even speak to me, then? She could have just . . . let me die. She's the mistress of the labyrinth, the keeper of the Minotaur, and she told me to *end it*. Why would she send me to find a sword and kill the creature she's entrusted with protecting? And why would she accept my sacrifice, and let me take the girdle, only to . . . to take it away and let Evelyn become her earthly vessel instead? None of it makes any sense. Why choose me, and then unchoose me, and then ask me to end this? What did I do to lose her faith in me?"

Joana made a noise in the back of her throat that sounded like a strangled groan. "Not this again," she muttered.

"Not what again?" Sam asked, bewildered.

Joana threw up her hands. "You're not always going to be the chosen one, Sam!"

Sam drew back sharply. "What are you talking about?"

Joana huffed out a breath. "You've always needed to be the best at everything you do, and you've always needed recognition for it. You needed to be Madame Iris's favorite in school, you always had to be the one to solve the final clue in Daddy's treasure hunt so *you* could be the one who presented what we found to him, and you made sure you always got the best finds from the dealers at Daddy's bookshop."

"That's not . . ." Sam trailed off weakly. "I didn't always need to solve the last clue. Sometimes I let . . . I mean, sometimes you figured it out first."

Joana rolled her eyes at Sam. "Don't get me wrong, I love that competitive determination. Kayla Granger cried every year when Madame Iris chose you to sit by her at the summer picnic, and she once started a rumor about me that I ate worms and dyed my hair. So she deserved what she got. But now you've been so fixated on getting Professor Atchinson to choose you that you've forgotten to choose yourself. You are young, poor, and female. Atchinson will *never* accept you. That's not your fault. That's his own crusty misogynistic fault. And now you're doing it with the goddess. She's trying to turn Bennett into her pet king and get us gored by her bull brother, and you're asking yourself why she didn't choose *you* to hollow out like a freshly shucked oyster?"

"I mean . . . it's not as if I wanted to be her earthly vessel," Sam muttered, shrinking into herself.

"Sure you didn't, but you really can't stand not being the best at everything," Joana said. "As someone who excels at failing, let me tell you something: If you let other people shape you, you will end up as hollow as an oyster shell anyway. You'll never be what everybody wants, but you'll lose yourself trying. Better to just be who you are, and anybody who doesn't like it can go chase themselves."

Had Sam lost herself? If she could be honest—and what better place to be brutally honest with yourself if not on death's imminent doorstep?—she could admit that she had felt out of sorts lately. Not just out of sorts—out of Sam. Joana was right; she had been so fixated on proving herself to Professor Atchinson, on proving herself better than his low opinion of her, that she had become the thing she couldn't respect. A thief, a treasure hunter, a desecrator of history.

Sam chewed at one corner of her lip. "You . . . might be right, Jo. I just . . . I lost so many years, being afraid. Afraid of the world, afraid of failing, afraid of losing. And I thought I could make it all up, if I could just win. I thought I could make Papa proud, show him that all our hard work had finally paid off. And when Professor Atchinson took that chance away from me . . ."

"You went a little crazy-eyed," Joana deadpanned. "Happens to the best of us. But I'm not dying in this bull run while Evelyn gets to play goddess and Theo Chapin steals our only form of protection. So pull yourself together and get us out of here. We're going to stop this ceremony, rescue that fool brother of mine, and then we're all getting drunk on the beach and promising to never raise another ancient deity again. Got it?"

Sam nodded, taking a deep breath that for the first time in days felt like it reached all the way down to the bottom of her lungs. "Got it. Sorry, Jo. For everything."

Joana waved her words away, facing the mural again. "Save your sorries for the tip jar at the taverna. So what are we missing?"

Sam looked around the chamber, trying to concentrate—to see it with her own eyes. "Everything up until now has been carefully concealed. The hidden chamber, the girdle, the labyrinth, even this chamber. All of it part of a puzzle meant to keep someone out. So why have the sword just lying there, out in the open?"

Joana shrugged. "Maybe the goddess got tired of playing hide-and-seek."

"Or maybe the sword was a test," Sam countered.

"Well, if it was, we failed spectacularly," Joana said.

"Hence the earthquake when Theo took it," Sam said. "There must be something, some connection that we're missing between all of these things. The Snake Goddess, the Minotaur, the labyrinth, all of it."

Joana huffed a breath. "So, at this stage, Bennett usually makes some point about there being another legend that says something entirely different from what everyone else believes, because my brother loves nothing more than to play the contrarian."

Sam nodded. "Bennett would say that's the thing about mythology, that it adapts and evolves to suit the societies it serves. Myths were simply stories created to explain the world around them. As societies evolved, their stories evolved as well. There's not one straightforward myth of the Minotaur and the labyrinth. Nor is there any clear mythology related to the Snake Goddess. There are the suppositions of Sir Arthur Evans, that she was some kind of mother goddess. But those are based on his own interpretations of the statues he discovered here at Knossos. And I don't know about you, but that didn't look like any mother goddess up there."

"So, if she's not a mother goddess, what kind of goddess is she?" Joana asked. "What's a different myth about her?"

"When we were in the museum, Bennett and I were discussing the myths related to the labyrinth," Sam said, digging through the tangled web of knowledge, trying to reach the snarl in the weave. "There was a myth, about Ariadne and Theseus."

"Oh, you mean the one where he tricked her into helping him escape the labyrinth and then up and abandoned her five seconds later when she had the audacity to take a little nap after betraying her father and fleeing the only home she had ever known for him?" Joana said.

"Yes! The island of Naxos!" Sam shot upright, forgetting for the moment the rolling floor beneath her feet as she crawled toward the far wall. "Look, there's a map!"

She pointed toward a section of the mural that depicted the Mediterranean Sea, hundreds of islands dotting the surface like flower petals strewn across a pond.

"All right, so which one is it?" Joana asked, stumbling after her. "There are about a hundred here."

"Bennett would know," Sam said despairingly.

"Sorry, my knowledge of Bennett-related things has been exhausted," Joana said. "I don't hold all of his obscure data about geography and history. I'm sure he'd know exactly where it was and would give us some fun, useless tidbit about how they had the highest production of wool or they made some kind of alcohol from tree roots or something."

"Wait, I know something obscure about Naxos!" Sam exclaimed. "I read about it when I was studying Linear B tablets. They were known in the ancient world as a source of emery, a type of abrasive rock."

She ran her hands over the islands in the mural, her fingertips scraping the surface of one island in the center of the mural, larger than the others. "It's rough, like there's something embedded here. I think this must be it."

Sam pressed hard on the island, and it gave immediately, sinking into the wall and leaving an island-shaped hole in its absence. She waited, watching that hole as if something great or terrible might appear from its darkness, but nothing emerged.

"Was something supposed to happen?" Joana asked, peering over her shoulder.

"I . . . don't know?" Sam said, looking around. It was hard to tell anything with all the rumbling in the earth. Perhaps they had opened another secret door, or another clue had appeared on a different section of the wall, or . . .

"The altar," Joana said, her few inches of height advantage allowing her to see the top of the altar. "It's open."

They clung to each other as they returned to the altar, the top that had so carefully cradled the sword of Theseus now gone. In its place was a small alcove, simple in construction. Within its confines was a flower as fresh and lush as if it had been picked from the fields only moments ago, the petals velvety soft and the pollen clinging to the stamen. It was an exquisite specimen, wide and open and inviting.

"A poppy," said Joana. "It's a poppy flower."

Sam looked to her in surprise. "What?" Joana said defensively. "A girl can't know her flowers? You never know when a suitor's trying to sell you roses on a carnation budget. You and Bennett haven't cornered the market on random knowledge. Why a poppy?"

"It's the Greek flower of sleep and death," Sam said. "They say Morpheus slept in a cave full of poppies as he shaped dreams."

"It's certainly dewy enough," Joana said practically. "Mama would kill to know what kind of watering program he uses."

"This must be what the goddess wants," Sam said. "This is what she sent me to find. She doesn't want to complete the ceremony. She wants to go back to sleep."

CHAPTER THIRTY-SEVEN

"**W**hat?" Joana asked in disbelief. "How is that possible? Isn't this whole thing happening because of her?"

"I'm not sure it is," Sam said, trying to piece together the puzzle. "She said, *End this*. What if she didn't mean complete it, but end it? Put her back to sleep before the ceremony was complete?"

"Why would she want that?" Joana asked. "I mean, if I were a goddess, I'd be epiphany-ing myself into every conceivable vessel. That's far too much power to just let it hibernate like a bear."

"It's a great deal of responsibility, too," Sam countered. "Maybe she doesn't want to feel the weight of her people's needs and tragedies anymore."

"That does sound an awful drag," Joana mused. "But then what about the snakes, and the singing, and the *snakes*?"

"I think they're all trapped in the machinations of the ritual," Sam said. "I think I started something, when I sacrificed the tin horse from my father and took the girdle. It caught us both, like a finger trap. Except one end was me, and the other end was a goddess. Maybe she's being forced to play this out as much as we are, unless we can find a way to interrupt it."

"Like putting her back to sleep and returning the girdle to the chamber," Joana said slowly. "Great, so how do we get the flower to her? We're trapped in the center of a labyrinth with a rabid man-bull on the prowl out there. Unless there's a spare ball of waxed yarn down here, we're still out of luck."

"Waxed yarn," Sam echoed, turning back to the section of the mural that depicted the events of Theseus's time in the labyrinth. There was the goddess, this time as Ariadne, handing the ball of waxed yarn to Theseus as he wielded the sword. But the yarn was attached to Ariadne at the waist, where the paint glittered gold and bright.

"The girdle," Sam said, tapping the image. "She's wearing the girdle here. And the yarn is spooling out from the girdle. Why?"

"Maybe we should have checked the inside of the girdle for a secret stash of yarn," Joana said.

"The inside of the girdle! That's it, Jo. You're a genius!"

"I know." Joana sighed. "You want to let me in on why I'm a genius this time?"

"The pattern on the inside of the girdle!" Sam scrabbled through her pockets, pulling out her field diary. "The symbols. I couldn't figure out what the numbers were meant to represent. But they're *steps*. The Snake Goddess is the mistress of the labyrinth, right? So she must be the one to hold the key to the labyrinth. The symbol we found in the cave—the same one we found to get into this chamber—it was also on the head of the girdle. I think the symbol represents the heart of the labyrinth, and the numbers are our ball of waxed yarn. They're the steps we need to take to get out of the labyrinth."

Joana nodded, looking toward the hidden door. "So we're . . . going back out there, then?"

Sam's enthusiasm withered slightly. "Oh. Right. I guess so."

"Well, I'm not going blind again," Joana said, peering into one of the burning bowls. "You think we could scoop this out with something?"

Sam studied the numbers she'd carefully transcribed in her notebook, doing her best to commit each one to memory. "I don't suppose there's a spare torch lying around somewhere?"

"Wouldn't that have been too convenient," Joana muttered, stalking the perimeter of the chamber. "You know, if this goddess wanted out of this business like you say, she could have given us a single light. A flashlight, something."

"She's a goddess," Sam murmured, softly repeating the first several lines under her breath. "I don't think things like light occur to her. But I can't remember all of these numbers in the code. There are too many steps. We need some way to see the book, even if it's just the butt of a cigarette. Something."

"Oh hell," Joana muttered, patting down her pockets. "I completely forgot."

"Forgot what?" Sam asked.

Joana held up her lighter, the metal gleaming in the firelight. "Panicked it right out of my head. We won't be able to see where we're going, but we should at least be able to read your notebook."

"That would have been helpful when we were searching the stones to get in here," Sam said.

"I was distracted," Joana sniped. "You know, the snakes, the goddess, the mindless worshippers, the damn Minotaur. Do you want it now or not?"

"Of course," Sam said hastily.

Joana looked to the closest basin of fire like she might risk scooping it out with her own hands. "Can we at least leave the door open?"

Sam tucked her notebook away in her pocket, dipping her hands into the small cavity in the altar to lift the poppy flower out. It had a surprising weight to it, nestling down in the dip of her joined hands. "Now who's afraid of the dark?"

"What can I say, I prefer to see my demise coming," Joana said.

They opened the hidden door again, pushing it as wide as it would go—which wasn't much wider than the crack they had originally passed through—but it did illuminate the walls of the tunnel just beyond. Sam repeated the numbers from her notebook to herself like the chorus of a song as they exited the chamber.

"What's first?" Joana asked, linking her arm through Sam's while being careful not to jostle the flower she held. She put her other hand on the wall. "You lead and I'll keep track."

"One hundred steps, then a left," Sam whispered.

They counted together, their words no more than a mingling breath as the firelight receded into the background. Every time Sam felt the overwhelming tug of panic try and draw her back to the center of the labyrinth, she thought of Bennett waiting above and steeled her nerves for the next turn in the sequence.

"Why is it so quiet?" Joana asked after they made their second right turn. "I haven't heard so much as a snuffle out of that thing since we left the center of the labyrinth."

"Maybe Theo is better with a sword than we thought," Sam said.

"I didn't care for all the roaring, but now I'm just imagining what's keeping the bull-man so occupied."

"Well, maybe don't imagine it out loud, please. I'm trying to concentrate on our next steps."

They fell into a rhythm, Joana measuring their steps as Sam counted off each line in her notebook. It wasn't until she had to stop and risk the light of Joana's lighter to check their next steps that Sam realized the key was actually working. They had their escape in sight, one carefully transcribed line at a time.

"We're almost there," Sam whispered, pointing to their progress on her key. "Look, just a few more turns and we'll be out of the labyrinth."

"Thank the godde—" Joana started, but she got cut off by a grunt, her arm tearing free and untethering Sam from the real world.

"Jo?" she whispered, freezing like a small animal. "Joana? Are you there? What happened?"

"I'm all right," Joana said. "I tripped over something."

"What is it? Do you have your lighter? Can you—"

"No, Sam," Joana said, her voice uncharacteristically tight. "You don't want a light. Trust me."

"Why? What is . . . ?"

But then Sam caught her meaning, her body recoiling while her mind processed Joana's meaning. "It's not . . . You don't think it's Theo, do you?"

"It would serve him right if it was," Joana said. Her hand found its way back to Sam's arm, her grip tight. "But I don't think it is. Based on my very brief and undesired contact, I think it was a woman."

Sam sighed in relief, before realizing the morbidity in it. Someone was still dead, no matter that it wasn't someone she knew.

"I . . . I lost my place," Sam said, panic gripping her. "I lost my count. I don't remember where we were."

"You said we were on the last few turns," Joana said.

"We were! I mean, we are. There were just a few lines left, but the last few lines are repeating. Ten steps and a left, ten steps and a right. Ten steps and a right, ten and a left. Ten, left, ten, right. Ten right, ten, left."

"Okay, so which ten is it?"

"That's what I don't remember!" Sam said, her voice rising in frustration. "We might have been on the first ten and a right, or the second ten and a left. I'm not sure we went all ten steps either. I lost count when you . . . when we . . ."

"All right, let's move on from that," Joana said. "Mentally and physically, please. Take a minute and think, Sam. Which direction do we go? Left or right?"

"I don't . . . I don't know," Sam said, pressing her eyes closed even though there was nothing to close out. But it seemed to help her gain some semblance of her sanity because her stomach stopped feeling like it wanted to eject itself through her throat. "I think . . . I think we went ten steps and turned left, then ten and right. And then ten and . . . and we hadn't gone left yet?"

"Is that a question?" Joana asked darkly.

"Jo, I'm sorry," she whispered. "It's the best I can do. I think we're meant to go left."

"And if you're wrong?" Joana asked.

"Then we retrace our steps and go right," Sam said. "Right?"

"Right or left, Sam?" Joana asked, her voice spiraling downward.

"Left, let's go left," Sam said, silently hoping she was right about left.

They followed the last few instructions from Sam's memory, each turn either leading them closer to freedom or back into the bowels of the labyrinth.

"Is that . . . ?" Sam said, squinting so hard it made her eyes water. She quickened her steps "Jo, is that . . . light? Up ahead? I think I see—"

But as they made the final right turn, a roar knocked them back, so close it took up every square inch of open space in the tunnel. It punched through Sam's chest with a force that made her ears pop. The physicality of it drove her back a step into Joana, sending the poppy flower tumbling from her hands. She cried out, her body shaking in the wake of the sound, her ears giving a high-pitched whining that didn't abate even as her chest stopped vibrating.

"Jo!" Sam called, her voice sounding like it was coming from under water. The meager light she had detected only a moment ago was suddenly gone, blocked by a looming presence before them. Something that filled the tunnel to an impossible height and breadth; something that growled in a voice that squeezed the remaining air from her lungs; something with horns that scraped the tall ceiling of the tunnel, leaving deep scores through the rock.

The Minotaur had found them.

CHAPTER THIRTY-EIGHT

Every single depiction of the Minotaur that Sam had ever seen had done him a disservice. Some depicted him as more man than bull, with the curved arms and thick legs of a warrior; others had shown him as more beast than human, with cloven hooves and a hairy hide all over. Some had painted him as villain, others as tragic victim. There had been so many artistic renderings of him over the millennia that he had become practically a household name.

But none of those depictions could truly capture the sheer *vitality* of the Minotaur. None of them could render the hot fog of his breath as it pressed on them in that underground space; none could capture the sharp movement of his bovine eyes as they assessed his next prey; none could properly convey the goose bumps that rose at the grating screech of his horns along the thick stones of the ceiling above. And none of them, not even the most detailed among the pack, could truly capture how fundamentally *wrong* the creature was, a twisted abomination of man and beast made flesh by a god's dissatisfaction.

Sam's scream was eclipsed by another roar from the creature, the force of it knocking her and Jo against the wall. A ringing set up in her ears, a nauseating mix of the Minotaur's battle cry and the impact of her head against the solid rock of the tunnel walls. And there was something else, dancing along the upper registers of the ringing. Something that sounded almost like . . . cheering.

"Jo, look!" Sam said, cringing back from the Minotaur's hot breath even as she pointed through a gap over his shoulder. "The light! I can hear the worshippers. We're almost there!"

"We're almost bull feed, Sam!" Joana said in a shout, her voice trembling. "We need to run!"

Sam shook her head. "If we do, we'll get lost. We're almost there, Jo. We just need to get past him."

"Get past him *where*? And *how*?"

"I don't—" Sam started, but the words caught in her throat as the Minotaur shifted position. His shoulders rippled, his head dipping and his horns tearing at the stones again as he lowered them directly at Sam and Joana. Sam had enough experience with barnyard animals to know what was coming next.

"Jo, he's going to charge us!" she said, grabbing her best friend's hand and diving out of the way as the beast bellowed, ramming his horns into the wall where the two of them had been only moments before. The impact shook the dust loose from the ceiling overhead, and the cheering filled the tunnel once again.

The Minotaur gave a great roar, twisting his head from side to side to try and pull his horns loose of the deep scores they had made in the stones. Sam tightened her grip on Joana's hand as she spotted a blossom of red behind the Minotaur's hoof.

"The poppy!" she said, lurching involuntarily toward the flower. "He's going to crush it!"

"He's going to crush *us* if we don't book it," Joana said, tugging her in the opposite direction. "Sam, I'm not going to go down in the history books as female victim number seven!"

"But if we don't get the flower, we can't stop the ceremony," Sam said, holding her ground.

Joana pressed back against the wall, looking longingly into the dark recesses of the labyrinth. "You're sure we can't just make a run for it?"

"Bennett needs us," Sam said. "And we need that flower."

Joana sighed. "Brothers are such a burden. Fine, I'll distract the Minotaur, you grab the flower, and then we run like hell."

"How are you going to distract him?" Sam asked. "We don't have anything to fight him."

Joana leaned down and pulled off her shoe, wielding the short heel like a battle-axe. "Never let it be said I'm not resourceful. I've beaten back more intent suitors with less. Just don't let me get gored. It would ruin this outfit."

They pressed in close together as the Minotaur finally freed his horns from the rock, rounding on them with a snarl. This close up, Sam could register every detail of his construction, from the stubby whiskers that vibrated as he breathed, to the fine coat of fur covering his human chest, to the deep stains flaking off the wicked points of his horns.

"Is that blood?" Sam whispered, not that she really wanted an answer.

"Just get that flower, Sam," Joana ground out.

Joana raised her heel, giving her own version of a battle cry, as Sam crouched low and prepared to dive for the flower. But before either of them could put Joana's shoe to good use, someone else came charging at them, filling the tunnel with his bellowing.

"Chapin?" Sam screeched, pressing back against the wall as the young man swung the sword of Aegeus over his head.

The Minotaur caught the attack with one of his horns, flicking his head in annoyance and sending the sword spinning off and clattering to the ground. Theo paused, stunned. The Minotaur lowered his head, horns pointed directly at the boy, and Joana gave him a kick with her bare foot.

"Go on, Chapin, pick it back up!" she hissed.

Theo shook his head, diving for the sword as the creature dove for him, both of them meeting their goal at the same time. Theo gave a grunt of pain as the sharp end of the Minotaur's horn caught him in the gut, lifting him a few feet off the ground before pinning him to the brick wall. He managed to keep his hold on the sword, bringing it down on the Minotaur's shoulder, where the blade bit through the thick hide and cut down deep into the muscle. The beast gave a roar of pain, his other horn screeching against the rock as he pushed deeper into Theo's body.

"Theodore!" Sam screamed, lurching forward as if she could help him.

"Sam, the flower," Joana said, grabbing her and pulling her back. "Get the flower!"

"We have to help him!" Sam said, her eyes glued to Theo's even as they glazed over in pain. He managed to pull the sword free and deliver another blow to the Minotaur, the cut shallower but no less impactful as the beast roared again. Blood streaked down his horn, pumping out of Theo's gut and cascading in waves.

"The only way we're going to help him is to stop this ceremony," Joana said. "And we can't do that without the flower, as you pointed out."

Joana was right—Sam knew she was—but it was still excruciating to pull her gaze from Theo's and locate the flower on the labyrinth floor. It was miraculously unharmed, and Sam scooped it up and darted out of the attack zone of the Minotaur. Theo looked to her helplessly as she paused, hesitating.

"Don't . . . leave," he said, blood now gushing up out of his mouth. "Dark. Please."

"Theo," she whispered, but the beast shook his head in fury and any remaining words were torn from Theo's midsection. Sam felt the earth tilt beneath her—or maybe that was her own sense of equilibrium abandoning her.

"Let's go," Joana whispered, grabbing Sam's hand and dragging her toward the opening filled with onlookers.

"We can't just leave him," Sam said, her voice thick. "Jo, we can't . . . Look at him. We can't leave him."

"He's already gone, Sam," Joana said, her own voice just as thick.

Once again, Sam knew Joana was right, but that didn't stop her feet from dragging and her stomach from roiling. Theodore Chapin was a lot of things, not many of them flattering, but he had just saved their lives.

"We've got to get up there somehow," Joana said, gazing up at the ring of onlookers. "You don't suppose they'd give us a boost, do you?"

The little bit of light Sam could see through the hole had an eerie tint to it, like the sky just before a storm. She held her trembling hands up, showing the worshippers the poppy.

"For the goddess," she called out. "Lift us out."

There was a hesitation among them, as if some unspoken communication passed through their ranks. Whatever was said—or unsaid—they seemed to reach a consensus, for soon one of them was lowering down a rope for Sam and Joana to climb out.

"A ladder would have been more expedient," Joana muttered,

but she stepped up to the rope as Sam held on, wrapping her arms around Sam to give her extra support as she cradled the poppy flower to her chest. Joana gave it a tug, letting the worshippers know to pull the two of them up as Sam pressed her eyes closed against the sight of the Minotaur making short work of Theodore Chapin. But she was sure the sounds would stay with her until her own dying day.

"I'm so sorry, Theo," she whispered as the worshippers lifted them out.

CHAPTER THIRTY-NINE

Sam crawled out of the hole, the worshippers grabbing at her clothes and helping her along. She turned her gaze skyward as Joana clambered out beside her, both of them squinting against the odd diffusion of light as they tried to make sense of it.

The sky was *wrong*. Dark and yellow, swirls of gray clouds hanging so low and heavy she thought she might touch one if she could stretch up on her toes high enough. It was like a gathering storm, but no storm she had ever encountered. This one was too portentous, too ominous.

"We made it out," Joana said, her voice strange and light. "Does that mean this whole nightmare is over? We beat the labyrinth."

Sam shook her head, looking around at the worshippers still in thrall. "I don't think it is. I think they only let us out on a trial basis, to deliver the poppy to the goddess. If we don't . . ."

"We're right back in the soup," Joana said glumly. "But where is my brother? And where is the goddess?"

Sam searched around the central court. The worshippers were still gathered, packed so densely it was as if all the neighboring villages had turned out. Maybe they had. But nowhere in their ranks did Sam spot the tall, powerful presence of the Snake Goddess. As she looked around, the worshippers were not looking at her. They were looking up.

Sam followed their gaze to where the clouds swirled and seemed to grow even denser at a point in the ruins far overhead. There the Snake Goddess stood, at the highest point of Knossos, her arms raised to the sky. Her presence was no less impressive at a distance; in fact, she seemed even more deified from the vantage point, flanked by her griffins and surrounded by kneeling worshippers.

"Oh boy," Sam said softly, her courage faltering under the weight of so much sky.

"I don't see Bennett," Joana said. "You don't think—"

"No," Sam said emphatically. "The ceremony isn't done yet. As long as we're alive, he's still Bennett. He must still be in the throne room. We just need to deliver the poppy and put the goddess back to sleep, and all of this will be over."

"Right," Joana said. "I'll get to Bennett, you get to the Snake Goddess. Let's end this business, now."

Sam nodded, steeling herself for the climb up those treacherous ruins. "Good luck, Jo. Tell Bennett . . . Tell him—"

"You'll tell him yourself," Joana said, giving her a quick, fierce hug. "When we put that goddess back to sleep. Go."

"More climbing." Sam sighed as Joana disappeared in the direction of the throne room, searching the edges of the central court for a path to reach the goddess. She spotted a set of stairs leading up, hurrying toward them as a great crack of thunder rattled the teeth in her head. Somehow, even though they were miles inland here, she thought she caught a salty taste of sea air.

But she made no more progress than the first step before someone gave a strangled cry to her left, barreling into her and gripping her tight. Sam yelped, afraid the Minotaur had escaped, but this creature was far too small to be the great bull-man. And it was blubbering far too loudly.

"The snakes!" the creature wailed, and in that crisp accent Sam identified its source. "Everywhere! Oh god, the snakes!"

"Professor Atchinson?" Sam said, hardly recognizing the man. His eyes were glazed and roving, his hair standing on end as if he'd been electrified. His mouth moved without speaking. His fingers gripped her shirtfront, giving her an unconscious shake.

"He was right, oh, how was he right?" the professor muttered. "Barnaby knew all along, how could he? How!"

"Professor!" Sam said desperately. "Pull yourself together, please. I have a very important task here, and you are keeping me from doing it."

The professor seemed to register her for the first time, his eyes coming together to focus on her. "Miss Knox! You must get me out of here. I cannot die like this, not by snakes."

He shook her again, the fabric of her shirt tearing a little at his insistence. She tried prying his grip loose, but that only seemed to invigorate his efforts. Finally, with no time and very little recourse left to her, Sam was forced to take extreme action. She shifted the flower to one hand, raising the other and slapping it sharply across the professor's face.

"Professor Atchinson!" she said, her voice cracking like a whip. "Let me go."

The man stumbled back, raising one hand to his cheek in surprise. "You struck me, girl," he said, the indignity of the assault bringing back a modicum of his former self. "You struck a superior."

"And I will do it again if you don't stay out of my way," Sam said firmly. She kept him in her peripheral gaze as she tucked the poppy flower into her shirt pocket to protect it from the professor's

predatory gaze. But his eyes alighted on the edge of a petal showing from the top of the pocket, his expression taking on a crafty
new sheen as he lurched for her once again. "Is that a means of
self-preservation?"

Sam wrestled her arm from his grasp, advancing up a few stairs
to put some distance between them. "Professor Atchinson, don't
even think of it. I have to get this to the goddess."

The professor scurried after her, surprisingly agile in his hunt for
said self-preservation. "Miss Knox, I demand you give over care of
that flower to me this instant."

"I can't do that, Professor. You should leave." Sam turned from
him to focus on her ascent. The stairs tapered into a narrow walkway with a sharp drop-off of at least twenty feet to the right. She
pressed closer to the large stones on her left, glancing back at the
professor while also looking for another way to ascend the remaining blocks to where the goddess held her court.

"How dare you speak to me so dismissively, you ignorant female!"
the professor said, his tone growing vicious. He grabbed at her
sleeve, pulling her shirt askew. "Give me that flower!"

"Professor, let me go!" Sam struggled, her impatience turning to
frustration as the professor continued his assault. For a small man,
he was surprisingly powerful. Sam gave a growl, the heat of rage in
her chest expanding until she felt as if smoke might puff out of her
mouth. In fact, she noticed a movement along the stones to her
side, waving like rolls of steam. Only, these waves were not white
but a striped brown and red, dipping through each crevice in the
stones and collecting at her feet.

"What on—" the professor yelped, stumbling back from the
warning hiss of the half dozen snakes rapidly gathering at Sam's
feet only to find another half dozen coiling on the path behind

him. They rose up, hissing in warning and nipping at the pleats of his pants as he pivoted and stepped and looked for all the world like a ballerina who had lost a toe shoe.

"You are doing this!" the professor exclaimed to Sam. "Make them stop! Call them off!"

"I'm not controlling them," Sam said. "I think they just don't like you. Or there's still enough of Evelyn in the goddess to make her feelings about you clear."

More and more worshippers gathered, forming a protective wall between Sam and the professor and driving him back toward the stairs leading down to the central court.

"You vile girl," the professor spat, the viciousness of his words undercut by the yelp of fright he gave as a wave of snakes advanced on him. "I shall not forget this injustice. I will make sure you and— Ah! No! Help me, you stupid girl! They are biting me!"

"I think you're better off trying to run," Sam called out, taking far too much pleasure in the professor's continued cries of pain.

"I shall do no such— Ah! Blast!" One snake had coiled around his foot, tripping him up as he reached the bottom of the stairs and sending him sprawling. The snakes swarmed, striking at every tender inch of exposed flesh. The professor wailed, curling into a tight ball, which only seemed to increase their furor.

Sam might have contemplated helping him, except the sky gave a loud rumble that echoed through the ground beneath her. She needed to get to the goddess. A few of the snakes started to climb again, showing her a series of cuts in the rough stone that were just wide enough that she could use them as hand- and footholds.

By the time Sam reached the platform where the Snake Goddess stood, her loyal servants coiled around her, the stones were slick with the unspent moisture in the air, the clouds above threatening to open up and pour down upon the worshippers who parted for

Sam's arrival. Sam slipped in her ascent, falling to her knees. The Snake Goddess did not acknowledge Sam, her attention on the storm collecting above them.

"Revered Snake Goddess!" Sam cried, lowering her head against the howl of the gathering wind. "Please! I know you don't want to do this. I know why you sent me down there, to the labyrinth. And I found it! I found the poppy flower, I have it right—"

But Sam's words died as she extracted the flower from her shirt pocket.

"No," she breathed, all her hope slipping out with that one whispered syllable.

In her struggle to extricate herself from Professor Atchinson's grip, the flower had somehow been crushed inside her pocket. All the life and vitality held within the petals had withered away, the pollen smeared along the inside and one of the gorgeous red petals torn at a jagged angle. It looked like a crumpled piece of children's paper art now, the edges already turning a deep red fading into black.

The flower was utterly ruined, along with her chances of ending the ritual.

CHAPTER FORTY

"**I**'m so sorry," Sam whispered, tears leaking out as she closed her hand around the ruined blossom. "Please, please don't let this be the end. I'll sail to Naxos and find another blossom! Or I will offer myself in Bennett's place. I . . . well, I know it's supposed to be a king-consort, but maybe you could make an exception just this once? Please, I'll do anything. Just don't take Bennett or Jo. Take me instead."

The Snake Goddess lowered her gaze from the sky, the weight of her attention settling on Sam like an iron mantle. She spoke in that magnificent voice now, churning like the sea. "Why would you believe I require your life in sacrifice instead?"

"I . . . Isn't that what all gods and goddesses require? A sacrifice? The labyrinth, the seven young men and women, the king-consort. All of this . . ."

"Is not of my doing," said the goddess, tilting her head in consideration as a curiously human expression crossed her face. "Do you truly know so much of our kind? I have touched the consciousness of the world since my awakening. Our ways are lost to you. Tangled in the stories of others. My people are gone, and their children believe twisted versions of our stories passed down by outsiders."

Sam looked around at the worshippers, their expressions gone slack. "I know what it's like to be judged on rumors and hearsay," she said softly. "You become trapped in it, trapped in the false expectations of others. Never able to share your true self."

The goddess lowered her head in a nod. "This world no longer knows the truth of me. I do not wish to remain where I am no longer needed, where I am misunderstood and misrepresented. I wish only to return to my rest."

"I'm so sorry," Sam said, knowing that her meager apologies meant nothing to an ancient goddess but needing to say them anyway. "For waking you up. For not knowing how to stop the ceremony sooner. For . . . for ruining our one chance."

She opened her hand, the flower losing all structure and falling apart in her grasp. She raised the delicate remains to the goddess.

"I tried, I really did," she said, her voice choked. "I tried my best, it just wasn't enough, in the end."

But the goddess's expression opened up, lit from within. "You found it."

"And ruined it," Sam said. "I tried so hard, but I failed."

The goddess glided toward her, her shadow enveloping Sam as she bent to examine the crushed remains of her only means of sleep. She scooped the flower out of Sam's hand, pressing it between her palms and rubbing them together until the petals and seeds formed a ball of paste. She held it out for Sam's inspection.

"Crushing the seeds releases their power," she said, her voice calmer and softer now. "You have not made a mistake at all, but rather a discovery. Do not let yourself be so afraid of mistakes that you do not undertake the journey at all. Mistakes are necessary on the path to wisdom."

Sam trembled with the ache of hope. "I haven't ruined everything? Bennett and Jo, they'll be safe?"

The goddess smiled at the crushed remains of the poppy flower, whispering an ancient word into its folds as she passed it through her lips. Sam didn't know the word, but she understood its meaning. *Serenity.* The goddess closed her eyes, lifting her face once again as the yellow leached from the sky, the clouds dissipating until swaths of blue peeked through. The earth stilled.

The goddess returned her gaze to Sam and held out a hand, her golden-headed snakes twining down her arm and depositing something in her outstretched palm. As they retreated, she held out the object to Sam. The melted tin horse from her father, the sacrifice that started this all. Sam took it gingerly from the goddess's grasp, the metal surprisingly cool.

"Know that I have taken measure of your worth," said the goddess, her voice turning soft and slow like the trickle of a stream. "It was the only reason you were able to initiate the ceremony, because you were worthy. Your sacrifice was worthy. Know your worth for yourself. Do not let others define it for you."

"Thank you," Sam said as the goddess closed her eyes once again.

Snakes came slithering out of the tiers of her skirt, sliding over her skin in an impenetrable barrier. The layers dissolved as the snakes slithered away again, leaving only Evelyn in their wake. The girl slouched down, pale and unconscious but still breathing, and Sam lurched forward to catch her before she fell. She lowered Evelyn carefully to the ground, tugging at the sacral knot binding the girdle to her midsection. It came away easily, unraveling and coiling in her hands. But the pull Sam had felt when she first touched the girdle was gone.

"It's over," she whispered, needing to say it out loud to prove it true.

The worshippers filling the ruins of Knossos slumped over as one, their ecstasy dissipating along with their goddess. Evelyn stirred in Sam's arms.

"Sam? What happened? Where am I?" she asked, her voice soft and hoarse. She struggled to sit up, wincing and slumping back down. "I feel as if I've been hollowed out."

"You sort of were," Sam said. "What is the last thing you remember?"

"I . . . I remember seeing you at the docks," Evelyn said, frowning as she struggled to recall. "Professor Atchinson had said there was some kind of raid, and they would need help moving stolen artifacts. But you were there, and Joana and Bennett. All dressed up. And there was a . . . a gold belt. It was so exquisite, the way it gleamed, and it was just lying there in the street. I needed to rescue it. And there was this incredible singing. I couldn't . . . But then I . . . It was . . ."

She shivered, sitting up suddenly in a panic. "Sam, what happened? What did I do?"

"It's all right," Sam said quickly. "What happened wasn't your fault, Evelyn."

"But . . ." Evelyn looked around helplessly. "But I don't understand. What am I doing here? Who are all these people? Where is the professor? Where is Theo?"

Sam shivered at the mention of Theodore Chapin, the memory of what happened to him still so fresh. Sam had experience with the pain of loss, however complicated the person was who was gone, and she took Evelyn gently by the hands. "Whatever happens, Evelyn, you're going to be all right. Be gentle with yourself."

Evelyn's eyes were wide, her lip trembling as she met Sam's gaze. "Why are you being so kind to me?"

Sam gave her a soft smile. "Because you deserve kindness. You deserve to be seen."

"Oh," Evelyn said softly, her eyes filling with tears.

"Sam!" came Joana's voice, just as she stumbled through the crowd of people waking in a similar state of confusion. She tackled Sam in a hug, giving her a fierce shake. "You did it, you absolute gem. You stopped her. Not that I doubted you would, of course."

"Jo, you're okay," Sam said, returning the hug just as fiercely.

"Oof, Sam, I won't be if you cut off my oxygen," Joana replied, though she didn't let Sam go.

"Bennett?" Sam asked, her heart in her throat as she pulled back.

"I'm here," Bennett said, appearing among the crowd. He gave Sam a rueful smile. "I wasn't as willing as Jo to step on people's hands and feet to get here."

Sam launched herself into his embrace, squeezing until she heard his ribs creak. She took a deep breath, inhaling his scent. "Bennett, I'm so sorry. I was wrong, about everything. I nearly cost you your life. I should have listened to you from the beginning, but I was stubborn and churlish and hardheaded."

"And clever, and brave, and loyal, and relentless," Bennett said, pulling back just enough to take her face in his hands. "I should be the one apologizing to you, Sam. I didn't believe you, when you told me about Atchinson having it out for you. I thought you were overreacting. I should have trusted you."

"But you were right," Sam pressed. "Jo helped me see that. I was so focused on gaining Professor Atchinson's approval, I lost my own sense of self. I stepped out of line, and you were only trying to pull me back on the straight and narrow."

Bennett gave her a soft smile. "Your passion for discovery and your sense of adventure are my favorite things about you, Sam. Truthfully, I was only afraid I couldn't keep up. I was afraid you would grow tired of me and leave me for some greater enterprise."

"Leave *you*?" Sam said, incredulous. "I was afraid *you* would leave *me* when you grew tired of my shenanigans."

Bennett laughed, the sound vibrating through her chest as his fingers slipped into her hair and dug into her scalp, lifting her face to his. He kissed her, his lips warm and strong. Sam sank into the kiss immediately, her breath catching in her chest and expanding from the heat caused by the pressure of his mouth against hers, until she thought she might burst.

"I will never *ever* tire of your shenanigans," Bennett said, pressing his forehead against hers. "I would expire from boredom and accumulated dust without the life you bring to every second of my day. I know when we were children you felt . . . affection for me. But that was a childhood infatuation. I am not that ten-year-old boy any longer, and neither are you a schoolhouse girl. I wanted you to be sure you wanted the me I am today, not some rosy-hued idealization of me."

Sam gave him a soft smile. All this time she had been so insecure in his attentions, when really it was Bennett who needed reassurances. "Bennett, I want any version of you. Even the bossy, tightly wound version. You can be many things, but never in all my life would I call you boring. And you shouldn't judge yourself by what girls like Helen Pickler or Edna Carter say about you. They couldn't put together an interesting thought if you shook all the contents of their minds out on a table and played jigsaw with them."

Bennett gave her a glorious smile. "And I want any version of you, even the one that raises an ancient goddess in her overenthusiasm. So long as you can always put her back to rest."

Sam held up her hands with a laugh. "My goddess-raising days are over, I swear it. From now on, I'll stick to pottery sherds and book restoration. But are you a little bit disappointed you won't be a king?"

Bennett chuckled. "It was hard to consider what economic policies I would enact when I was being guarded by flesh-melting snakes. I believe I will leave the monarchy to the British."

"You'll always be a king to me," Sam said, grinning up at him as he lowered his head to kiss her again, thoroughly and without reserve.

"Save it for when I'm not around," Joana said, but she smiled at the two of them as they parted. She caught sight of the girdle coiled in Sam's hand, her shoulders tensing. "Why do you—"

"It's all right, Jo," Sam said quickly, unraveling the girdle and holding it up for inspection. "She's gone. Back to where she came from."

"Mmm-hmm," Joana said, still eyeing the belt. She glanced at Evelyn. "And this one?"

"Be kind," Sam said softly. "She has a lot to process still. What about the Minotaur? And . . . and Theo?"

Joana shook her head tersely. "The central court was all closed up by the time we made it out of the throne room. If the Minotaur is still kicking around down there, it's where he'll stay. Along with poor Theo. What are we going to do with that thing?"

Sam wrapped the girdle around her hands. "We need to return it to Skotino cave."

"Or, counterpoint, we take a cruise and toss it in the middle of the sea where no one could ever possibly find it again," Joana said.

But Sam shook her head. "We need to put things back to right. It belongs in the bench shrine in the cave."

They descended the ruins carefully, doing their best to avoid the questions of the worshippers who gathered now in little clusters to discuss their experiences. They had to pause as they reached the central court, however, as they found Professor Atchinson bemoaning his fate at the foot of the stairs. Angry red welts covered his skin, none of them fatal but all of them looking quite painful.

"Professor, are you all right?" Sam asked.

"You wretched, horrible girl!" the professor wailed. "This is all your doing. You and those infernal creatures. I will have you all— Oh! Oh, it stings! It burns!"

"He seems fine," Joana said dryly. "Back to spelunking."

It was full dark by the time they returned to Skotino cave, their flashlights casting long shadows over the trees and stones as they made the sharp descent toward the entrance.

"You know," Sam huffed as they climbed their way down to the inner caverns. "I really do think I'm getting the hang of this whole cave-diving business."

"Not me," Joana grunted. "After all this, I plan on getting as far from underground as possible."

"How will you do that?" Bennett asked.

"I think I'll take up flying," Joana said, sliding down the last bit of terrain before the hidden chamber.

"We're here," Sam said softly, the glow of the girdle overtaking the light from their flashlights as it illuminated the symbol of the goddess.

The chamber was no less impressive, even with the departure of the Snake Goddess. Her presence lingered in the mural overhead, her shadowy face no longer hidden from Sam's view. Sam approached the altar slowly, holding up the girdle.

"Thank you," she whispered, surprised at herself. "For knowing my worth, even when I didn't."

She looped the girdle over the horns of consecration, the tail end wrapping neatly in a figure eight. The chamber gave a scraping sigh, the panels of the skirt in the wall returning to their original position and hiding the girdle from view. The walls of the chamber continued shaking, a grinding sound coming from the door at the top of the stairwell.

"I think the cave is bidding us adieu," Joana said.

"We'd better go," Bennett said, taking them both by the hand and leading them quickly up the stairs out of the hidden chamber.

They just managed to slip through the opening before it closed up completely. But the walls didn't stop shaking, driving them out of the lower chamber to scrabble up the rope as the rock overhead gave way, crashing down and filling the chamber with debris. They huddled together as more and more rocks fell, until finally the earth settled again. In the wake of the small quake, the entire lower chamber was buried.

"And good riddance," Joana said. "Now, I believe I was promised sand and alcohol. Preferably somewhere far, far from here."

"For once, I am in agreement with you," Bennett said.

"About sand and alcohol?"

"About somewhere far, far from here," Bennett said dryly.

Sam paused as Joana and Bennett continued their climb, considering the narrow seams in the rubble and the secrets now buried beneath them. "Rest well, goddess."

She touched the rocks softly, before following after her friends.

EPILOGUE

"**Y**ou know, I think I am finally acquiring a taste for this stuff," Sam said, taking a tiny sip of the clear liquid in her glass. She did her best, but she couldn't help a small wince as the rough flavor hit the back of her throat. "It's certainly better than the raki on Crete."

Joana chuckled, kicking her ouzo shot back like a seasoned professional. "They have wine, too, Sam. Don't be a hero. Again."

Sam gave a sigh to the heavens. "Will you ever move on from that? We were all being quite heroic."

Joana leaned back in her wicker chair, taking a deep breath of warm sea air as she dug her toes into the soft sand. Her sun hat dipped over her eyes, lending her an air of mystery that drew the eye of several sunbathers nearby.

"Everything I do is heroic, Sam," Joana said, pursing her lips. "You'll have to be more specific."

Sam smiled, mirroring her movement and closing her eyes as she turned her face toward the delicious Mediterranean sun. She might not have really acquired a taste for ouzo in the past two weeks since they returned to the mainland in Greece, but she had a certain appreciation for the languorous warmth that spread through her limbs as the liquor worked its magic.

"You know," she said suddenly, her eyes popping open. "I think this is the first vacation I've ever taken. Is this what they're all like?"

"Some of them have handsome young men as well, though I don't suppose that would interest you," Joana said. She cracked one eye open to survey Sam. "But if this really is your first vacation, I've failed you as a best friend. Didn't you come along on that one summer in Maine?"

Sam laughed. "No, but I got an earful about it when you all returned."

Joana groaned. "It took three weeks for the rash to go away. I've been traumatized by nature hikes ever since."

"I told you to stick to the trail, Jo" came Bennett's voice from behind them. "But you insisted on taking the path less beaten."

"Bennett!" Sam exclaimed, the ouzo buoying her up as she threw her arms out to him. He smiled indulgently, grunting in surprise as the force of her embrace tipped him off balance.

"I see you two got started early." He laughed, catching himself on the edge of her chair to keep them both from tumbling into the sand. His raven hair was streaked with tinges of softer brown from their two weeks in the sun, his skin a deep bronze that made his eyes pure gold. Sam gave him a hearty kiss, mussing some of that perfectly waved hair. When she pulled back, his cheeks were slightly flushed.

"Mmm, right," Bennett said, clearing his throat.

"Hello, brother," Joana said, reaching for Sam's ouzo glass and tossing back the rest of the shot. "What's the good word?"

Bennett took the vacant wicker chair beside them, his linen

suit perfectly pressed despite the heat of the day. He had allowed Joana to choose the hotel when they returned to the mainland, and she had not squandered the advantage. Sam was almost embarrassed to have someone doing all her chores for her—especially her laundry—but Joana had insisted.

"I was finally able to get in touch with the new university president elect. Professor Atchinson is still in hospital recovering from what the president said was an 'unprecedented number of nonvenomous snakebites.' The doctors think he stumbled on a breeding nest. He's apparently not making much sense, though. Babbling about a goddess and a cursed undergraduate female. They've had to remove him from his post temporarily until they're sure he can recover. And he'll be subject to an investigation in Theo's disappearance, since he insisted on one for Professor Wallstone when Phillip went missing in Ireland. Set his own precedent."

"Atchinson should be happy to know he's finally making the department policies," Joana said, lifting her raki glass in a hollow cheers. "And I can't think of a more fitting tribute to Theo than to have Atchinson finally be forced to acknowledge him publicly."

"So no one is in charge of the department now?" Sam asked. "What will we do when we return for the fall?"

"Ah, well, with Professor Atchinson incapacitated, the board has seen fit to fully reinstate Professor Wallstone," Bennett said with a smile. "Apparently he's quite back to his old self, without Atchinson there to constantly agitate him."

"I would think Atchinson might be more sympathetic to old Wally right about now," Joana said.

"I don't think that man is capable of sympathetic thought," Sam said, standing and stretching. "Though I am happy at the prospect of returning to a Wallstone-run department. Perhaps I'll get my chance at the Kincaid Mounds after all. I think I want to swim in the ocean again. It's shockingly cold."

"I believe I'll stay up here on dry land, where it's shockingly warm," Joana murmured into the fresh glass of ouzo a waiter had dropped off for her. But she gasped, splashing it everywhere as she gave a strangled cry. "Sam, your foot!"

Sam looked down, something dark and green and slithery running over her bare foot. She screamed, kicking out her leg on instinct, only to land the slimy strand of seaweed directly in Bennett's lap. She clapped her hands over her mouth in horror.

"Oh, Bennett, your suit! I'm so sorry, I thought it was a sn—"

"It's all right, Sam," Bennett said, lifting the seaweed and tossing it far away from them. He frowned at the greenish stain it left behind. "My mother would say it was time for a midafternoon ensemble change, anyhow."

"That's the spirit, brother!" Joana said, lifting the remains of her glass and tossing it back. She shuddered at the impact of the alcohol. "If I never see another scaly creature again, it will still be too soon. Maybe I'll take myself off to the mountains instead."

"They have snakes in the mountains, Jo," Bennett said.

"Well, then flying it is," Joana said with a smile. "They don't have snakes on planes."

"I shudder to think of you in charge of large machinery," Bennett said.

Joana turned a wicked grin on him. "As well you should. It might be a mistake, but I'll certainly make it a glorious one."

Sam smiled out at the glittering expanse of the ocean before her, the horizon as open as her future. "Someone once told me mistakes are necessary on the path to wisdom. Do not let yourself be so afraid of them that you do not undertake the journey at all."

"That's quite profound," Bennett said. "Who told you that? Was it Wallstone?"

"Oh, just a goddess," Sam said, her smile widening. "Shall we swim?"

ACKNOWLEDGMENTS

I t's always a bit of a shock and a thrill to make it to the acknowl-edgments stage of things, never more so than for the book you wrote during a pandemic with two kids at home on virtual learning. This book took everything out of me, but it put back something indelible, and I'm incredibly grateful to have gone on another jour-ney with Sam, Jo, and Bennett.

As always, my eternal gratitude to Lindsay Funkhouser, Christina Frost, Bryn Shulke, and Anna Sargeant for making sense of my nonsense. You ladies keep me grounded, keep me sane, and taunt me with your Tuesday night wines.

Thank you to my agent, Elizabeth Bewley, for always being one phone call away when I'm too in my own head. You're a true cham-pion, and we make a great team.

To my editor, Kieran Viola, I said it before and I'll say it again here in print—you saved my soul on this book. I'm incredibly proud of what we created together, and I know your insight got us over the finish line. Thank you.

To the entire team at Hyperion, who worked their butts off dur-ing a pandemic to keep making books and getting them into the hands of readers. Thank you to Cassidy Leyendecker for always keeping me in the loop. Thank you to Guy Cunningham, Dan Kaufman, Martin Karlow, and David Jaffe for putting up with my complete lack of understanding of how commas work. Thank you to Phil Buchanan for the always top-notch designs. Thank you to Sammy Yuen for the absolutely gorgeous cover art. I didn't think you could top the first one, but you absolutely did. Thank you to Seale Ballenger and Christine Saunders for all the ideas, calls, and emails, and for giving me the perfect answer to "How was your weekend?" My thanks also to Sara Liebling, Marybeth Tregarthen, Dina Sherman (woot librarians!), Elke Villa, Holly Nagel, Monique Diman, and Vicki Korlishin for championing Sam and Co. in the best way.

To my family—Joe, Max, Lily, Mom, Dad, and Matt—thanks for being better at selling my books than I'll ever be. You're all professionals and I'd hire you in an instant, but I only pay in hugs and elaborate breakfast spreads.

And finally, to my readers—thank you for loving Sam and her crackpot adventures as much as I do. You know the old saying: Every time a glowing review gets posted on the internet, an author gets their wings. I'm pretty sure that's how the saying goes, don't fact-check me, though.